A GAME

WORTH

WATCHING

Rick —
As I start my new adventure, I'm giving you
a signed copy of my book because I FULLY
expect one from you in return! Here's
to having our writing dreams come true.
Thanks for everything.

Samantha

SAMANTHA GUDGER

Cover Design: Michelle Preast
        http://www.michellepreast.com
Interior Formatting: Ellen C. Maze, The Author's Mentor
        www.theauthorsmentor.com

ISBN-13: 978-1483964867
ISBN-10: 1483964868
Also available in eBook publication

Dedication

For my husband Ian.
And for anyone who's ever been told
you are not good enough,
strong enough,
or smart enough.
Because you are.

Table of Contents

One

I f looks could kill, the new guy would be dead already. Emma took a step towards him, her glare firmly in place.

"Excuse me?"

Mike—the new guy, the arrogant guy, the guy who needed to learn that Saturday morning basketball games at the park didn't start with him circling Emma like he was the wolf and she was the prey.

"I said you don't look like much."

The disgust in his eyes was enough for Emma to know he was the kind of guy who wouldn't share a court with girls, much less play basketball with them. His arrogant smirk didn't help.

"Why don't you let us guys play basketball and you can cheer for us from the sidelines?"

Tom closed his eyes and shook his head. Jerry winced, and the rest of the guys suppressed their laughter as Riley grabbed the back of her sweatshirt and pulled her away from Mike. Emma's face burned with anger, her hands balled into fists, and her mouth clamped shut to prevent a stream of vicious words from spilling out.

"Em," Riley said, unable to hide his smile, "take it

easy."

"Take it easy?" she growled. "First he says I don't look like much and then he says I should be a cheerleader. Who does he think he is?" Emma took a step in Mike's direction with the intent of having her fist speak on her behalf, but Riley yanked her back to his side.

Why were the new guys always so against playing basketball with a girl? One thing she knew for sure was that she *did* belong on a basketball court full of guys. If Mike wanted a cheerleader, he could put on the skimpy skirt and pompoms and cheer for himself.

Jerry cleared his throat. "Now that we've all met, how about we play?" He tossed the basketball to Emma and turned to Mike. "And just for fun, you can guard Emma," he said, unable to hide the grin on his face.

Her mouth twisted into a smile. Payback. Nice. She would love nothing more than to prove to Mike that not all girls were cheerleaders, and boys weren't the only ones who ruled the basketball court. She pulled free from Riley's grip to meet her victim at half court. Riley followed.

"Em." The warning in his voice tried to pull her back.

"Yeah, yeah, I know," she said, waving him away, "behave."

He stepped in front of her, forcing her to look at him. "Actually, I was going to say be careful. This guy looks like he could crush you with his bare hands."

Emma glanced at Mike. Sure, he was the size of a lumberjack with hands as big as her head and muscles the size of her entire body, but she didn't care. He deserved to be taught a little humility. "You know what they say," she said, squeezing the basketball in anticipation of the challenge, "the bigger they are, the harder they fall."

Riley shook his head and joined the rest of the guys as they cleared the court. The guys included Riley, Tom, Jerry, Ben, Alex, Cy, Carson, and Emma. Yep, she was one of them. This fact had less to do with her being a girl and more to do with her skills on the basketball court and how hard she punched. If Mike knew that, she wouldn't be facing off with him to prove she was a basketball player, *not* a cheerleader.

Mike noticed the guys lining up along the sideline instead of matching up on the court. "Hey, what are you guys doing? I thought we were going to play."

"The first one's all you." Tom waved him toward Emma. "Consider it your initiation."

Holding the ball in triple-threat position, Emma stared into the eyes of her defender. Poverty child. Loser. Poor girl. Tomboy. She was well aware of the labels people placed on her. She saw their looks as she weaved through the halls at Bradshaw High School; she heard their whispered insults, felt their judgments. In a school where ninety percent of the students came from families with money—lots of money—Emma stood out like a porcupine among swans, and not in a good way.

Emma knew she wasn't much to look at. Boys basketball shorts hung on her hips, her faded sweatshirt was a size too small, and her blonde hair was secured in a wad behind her head, the ends poking out in random directions. Yes, her family was poor. Yes, she wore her brothers' hand-me-downs. Yes, most of the kids at school hated her for reasons she didn't understand. Emma didn't care. She could play basketball—that's all that mattered to her.

She glanced at Riley. He stood on the sidelines, arms crossed and eyes glued on her in case things got rough and he needed to intervene. It had only happened once or twice—the new guy charging her with the intent to cause bodily harm because he couldn't take losing to a girl. Thank goodness she had Riley.

"We playing or what?" Mike asked.

"Absolutely." She spun the ball in her hands, waiting for Mike to step up and play defense, but he kept his distance. Mike's stupidity was Emma's opportunity. From

3

behind the three-point line, she shot the ball, her smirk in place as the ball dropped through the net.

"Lucky shot," Mike muttered before Tom yelled from the sideline, "Watch the long shot. She'll sink it every time."

The rest of the guys laughed, knowing only too well the truth to Tom's statement. She'd scored way too many three-pointers during their games to let them forget it.

Mike scowled at her, snatched the ball from the ground, and set up for his turn on offense. Revenge was written across his face. She smiled inwardly. Bring it on.

He jabbed left before dribbling right. Emma shuffled her feet, staying with him. Mike attempted a crossover to change direction, a slow crossover. Not between the legs or behind the back or anything more sophisticated than Basketball 101, but a crossover right in front of her. He had a lot to learn. Her hand struck out like a viper, flipping the ball away from him and into her possession. This time, when she set up at the three-point line to drive right, Mike didn't give her the extra step. He forced her left instead. Not a bad plan, but Emma didn't have a weak side, so if he wanted her to go left, she'd go left.

One dribble, two dribbles, between the legs to the right, spin move to the left, all executed to perfection in under two seconds. She faked the shot. Mike flew through the air trying to block the ball, but she stepped around him for the easy lay-in.

The guys clapped. Mike growled. Emma grinned. It was the second basket of many. Mike and Emma battled one-on-one for the next ten minutes. Mike desperate to beat the girl; the girl determined to prove, beyond a doubt, that she was a basketball player, not a cheerleader. Considering she outscored the guy five to one, Emma figured she'd gotten her point across, especially when Mike slammed the ball on the ground and turned to the guys.

"Okay," he growled. "I get it. The chick can play."

"That's my girl," Riley said with a smile, joining Emma on the court to give her a high five. The rest of the guys averted their eyes from Mike, trying not to laugh, and started picking teams.

If she hadn't been so caught up in her victory and entertained by Mike fuming over his loss, Emma probably would've seen the woman slip through the fence behind them and step onto the court. She would have sensed how her life was one moment away from changing. Again.

Two

"Excuse me."

The voice was not one of their own. Emma and the guys turned to look at the woman who'd inched her way onto their court.

Eight guys and one girl stared at the woman, but the intruder only had eyes for Emma. Emma took a step back. With her black running suit, her brown hair pulled back in a ponytail, and her perky smile, the woman didn't look like a police officer or a social worker, but that didn't mean she wasn't one. Growing up in a single-parent family with four brothers, Emma had seen her fair share of authority figures and knew enough not to trust anyone. Except Riley.

The woman took a step forward. "Are you Emma Wrangton?"

Emma tensed. She had never met this woman in her life, so why had she thrown Emma's name out there like she already knew the answer? The temperature seemed to drop ten degrees. Emma shivered.

Riley grabbed Emma's hand and pulled her behind him, blocking her from the woman's stare. "Depends on who's askin'," he said, his voice hard and filled with caution.

The woman stepped closer. "I'm Jen Knowles. I'm the new girls' varsity basketball coach at Bradshaw High School." She answered Riley's question but stepped to the side and craned her neck to reconnect her eyes with Emma's.

Riley glanced over his shoulder at Emma. She could only imagine what he was thinking. *Girls' basketball coach looking for you? That's a first.* The curiosity in his eyes didn't match the fear in hers. He stepped aside but remained close.

"Word has it you're the best female basketball player in town," Jen said.

A few of the guys whistled and hollered their approval, but Emma remained skeptical of the woman's motives and stayed on guard. Call it intuition, paranoia, or complete distrust of the female population, but something in the woman's voice didn't sound quite right.

Jen nodded toward the basket. "From what I've seen, I'd say the rumors about you are true."

Poverty child. Loser. Poor girl. Tomboy. Not exactly the kind of rumors a real coach acted on to go in search of some girl. If there were rumors circulating about her basketball abilities, Emma hadn't heard them and didn't know who would have started them. Aside from Riley's parents and the guys, no one knew she even played. Even if this woman was different, Emma recognized the look on her face. The plastered on smile and hopeful eyes couldn't hide Jen Knowles' caution over Emma's appearance. Add Emma's lack of eye appeal to the fact she'd never played on a real team, and people automatically assumed she was plagued by bad habits and wasn't worth their time.

Until now.

"I want you on my roster." Jen's comment left no room for misinterpretation.

"I don't play organized sports," Emma shot back. No room for misinterpretation there either.

"Why is that?"

Emma shrugged. She wasn't about to explain herself to anyone, least of all to a stranger whose presence delayed a much anticipated basketball game.

"The team could use you." Jen kept her eyes fixated on Emma, waiting for her to respond, but Emma remained silent. No way would she ever consider playing for the girls' team. Not even if someone paid her. Her one goal in life was to graduate high school with her sanity intact, not sacrifice herself to be at the mercy of cruel and heartless girls. Besides, the girls at school had proven a long time ago that Emma didn't belong in their cliques. Between the glares, accusations, and rumors they had spread to embarrass her, Emma stayed as far away from them as possible.

"No offense," Emma said, regaining her confidence, "but the girls' team is a joke."

"Emma!" Riley snapped.

"What?" She shrugged. It wasn't a secret. "They haven't won more than two games a season in over a decade."

"Maybe this year will be different," Jen Knowles challenged.

Emma almost laughed, but she knew Riley would smack her if she did. "Maybe it won't."

Jen pressed her lips together and nodded once, as if sensing the more she tried to persuade Emma to join the team, the more Emma would resist. "I'd appreciate it if you would at least consider coming out for the team. The first practice is a week from Monday."

Tom grasped Emma's shoulders from behind. "If Emma tries out for any team, it will be the boys' basketball team."

Jen's shoulders slumped, as if all of her dreams for the season had vanished, but Emma was with Tom. The guys' team sounded a lot more appealing than the girls' team. At least the guys won a game once in a while.

Jen Knowles continued to stare at Emma, probably hoping to infuse her with enough school spirit to propel her to join the girls' team.

Emma crossed her arms and stared back. Not happening.

"Please," Jen said. "Just think about it." She finally turned to leave.

The guys retreated to the basket to shoot, while Emma watched the woman cross the court and disappear into her car. What right did she have to intrude on their court and beg for Emma to join Bradshaw's girls' basketball team? Their reputation alone was enough to deter Emma from ever stepping foot on the court, and the team consisted of—gulp—*girls*. The mere thought made her want to gag.

"Are you going to do it?" Riley asked.

Emma laughed. "No."

"Why not?"

"Because only losers play for the school team."

"Hey." Riley pointed to his chest with both hands. "I play for the school team."

Emma patted his chest. "Exactly my point."

One by one, the guys drifted off the court to go home or to work or wherever else they went on Saturdays. Four hours of basketball was enough for any of them, but Emma sometimes wished the hours would stretch a little longer to reduce the amount of time she had to spend at home.

"You want to stay and shoot around?" she asked Riley before he could follow the others and abandon her too.

"Can't." He put up one last shot before snatching his water bottle from the bleachers and taking a swig. He swiped the back of his hand across his mouth to catch drops of water dripping from his chin and snapped the lid of his bottle closed. "My mom told me if I wasn't home in time for dinner, she'd skin me alive."

"Ah, the old parental threat. You better get going then."

Emma bowed her head, trying to hide her disappointment. Time always seemed to steal so much of the day. She thought for sure Riley would stay longer, but Mrs. Ledger's threats were not to be taken lightly. Sometimes Emma wished her dad would use a parental threat, if for no other reason than to show he cared.

"Well, come on," Riley said impatiently from the sideline. "You're invited too."

Her eyes lit up. "Really?"

"Yes, really. My mom's making your favorite."

"Homemade macaroni and cheese?"

"Yep."

"With little broccoli pieces and chicken?"

"Yep and yep."

Her mouth started to water. She hadn't had Mrs. Ledger's macaroni and cheese in months. She retrieved the basketball and fell into step beside Riley.

Darkness came early in November, and with no sun to indicate the transition from day to night, the park faded from gray to black as Emma and Riley stepped into the street and headed toward home. She couldn't prevent the bounce in her step or the smile on her face. Dinner at the Ledgers'. There was no better end to her day.

He shook his head at her excitement and settled his arm around her shoulders. "My mom loves you more than me, and I'm her only child."

"And my dad loves you more than me, and I'm his only daughter, so we're even," she said, determined not to let him make her feel guilty.

"He does not."

"Oh, please. My dad would kill for another boy in the family rather than be stuck with me." As if four sons weren't enough already.

Riley stopped walking, and his voice turned serious. "Em, that's not true."

"It is true, and you know it." She poked him in the

chest. No matter how wrong it seemed or how much they wanted to deny it, they both knew her dad preferred Riley to her.

Riley studied her, trying to decide if he wanted to fight it out or let her comment slide. He took a deep breath and exhaled through his nose. "Whether it's true or not, I'll never be able to understand why he'd want to get rid of you when you have the most squeezable cheeks." He grabbed her cheeks with both hands and pinched them like his grandma used to do when Emma was little, except with more pinch.

She swatted his hands away, and he took off running. She heard his laughter echo down the street as she chased him the last two blocks to his house. They burst into the house just as Mrs. Ledger set the pan of steaming macaroni and cheese on the dinner table. The smell of cheesy goodness was enough to fill Emma's stomach for a week.

Mrs. Ledger took one look at them, set her hands on her hips, and started barking out orders. "Shoes off. Wash up. Don't even think about starting a water fight."

Riley and Emma exchanged a look, forcing back laughter, before doing as they were told. After eight years of friendship, Riley's mom knew what kinds of disasters to plan for before they even happened. It wasn't fair, but tonight it didn't matter because it was mac and cheese night.

The love of macaroni and cheese. How to explain it? It wasn't the boxed kind with the powdered cheese or the creamy sauce that left a layer of residue on the top of your mouth and on your teeth or anything. This stuff was the real deal. Freshly grated cheese sprinkled over noodles and vegetables and chicken, baked to perfection, and delivered to the table in one delicious cheesy-melted meal.

Unlike Emma's family, the Ledgers ate meals together at the table with napkins and matching dishes. At the Wrangtons', dinner was rarely anything beyond frozen pizza or TV dinners. Dinner with the Ledgers not only consisted of food—really good homemade food—but civilized conversation too.

"So," Mr. Ledger said. "Anything interesting happen today?"

Emma's fork froze halfway to her mouth. He knew. He knew about the stranger on the court asking her to try out for the girls' team. Why else would he ask such a pointed question? Okay, so maybe he always asked the same question whenever she came to dinner, but tonight it seemed to hold more weight than usual. She cast Riley a don't-you-dare look from across the table, knowing he would reveal details just to aggravate her. The last thing she wanted was everyone knowing her business.

Riley grinned at her. "Actually," he drawled out.

Shaking her head slightly to avoid parental detection, Emma scolded him with her eyes.

Riley shifted his gaze to his dad. "Emma beat another new guy on the court today."

She breathed a sigh of relief. Maybe she should give Riley more credit. It wasn't like he was out to intentionally ruin her life.

Mr. Ledger looked at her with a downturned head and upturned eyes. "Emma, you should give those boys a chance."

He only said this because he felt obligated as a parent. She knew for a fact Mr. Ledger found her ability to humiliate guys on the basketball court amusing—he took after his son in that regard. Plus, the effort it took him to hide the smile trying to burst forth on his face was another giveaway.

"Sometimes boys need more time to prove their worth," Mr. Ledger said.

"Not this one." Emma speared a piece of chicken with her fork. She remembered Mike's remarks, his cocky smile, and his intent to embarrass her. He deserved what he got.

"Oh yeah?" Mr. Ledger winked at his wife. "What did

this one do?"

"He told me I should be a cheerleader for the guys."

Mr. Ledger's booming laughter joined his wife's giggles. Emma didn't understand what was so funny. They knew how much she hated guys who didn't respect her on the court.

"I think it's great." Mrs. Ledger patted Emma's hand. "Those boys need to learn not to underestimate girls. I'm surprised my own son lets that type of thing happen to you." She cast Riley the kind of disapproving look only a mother could pull off.

"Me?" Riley exclaimed, dropping his fork on his plate and leaning back in his chair. He glanced at his dad and then back at his mom. "How did this whole thing become my fault?"

Emma laughed. She loved it when Mrs. Ledger took her side. "Your mom's right," she teased. "If you stuck up for me like a real gentleman, I wouldn't be forced to humiliate boys and ruin their dreams of becoming arrogant basketball players."

Riley glared at her from across the table. An evil grin flashed on his face as he turned toward his dad. "Speaking of basketball players, the girls' varsity coach asked Emma to join the school team today."

Emma's grip on her fork tightened as she tried to decide whether or not to use it as a projectile weapon on her best friend. Why did she always give Riley a reason to seek revenge? She loved Riley's parents—they were the only adults who cared about her—but they had a tendency of being overly supportive because they loved their son and she was his friend. Support she didn't deserve considering she wasn't their child, and not even her own dad gave her the time of day.

Besides, she hated when people made a big deal out of nothing, and Riley's parents made a big deal out of everything. Like the time Riley told them she won the sixth grade spelling bee, and they threw her a party to celebrate. Or the time she scored her first three-pointer in a game against the guys, and they bought her a brand-new basketball. Or the time she got into a huge fight with her dad, and she fled to the Ledgers' where they called a family movie and pizza night.

Yes, she loved Mr. and Mrs. Ledger, but she hated how guilt consumed her every time they went out of their way for her. Riley knew this, of course, but did he care about her feelings? No. He just stared at her with his lopsided grin.

"That's great." Both of Riley's parents radiated smiles toward her.

Emma glared at Riley. "I hate you."

Riley chuckled. "I know."

"Are you going to do it?" Mr. Ledger asked, sounding exactly like his son.

Emma's "No," battled Riley's "Yes," as they answered simultaneously.

She could feel Mr. and Mrs. Ledger watching the two of them. It was only a matter of seconds before they chose sides for the debate. Would they side with their one and only son who was determined to bully Emma into joining the girls' team, or would they side with his best friend who was determined to live a girl-free life? Confident they would join forces with their son, Emma quickly took control of the conversation.

"No," she said firmly. "I'm not."

Riley cocked his head to the side. "Why not? You used to talk all the time about being part of a team. Now's your chance."

"Yeah, well, things change." She used to talk about being a lot of things as a kid, but she gave up dreaming when she realized nothing good ever happened to her. "Besides, I am part of a team. The guys are my team."

Riley rolled his eyes. "A bunch of guys shooting hoops at the park is not a team."

Emma dropped her eyes to the food on her plate. "Maybe not to you."

She didn't know where the words came from or why her chest tightened at Riley's comment. Having never played on a real team with a real coach, Emma didn't know what it was like to form bonds with a group of individuals who worked hard to achieve a common goal, but she could imagine. Loyalty, commitment, determination, faith, and trust. The qualities expressed by teammates were endless—a lesson Emma learned from playing with the guys. When her home life crumbled, the guys were the ones who helped her escape from it.

For Riley, Saturday games with the guys meant hanging out with friends and goofing off. He'd played on sports teams since the day he could walk. He didn't know what it was like to not have the money to pay for registration fees, summer camps, travel expenses, and equipment. Sometimes he forgot about the world she lived in.

Regret flashed in Riley's eyes as he recognized Emma's mood slip, realizing how much more important Saturday games with the guys meant to her. "Em."

Even after eight years of friendship, she still couldn't figure out how Riley could encompass the depth of a sincere apology just by saying the first syllable of her name.

Before he could say anything more, Emma held up her hand to cut him off. "The last thing I want to do is spend the next three months playing basketball with a bunch of girls and getting slaughtered by every team in the league. I'm sorry, Riley." She did her best with an apologetic smile. "I just don't think the girls' team is for me."

She expected Riley to put up a fight and tell her all the reasons why she should join the team, but he didn't. Somehow rendered speechless, Riley held her gaze in silence. She figured the conversation was over, and they could all go back to enjoying the mac and cheese cooling on their plates, but Mr. Ledger took up where Riley left off.

"Look, Emma," he said gently. He wiped his mouth with a napkin before resting his elbows on the table and leaning forward. Emma held her breath, waiting for the words of wisdom he always shared in moments like this. "I get it. Some stranger shows up and asks you to join her losing team, which is made up of all those cheerleading type girls you despise, and you think, 'Why should I play? What's in it for me?'" Mr. Ledger shrugged. "Maybe nothing. But the reason the coach found you is because she needs a leader—a leader who is strong and confident and not afraid of what the rest of the girls will think of her. Not everyone can fill that kind of role. But you…"

His words stopped there, forcing her to fill in the missing pieces. Emma loved when Mrs. Ledger took her side, but she hated when Mr. Ledger took Riley's. She hated disappointing both of them. "Mr. Ledger, I—"

He held up his hand to stop her. "I don't know if joining the team is the right thing for you or not, but I do know you are an amazing basketball player. I'd hate to think you're limiting your talents to beating and humiliating guys in the park when you could be a real asset to the school team. The decision is yours, but before you decide, maybe you should think about it a bit more. There's no harm in that, right?" His smile of encouragement made Emma squirm. The last thing she wanted to do was waste time thinking about it. It wasn't like her decision would change over time anyway.

With both Riley and his dad staring at her expectantly, she couldn't bring herself to do anything but nod and agree to think about the stupid girls' basketball team.

Mr. Ledger leaned over and squeezed her arm before returning to his meal. From across the table, Riley winked at her. She looked away. This evening had started out so good with the promise of her favorite meal, but now she was outnumbered two-to-one over some girls' basketball team.

"If you do go out for the team, we'd love to come see

you play," Mrs. Ledger said.

Emma choked on the noodle halfway down her throat. Make that three-to-one. "That's not necessary," she said. On the slim to none chance—with heavy emphasis on the none—she did go out for the team, the last thing she'd want is a cheering section. She had never been good in the spotlight. Invisibility suited her just fine, especially since nothing good ever happened when attention was thrown her way. Why couldn't the Ledgers understand that? No way would she allow her best friend and his family to force her into making the biggest mistake of her life. It was best to stand her ground with an irreversible no.

◆◆◆

Emma slipped into her house unnoticed. Her two younger brothers, Lucas and Lenny, were wrestling on the brown shag carpet of the living room floor, and Lance, her older brother, sat beside their dad on the couch watching some football game on television. Logan, the oldest of the pack, sat in the old wooden rocker reading a book.

She poked her head into the living room. "I'm home."

"No one cares," Lance responded. No one else said anything.

She had given up a long time ago thinking her dad or brothers worried about her when she wasn't home. They made it clear that being the only girl didn't afford her specialized treatment. After all, if it weren't for her, the house would be an all-male lair. She couldn't shake the feeling that her dad wished one day he would wake up and she would have disappeared just like her mom had done five years ago. Growing up with four brothers had hardened her; growing up without a mom had hardened them all.

She retreated to the garage, ignoring the smell of must and mildew that refused to go away no matter how many air fresheners she used. She weaved through stacks upon stacks of boxes, an old weight lifting set, bikes with flat tires and bent spokes, broken furniture and lawn tools, and every other type of artifact her family had discarded over the years, until she finally came to the corner of the garage that served as her bedroom. Boxes stuffed full of her family's possessions built her makeshift walls. A three-bedroom house wasn't big enough for a family of six, especially when only one of them was a girl. Her dad figured she needed the most privacy, and what was more private than a garage—graveyard—full of broken toys and tools?

Her bedroom consisted of everything a bedroom should have including a dresser with missing knobs and drawers that refused to close all the way, a single bed that squeaked when she applied pressure, a wobbling bedside table, a lamp with a missing shade, and a scrap of gray carpet to separate her feet from the concrete floor. A few items of clothing hung neatly on hangers from the tops of boxes, and she made sure all of her girl-related items were safely hidden in a cardboard box where Riley wouldn't stumble upon them. What more could a girl ask for?

After switching on the space heater that kept her just above freezing in the winter, Emma changed into a pair of sweats and a long-sleeve shirt for bed. The springs squeaked their goodnight as she climbed under the covers. She stared at the ceiling she couldn't see in the dark and listened to her dad and brothers. Laughter and shouts of triumph over the game filtered through to her from the other side of the wall.

Sometimes privacy was synonymous with loneliness.

"Goodnight," she whispered to her family, separated from them by so much more than a wall.

Mentally drained from the day's drama, Emma's eyelids drooped closed within minutes. The space heater hummed along with the voices of her family, and the warm current of air stroked her face as it mingled with the draft of cold winter air slipping in from the crack under the garage doors. She felt herself slip a few notches toward sleep.

Footsteps. The sound of feet shuffling against pavement. Something about that particular sound seemed off as Emma tried to fight sleep to place it. Did it come from the world around her or from her dreams? In her sleep-induced state Emma tried to make sense of it, but before she could, a hand clamped down on her mouth. No matter how hard she struggled, she couldn't scream for help.

Three

"Shh. It's me," a voice whispered in the dark.

Emma grabbed the hand covering her mouth and pulled it away, her heart pounding. "Riley?" she gasped. "What are you doing here? You scared me half to death."

She heard him chuckle in the dark.

Emma seriously regretted telling him where the hidden key was to her garage bedroom. Sure, he'd snuck in before, but usually he warned her first.

Before she could pull her arm back to punch him, Riley shoved something into her hands. "Put this on."

From the feel of it, she knew it was her favorite sweatshirt. It was a hand-me-down like everything else she owned, but it fit perfectly and had stood the test of moths and basketball. Plus, it was green, her favorite color. She pulled it on and slipped her feet into the shoes Riley tossed to her.

He waited in the doorway leading outside. She stopped and leaned against the opposite side of the doorframe to secure her hair in its usual wad, preparing for their sprint to safety.

Riley reached over and brushed a stray hair from her face. "You ready?"

"Why do you ask me like I haven't done this a million

times before?"

Smiling, he slipped his hand in hers. They were twelve the first time they snuck out together on a night when no moon lit their path. Riley had gone one way and Emma went another. For a girl whose mom had disappeared with no warning, fear of separation did funny things. By the time Riley found her, she had already fallen victim to the tears over his absence. From then on, Riley ensured her hand was secured in his whenever darkness or anything else tried to separate them, even after she grew old enough to take care of herself.

Hand in hand, they snuck between the houses and bushes until their feet slapped the pavement. They walked a few blocks before ducking between two evergreen trees, finding the path through the woods, which would lead them to the water of Puget Sound. Outstretched tree limbs brushed at them in the dark. Their feet, familiar with the route, automatically stepped around tree roots poking through the ground. With no moon or flashlight to illuminate their path through the trees, only Riley's soft humming guided Emma forward until the darkness of the forest parted to reveal the night sky and rocky beach. They walked along the water's edge and climbed onto their fallen tree trunk to sit side by side, looking out over the water. Emma reclaimed possession of her hand and shoved it in her pocket to stay warm.

The Narrows Bridge towered above them, the current surging beneath it. Aside from cars whooshing across the bridge overhead and the occasional boat puttering by, the night was quiet. During the day, people littered the beach and walked for miles along the shore at low tide. Kids dug holes and upturned rocks looking for crabs, dogs swam after sticks, and young couples hid among the rocks for privacy. Now, as millions of stars looked down on them and lights from the opposite shore reflected on the water's surface, it was just Emma and Riley. She watched the moonlight glisten on the water and thought about how perfect the moment was…until Riley spoke.

"So, have you thought any more about trying out for the girls' team?"

His nonchalant tone didn't fool her. Tonight's excursion wasn't about spending time with his best friend. He'd planned the evening for one simple reason—to convince her to play for the girls' team. She should've known. For Emma, the thought of joining the girls' basketball team at school was just as absurd now as it had been when Jen Knowles invaded their court this afternoon. Emma refused to be swayed with time. "No," she said firmly.

When Riley responded, his tone matched hers. "I think you should do it."

She sighed. "I'm sure you do, but I already told you I wasn't."

"Why not?"

"Because they're girls." She could have said they were diseased and it would have sounded less horrific. Her life was, and always had been, one hundred percent *Matchbox* cars, mud, grass stains, and *Transformers*. No dolls, no dresses, no lace, and no pink. "I don't know anything about girls."

Even in the dark, she could feel him smile. "You do know *you* are a girl, don't you?"

She punched his arm. "Very funny." Yes, she was a girl, but she wasn't a normal girl; even he could attest to her uniqueness. She was just another one of the guys. She didn't care about popularity status or making herself look beautiful for the male population or being America's most beloved princess. What she did care about was the accuracy of her jump shot, hanging with the guys, and staying as far away from girls and all things girl-related as possible.

She listened to the water lap at the shore and shivered. Winter was definitely approaching. The breeze blowing off the water, smelling like salt and seaweed, didn't help her stay warm. She pulled the hood of her sweatshirt over her head and stuffed her hands into her sleeves to hide from the cold, but it bit into her anyway.

Riley looked at her, expecting more of an explanation for why she refused to step on the basketball court with a bunch of girls as her teammates. She knew he wouldn't move past the ridiculous idea, but she couldn't tell him the whole truth: girls scared her. She'd seen plenty of movies and overheard enough girls at school to know the truth about them. Girls could be your best friend one second and your worst enemy the next. They revealed secrets during moments of distress and sacrificed bonds of friendship for boyfriends and popularity. They used and humiliated people for their own personal gain. They claimed to care about you only to flee in the middle of the night never to return. Girls couldn't be trusted, and Emma refused to be thrust into the middle of their drama, knowing she'd only get hurt in the end. Joining the girls' basketball team would be like entering piranha-infested waters. No thank you.

Riley wouldn't understand. He'd accuse her of overreacting and tell her not to always expect the worst in people. Maybe he'd be right, but he didn't know what it was like to be hurt, unloved, and abandoned.

She took a deep breath before plunging ahead with an answer to satisfy him. "I've been surrounded by guys my entire life. I can't just cross over. It would be like going to a foreign country without speaking the language or appreciating their culture." Aside from the whole girl phobia thing—or maybe because of it—Emma was as bad as a guy at understanding her own species.

Riley studied her profile. "It could be good for you."

"Says the guy with the perfect life."

"My life is not perfect."

She rolled her head in his direction, her eyebrows raised in question. Unlike most of the kids at school, Riley didn't flaunt his lifestyle, but that didn't mean he couldn't hold his own against any of them. He had plenty of money in the bank, two great parents, a huge house, and a nice set of wheels. Plus, he was an all-around nice guy, and everyone loved him. Truth be told, Riley Ledger had it good, and he knew it.

"Okay," he finally conceded. "Compared to your life my life may *seem* perfect, but only because you have enough problems for the both of us."

"Exactly," she said. "Which means I don't need any more, especially not in the form of a girls' basketball team."

Riley hopped off the log to stand in front of her. She hated when he peered up at her with his blue eyes, looking all innocent and trusting, like there was nothing in the world he wouldn't do for her. It only made it more difficult for her to stand her ground.

"You can fight me all you want, Em, but the truth is you'll never get a college scholarship to play on the *boys'* basketball team. This could be your shot."

The mere mention of college put her on edge. "My shot for what? College isn't for people like me. It's for people like you." He knew the limitations she faced with no money to pay for college and no support from family. Education wasn't exactly a high priority for her. As much as she wanted to believe Riley, it was hard to think seventeen years of nothing would miraculously unfold a future of possibilities for her.

Leaning against her knees, Riley rested his arms in Emma's lap and looked up at her. "What's so different about you and me, huh? And don't you dare say anything about household income because you know I won't buy it."

Emma didn't respond. She didn't want to rehearse how the world treated them differently or how she was so much less than him. Of course, Riley didn't see, or maybe he chose not to acknowledge, how the two of them were from two different worlds. Just because they were friends didn't mean the future would bring similar paths for them. It had always been her expectation that Riley would go to college and earn some fancy degree while she stayed behind to perfect her would-you-like-fries-with-that speech for a living. Household income wasn't the only thing separating them, but it sure was a huge factor.

"Em, as soon as colleges see you play, they'll—"

"Riley, stop," she snapped. She didn't want to hear any more about girls' basketball teams and colleges and how much he thought she deserved some bright future. His biased opinion would do nothing except give her false hope. "I'm *not* going to college."

He grew quiet and still, studying her in the moonlight. When the seconds stretched into an eternity, she bowed her head, unable to look at him any longer. She could only imagine what thoughts he entertained in that stubborn head of his.

He leaned in to look at her downturned face. "You deserve this opportunity, Em," he said softly. "Who knows where it will take you?"

When she lifted her eyes to his, he put on his you-can't-resist-me puppy dog face. "For me?"

Why did he always have to make things so complicated? Did it really matter if she didn't go to college or play on some stupid girls' team?

She growled in frustration and jumped off the log to escape. Wrong move. Riley's arms shot out, trapping her between his body and the log, forcing her to face him and the conversation.

"Will you at least seriously consider it?" he asked. "Please?"

"The girls' team is horrible." It was a fact and everyone knew it.

"Maybe they wouldn't be so horrible if you played for them," Riley challenged.

"I'd be playing with girls who have hated me and

teased me since elementary school." Merely picturing their faces made her stomach churn.

"Since when are you afraid of a challenge?"

Emma injected as much pain as she could into her eyes to gain the pity vote. "I'll be miserable."

He secured her face between his hands. "I'll support you every step of the way."

She stared into his eyes, ready to voice her objection with a final no and close the topic of her joining the girls' basketball team once and for all. But that was easier said than done. She wasn't talking to just anyone; she was talking to Riley. The boy who taught her everything she knew about basketball. The boy who looked out for her, protected her, and believed in her. The boy she'd do anything for—even if it meant joining a stupid girls' basketball team.

She felt her resolve weakening.

Ugh! How did he do that? Her decision to stay away from the girls' team had been ironclad not two seconds ago. She glared at him. "I hate you."

A smile tugged at his lips. "I know."

They both knew he'd get his way, and come Monday, the Bradshaw High School girls' basketball team would have one new girl to add to the roster, but she didn't have to be happy about it.

◆◆◆

The next week passed quicker than a baseline-to-baseline wind sprint. Emma tried to forget about girls and basketball tryouts and her promise to Riley to go out for the team, but the guys wouldn't let her.

"You don't have to wear a little skirt to play on the girls' team, do you, Emmy?" Tom had mocked her.

"You don't want to wear my fist in your face, do you, Tommy?" she'd responded. If Riley hadn't been there to laugh off their jokes and keep her in line, she probably would have picked a fight with Tom or any of the other guys to prove she wasn't growing soft.

To make everything worse, Riley insisted she spend the week getting in shape for real practices, threatening they weren't anything like Saturday games with the guys. No, she'd never played on a real team before, so the whole practice thing was foreign, but how hard could it be? Even if she refrained from basketball and slept through the week, she'd still be the best player on the team. She knew the game of basketball inside and out and could play it in her sleep. Basketball wasn't what kept her up at night and made her defensive and irritable as Monday approached. No, her problems were so much bigger.

Take girls for instance. She couldn't remember the last time she'd spent any amount of time alone with one, and the thought of spending two hours locked in a gym with a group of the drama-stricken species nauseated her. Riley wouldn't be there to hold her back if Lauren or one of her clones picked a fight.

Lauren. If Emma had a polar opposite, Lauren would be it. Lauren was the epitome of the boy-obsessed, attention-craving, high-squealing type girl Emma despised. Not to mention the perfect blonde had made Emma's life miserable since elementary school. She'd spent the majority of her life avoiding Lauren only to have to figure out how to exist on the same court with her during their senior year. Talk about a nightmare. But before she came face-to-face with Lauren, Emma had to ask her dad for the one thing she needed.

She had postponed the talk with him as long as possible. Although the rush hour before school wasn't the ideal time, it was now or never. Procrastination didn't keep many options open. It couldn't be easy being a single dad raising five kids. Sure, Lance and Logan were out of high school, but they still lived at home working dead-end jobs and acting like sixteen-year-olds.

Taking a deep breath, she opened the door from the garage into the house. Lucas and Lenny were at the table fighting over cereal boxes, Lance was pouring over the sports section of the newspaper, and Logan was shoveling food into his mouth with one hand and holding a book in the other. Her dad stood at the sink attempting to wash a week's worth of dishes. Emma walked over to him and looked up at his weathered face.

She often wondered what her dad had been like before. Before he had five kids. Before he had to work two jobs to support his family. Before his wife left him. Had he ever laughed so hard he cried? Had he ever brought home flowers to his wife for no other reason than to say he missed her? Had he ever looked into the eyes of his children—into the eyes of his only daughter—and felt an ounce of love? There were so many things about her dad she didn't know, so many things she was afraid to ask.

"Dad?" she said, preparing to ask the question on top of her current priority list.

He didn't answer. She hated asking her dad for anything, but since he refused to let her get a job, for reasons he had yet to explain, how else was she supposed to obtain money to buy what she needed?

Nothing Emma owned was new. Being the middle child of five and the only girl, none of her needs ranked as a top priority in the Wrangton household. Over the years, she'd learned to watch her brothers and notice when clothes no longer fit them so she could be first in line to snag decent clothing before it continued down to her younger brothers. Without a job, she'd learned to scour for change anywhere from couch cushions to gutters. Aside from Riley's parents creating summer cleaning and painting jobs for her, it was the only way she could earn money. It didn't hurt living with boys who ripped holes in their pockets faster than they could tie their shoes. But collecting change didn't build her savings very fast, especially when most of it was spent on supplying her basic needs.

Keeping her voice down to avoid detection from her brothers, she tried again. "Dad?"

"Yeah?" he asked, scrubbing a plate that refused to give up its hold on the encrusted food. The sight of her six-foot-two muscular dad losing a battle with dirty dishes was almost humorous.

"I'm...uh...trying out for the basketball team at school, and I could really use some new shoes." She glanced over her shoulder at her brothers, trying to determine if they were eavesdropping. "Nothing fancy, but—"

"What about Lance's old ones?"

At least he was listening. "Those are the ones I'm wearing now and there's a hole in the sole."

"What about Lenny's?"

Lenny looked up at the sound of his name.

"He only has one," Emma muttered. "He lost the other one in the creek."

"Logan's?" her dad tried one more time.

She frowned at him. "More duct tape than shoe."

She saw her dad sifting through options, knowing there weren't any except to give in and let her buy a pair of shoes for herself. Shoes that molded to her feet instead of the other way around. "Dad, I—"

"What do you need shoes for?" Lance slapped the newspaper on the table and joined the conversation. "It's not like you're good enough to play, even if it is for the girls' team."

Lenny and Lucas laughed, their cereal boxes forgotten.

"What would you know?" Emma spit back. She hated how her brother made assumptions when he'd never seen her play. "At least I'm not the one who got kicked off the school team for flunking three classes because I was too lazy to do the work."

The chair groaned against the floor as Lance shoved it back and stepped toward her. She saw his hand form a fist and wondered if he would hit her with their dad watching. It wouldn't have been the first time he'd laid his hands on her.

She used to love watching Lance play basketball when he was a freshman and sophomore in high school. He dominated the court with swift feet, a killer jump shot, and the best defense the league had ever seen. His twisted smile let defenders know he never lost in a one-on-one competition. Everyone said he'd go pro. But when the school put him on probation for grades, rather than stepping it up, he blamed the world for its unfairness and gave up. He could have been great. Not exactly something he wanted to be reminded of, especially by his little sister.

"Hey." Their dad spun away from the sink and stood between Lance and Emma before anything could erupt between them, his eyes burning with warning. "Enough."

Lance and Emma glared at each other as their brothers looked on. Lenny and Lucas were always interested to see a fight, whereas, Logan hid behind his book, avoiding conflict at all cost.

"Go on." Her dad nodded toward the living room to tell Lance to get going. Lance, for once, obliged.

"Listen," her dad murmured, turning his back on the boys to face her without completely making eye contact, "I'm a little short this month." He held his hands out to the side in defeat. "I'm sorry."

"Oh, no problem." She forced what she could of a smile. "I'll figure something out."

Not wanting him to see her disappointment, she muttered goodbye, grabbed her recycled backpack with the broken strap, and left for school, making sure she didn't cross paths with Lance. She hoped her shoes would last a few months longer. Thankfully, her dad bought duct tape in bulk.

◆◆◆

The final bell came way too soon. Final bell meant school was over and practice began. Basketball practice. With girls. If someone had asked her a month ago what her future looked like, Emma's answer would not have included standing outside the auxiliary gym trying to gather enough courage to push through the door.

They were just girls, she told herself. Evil girls. Girls who despised Emma for existing in a world not big enough for all of them. Girls who carried the legacy of the world's worst basketball team ever. Girls. That's all they were. Nothing to be afraid of. Besides, she'd promised Riley.

Emma pushed through the door, sucking down one last breath of fresh air, and stepped into the gym. The panic attack started seconds later. Girls were everywhere. Okay, maybe not everywhere considering there were only seven other girls present, but having spent absolutely no time isolated in an all-girl environment, they might as well have been everywhere. Emma's heart pounded in her chest and her breathing shortened into rapid gasps. Was suffocation a normal reaction to the female population? The air must have been poisoned by *them*. With their designer clothes, painted faces and decorated claws, they acted as if they owned the place. She didn't belong in their world. Not with her baggy shorts, messy hair, and hand-me-down shoes, insignificant in every way except for maybe basketball.

Emma scolded herself silently. No way would she allow these girls to hold such power over her. She forced down a deep breath and ignored the voice in her head telling her to run while she still had the chance.

Coach Knowles and a handful of girls turned to stare at her as the door slammed closed.

Unlike the rest of the girls, Coach Knowles smiled at Emma, relief on her face. "Emma, it's good to see you."

Let the torture begin.

"What is *she* doing here?" Lauren asked, her tone filled with disgust.

31

Coach Knowles ushered Emma over, unable to resist giving her the head-to-toe assessment again. Her gaze fell to Emma's feet and settled there. "You're going to need new shoes at some point."

Emma's face burned as Lauren's laughter cut through Coach's final words. "The day Emma buys new shoes is the day her family starves."

Only a rich kid would find that comment funny. Once you experience a hungry stomach with only an empty plate to look forward to, all humor vanished. It didn't help to have to stare at all the top-of-the-line athletic shoes in the room and wish for a different life. They may not be able to play basketball if their lives depended on it, but they sure did look the part. As for Emma, she had no other choice but to play the hand she was dealt and not let Lauren beat her down before practice even started.

She straightened up and addressed Coach Knowles. "You get me as is, or you don't get me at all."

Coach smiled and patted her on the shoulder. "Welcome to the team."

The gym door banged open and the sound of running feet thudded against the wood floor. Emma turned, fearing more girls, and found herself face-to-face with Riley.

"What are you doing here?" she asked, overwhelmed by gratitude for his presence. Maybe he'd come to take her away. Maybe he'd talked to the boys' basketball coach and there was a place for her on their team after all. Anything was possible.

Without answering her question, Riley apologized to Coach Knowles and pulled Emma aside. "Here." He handed her a box—a shoebox.

"What's—" Comprehension dawned on Emma, and she shoved the box back into his hands. "No, I can't take these."

"They're from my parents."

She threw him a look, not believing his lie.

Riley rolled his eyes. "Okay, fine, they're from me, but

they wanted to help."

"I still can't take them." It was one thing to ask her dad for money to buy a pair of low-end shoes but completely different when her best friend and his parents bought them for her as an act of pity. Especially considering they'd never bought anything low-end in their lives and probably hadn't started with her. "No." She shook her head. "I'm sorry, I can't—"

"Emma." The force behind his voice silenced her. "No is not an option. You take these, you wear them, and you remember what I said the other day. Seize this opportunity. Hold nothing back."

She continued to stare at him. Accepting the shoes went against everything she'd ever promised herself regarding their friendship. She didn't want to be a nuisance or a charity case. Sure, she snatched fries from his plate at lunch sometimes and accepted small presents from him at Christmas, but a pair of brand-new shoes took things to a whole new level. No matter how desperate she was, it just didn't feel right.

He took a deep breath and exhaled through his nose, his patience wearing thin. "Fine. We'll figure out a way for you to pay us back through slave labor. Satisfied?"

"I guess." It wasn't a perfect solution, but she knew she needed shoes, and so far it was the only option she had. She accepted the box from Riley and opened it. Her first pair of brand-new shoes. Ever.

"I thought about getting you the pink ones," he said with a laugh, "but I figured you'd kill me, so I went with these instead."

Black was definitely better than pink and he was right, she would've killed him. The opportunity to thank him was interrupted by Lauren's screeching voice. "How sweet! Riley gave his charity case a new pair of shoes."

Riley, unfazed by Lauren's insult, kept his eyes on Emma and fought back a smile. "You're going to have your hands full."

Emma glared at him. She'd already had more of Lauren than she could endure and practice hadn't even started yet. "Just remember, you forced me into this."

"Don't hate me for too long." He squeezed her into a hug. "You've got this."

Overcome with appreciation for his friendship, Emma did something she'd never done before. Rising on her toes, she kissed his cheek. "Thank you."

What was that? she screamed at herself. Never in her life had she kissed him in any way, shape, or form, nor would she have if she'd put an ounce of thought behind her action. Sure, a sign of gratitude was required for his generosity, but how about a handshake, a punch on the arm, a head nod, a grunt? Not a kiss! It was such a girl thing to do. She almost died right then, wondering if Riley was two seconds away from calling off their entire friendship over a stupid kiss.

Riley's face turned red, and he cleared his throat. "I…uh…better get to practice."

Grrr. He was disgusted. She knew it. They were friends, yes, but not the kissing on the cheek kind. "Me, too," she muttered. It must have been the atmosphere. Outnumbered by girls high on emotions. Stupid girl behavior must be contagious.

She turned away to join the herd of girls, so she wouldn't have to watch Riley flee from the scene—flee from her.

"And Em?"

She spun back around, hoping he'd give her another chance to never gush with girly gratitude toward him again. "Yeah?"

He gave her a lopsided grin. "Try to be nice to the girls. Don't hurt any of them on your first day."

Four

Boys had tryouts.

Girls had practice.

During the first hour of practice, Emma gained a deeper understanding of what that meant. The losing history of the girls' team was not an incentive to spend every evening during the winter to be all you could be on the basketball court surrounded by girls who disgraced the name of the game with their lack of talent. And people wondered why Emma was so opposed to school athletics, especially girls' athletics.

She didn't know why she despised girls so much. Maybe it was because she had four brothers and didn't know any better. Maybe it was because she'd accidentally smacked Lauren in the head with a soccer ball during fourth grade PE class, and the girl and all her friends had hated her ever since. Or maybe her mom's abandonment had taught her to never trust the female population. Staring at the group in front of her failed to give Emma the boost of confidence she needed to even think about befriending these girls.

Coach Knowles waved her hands in the air. "Gather around everyone."

Eight girls. Final count. Barely enough for a complete team. If she hadn't promised Riley, Emma would have run out the door and never looked back. She pulled her eyes away from the exit sign and focused on Coach.

Coach Knowles looked barely old enough to have graduated from college with her big brown eyes, bobbing ponytail, and a smile that seemed to say the world was a super happy place 24-7! Talk about repulsive. The woman had no idea what she was getting herself into. Even a newbie could tell Jen Knowles had no real coaching credentials to her name. She didn't take charge, her presence did not demand respect, and it was questionable whether or not she would last an entire season.

Emma wasn't the only one who sensed Coach's let's-all-be-best-friends-forever attitude. Lauren and Madison did simultaneous eye rolls every five seconds as Coach droned on about how happy she was to be here and how great the season would be and how teamwork was the most important aspect of basketball. The Bradshaw girls' basketball team had eaten through more than their fair share of coaches over the years, and Jen Knowles was just one more coach passing through their school. The woman needed to wipe the smile off her face. Ten years of losing would not change just by her standing in front of them.

"Why don't we start off with some introductions?" Coach Knowles clapped her hands and turned to Emma with eyebrows raised, looking way too eager and way too clueless for the first day of practice.

Emma bowed her head, hating the way everyone thought saying your name in front of a group of people was the easiest task in the world. "I'm Emma," she mumbled.

"Poverty child," Lauren muttered.

Like Emma hadn't heard that one a million times before. At Bradshaw High School, ninety percent of the kids believed if your parents didn't earn triple digit salaries, you lived in extreme poverty and weren't worthy of attention. If she attended any other school, she may have had a shot at being normal, but with the whole single parent, hand-me-downs, hate-girls mentality, normal was out of the question.

Lauren's words were meant for everyone to hear and a few of the girls laughed as Lauren and Madison high-fived. Emma ignored them and waited for the attention to move to the next girl. Aside from Lauren and Madison, Emma didn't know any of their names, nor did she exert the effort to try to learn them. Poverty child. Loser. Poor girl. Tomboy. That's what they all knew of her. They were all label believers. Good. It was better that way. Less personal, more basketball. The last thing she wanted was to bond with any of them.

Warm up laps and stretches could be better defined as clique social time. Emma held back to gauge the rest of the girls, but considering she could walk faster than half of them ran, it wasn't long before she pulled in front of the pack without even trying. After the first lap, half the girls started walking. Walking! Like they were in some first grade PE class.

Dribbling drills came next. The object of the first drill was to dribble the ball from one end of the court to the other and back, remaining in control at all times. Bored already, she grabbed a ball from the rack and took her place in line. The first girl took off from the baseline. Emma had never played on an actual basketball team before, but she was pretty sure slapping at the ball wasn't considered dribbling, and if a person couldn't dribble without taking her eyes off the ball long enough to look for an open player, then it would be a long season for all of them.

Lauren and Madison fixated their destructive criticisms on the runt of the group. The runt could pass for a twelve-year-old kid. Maybe. The kid had yet to grow into her body and it showed. Trying to figure out how not to trip over her mammoth feet, the kid hit the ball off her foot after the second dribble and raced after it as it rolled the length of the gym. The girl tripped at the opposite baseline, and the ball, having bounced off the wall, rolled into her head. No wonder she was Lauren's pick of the litter.

Coach Knowles clapped her hands for each girl, shouting encouragement while the rest of the girls clustered in groups of two to continue their conversations from warm ups. Even if Emma had the urge to attempt civilized conversation with any of them, she knew she would get shot down faster than a hunted duck. Why were guys so much easier to be friends with? Forget friends, they were easier to associate with in general. Less judgmental, less critical, less evil. Sure, guys had a tendency to be cocky, conceited, and rude, but Emma still preferred them to girls any day.

Emma shook her head. *Kill me now,* she thought.

Basketball had never been something she could do halfway. It was all or nothing—for better or worse. She stepped to the line to take her turn and took off at a sprint, dribbling the ball with her right hand and then switching to her left on the return trip. She wasn't even breathing hard when she crossed the line.

The side conversations had ceased, and eight sets of eyes stared at her like she was a freak show at the circus. "What?" she asked.

"Showoff," Lauren muttered.

"Slacker," Emma shot back.

The next thing Emma knew, she was Jen Knowles' new coaching tool. For the rest of practice, Coach started every drill with, "Watch Emma."

"Watch Emma dribble."

"Watch Emma shoot."

"Watch Emma pass."

Watch Emma scream!

Being put on display like some prized honor student wasn't her idea of productive practice time, and it certainly wasn't the way to build team unity. Seriously, did the woman know anything about coaching? These girls wouldn't improve by watching Emma demo everything and then replicating her. They needed skills broken down and explained in detail at the kindergarten level. They needed individualized instruction, repetition, and discipline. No wonder Bradshaw was the worst team in the league.

The girls watched her execute every drill to perfection, but they proceeded to air ball half their shots, throw passes out of bounds, and trip over their own feet. Coach tried to give pointers to each girl, but they were all so incompetent, one comment did more harm than good.

By the time Coach put an end to her humiliation, Emma was ready to quit. She felt the resentment of every girl in the room, and if they hadn't hated her at the beginning of practice, they sure did now. Nothing was worse than a know-it-all.

Emma wouldn't last the week. Basketball she could handle. Guys she could handle. She could even handle her own family, but girls would destroy her.

Practice ended with a few harmless wind sprints. She thought half the girls were dying by the way they clutched their sides and groaned in pain every time down the court. Emma shook her head and laughed. She'd never heard anyone wheeze so loud before. Didn't they know ninety percent of basketball was running? It was day one of basketball practice. How would these girls survive the season?

The runt of the group was the quickest, but she tripped over her feet twice and face-planted both times. She almost fell a third time, but she grabbed at Emma for balance and saved herself. The same could not be said for Emma who sprawled across the floor, receiving floor burns on both elbows and knees.

"Sorry," the kid squeaked.

Emma growled in response. Pushing her body off the floor, she attempted to stand when something slammed into her from behind, sending her sprawling onto the floor again.

"Stay down, loser."

The voice was unmistakably Lauren's, as were the

hands that had shoved her. She jumped to her feet, ready to charge after Lauren and settle the score, but the freshman leaped in front of her.

"Don't do it." The kid's forehead scrunched with worry, her eyes wide with fear. "She's not worth it."

Emma's hands balled into fists and her body shook from the effort to cage her anger. If it weren't for the kid's voice reminding her of Riley's order not to hurt any of the girls on her first day, she wouldn't have thought twice about taking action.

She took a deep breath and exhaled loudly as she looked down at the kid staring up at her.

"I'm Ashley," the kid said, offering her hand to Emma.

"Stay out of my way." Emma pushed the kid aside without a handshake and resumed her sprints, staying clear of Lauren and the rest of the girls.

The whistle ending practice couldn't have come soon enough. Five minutes longer and Emma would have punched something. Or someone. Spending so much time with girls was hazardous to her sanity. It had to be. Gritting her teeth, she snatched her bag from the sideline and bolted for the exit.

The day had already surrendered to night, so the only light in the parking lot came from two lone streetlights. All she wanted was to get as far away from the girls as possible. She bowed her head against the wind and headed for home. A car horn honked twice before she looked up to place it. Riley's jeep was parked at the curb, his face lit by the interior dome light.

She practically sprinted to the getaway car. She threw her bag into the backseat before climbing into the passenger seat next to him.

He put the car in gear and stepped on the gas. "So, how was it?" When she kept her eyes fixed on the darkness beyond her window rather than answer, he risked a glance in her direction. "Ah, Em," he groaned. "Don't tell me you caused trouble on the first day."

Jerking upright in the seat, she shifted her body toward him. How dare he accuse her of causing trouble. If he wanted to blame someone, he could point his finger at the other seven girls and a coach. "I didn't cause anything. I told you they hated me and would never accept me as part of the team, and I was right. I mean, is it my fault I was the only one who could dribble the ball?"

Riley laughed. He had no idea. Even if she described practice in detail, he'd never believe how horrible the girls' team was and how they'd never win a game in a million years.

"This is all your fault." She slouched in her seat, regretting every second she'd spent holed up in the gym with all those girls. "I can't believe I let you talk me into this. Do you have any idea what it's like playing basketball with girls? It's an absolute nightmare."

"I don't know." He grinned at her. "I kind of like it."

She rolled her eyes. Riley's only experience with girls and basketball consisted of Saturday basketball games with her and the guys. Not a good comparison. "Trust me. No other girl out there is like me. They're prissy and conceited and have absolutely no athletic ability. And they complain about *everything*."

"Kind of like what you're doing now?" he teased.

She glared at him. "Not helping. In fact, I may not go back tomorrow."

"Whoa, okay." His hand shot over to grasp her arm. "I'm sorry."

She froze. His touch reminded her of her idiot kiss move earlier. All she could do was stare at his fingers on her arm, her cheeks burning in embarrassment, and hope he wouldn't feel the need to have a little heart-to-heart chat about what the kiss meant. It meant absolutely nothing.

"You're right," he said, breaking into her thoughts. It took her a second to realize he was talking about the girls and not agreeing with her about the kiss. "I don't know what it's like for you, but I'm sure it will get better."

"Doubt it," she mumbled, knowing she'd be at practice tomorrow and hating how Riley had so much power over her. "Why is this so important to you anyway? Considering it's my life, shouldn't I at least have a say in decisions affecting me?"

"Sorry," he said unconvincingly. "But you don't have the best judgment on what's best for you, which is why you have me. And I've told you why this is important; this could be your ticket out of here. I don't want to see you follow the same dead-end path as the rest of your family."

Emma tensed.

The smile faded from Riley's face, and his eyes shot in her direction. "I'm sorry, that came out wrong."

No member of her family was on the fast track to success. It was a fact, not a secret. But family was family. If she didn't defend them, who would? "My family's not all bad," she said quietly, keeping her focus on the floor. Sometimes it was difficult to see past Logan's passiveness or Lance's hatred of the world, and she couldn't remember the last time she'd spent five minutes of uninterrupted time with her dad. But they hadn't left her. That had to count for something.

"I know." Riley glanced over at her again. "I'm not all bad either. I just have dreams for your future."

She snorted. "My future." When she thought about her future all she saw was a job with a hair net and grease stains. Not exactly the dream occupation. She didn't have to look at Riley to know he was rolling his eyes, thinking very different things for her future.

"You'll see."

His tone made Emma look at him, believing for a moment that everything he dreamed for her could come true, that it was all within her grasp if she just reached for it. It was only an instant. The feeling disappeared when he pulled into the driveway of her house, and she watched Lance slam the front door and storm down the porch steps. He threw himself behind the wheel of his CR-X, which only worked half the time, and Emma heard the engine cough and sputter a few times before finally turning over. Gravel shot out from beneath the tires as he reversed and sped past Riley's jeep.

She saw her dad's silhouette in the window, his head bowed into his hands. Fighting with his son took more out of him than an entire day working two jobs. She longed to comfort him, to assure him everything would be all right and to tell him he wasn't the world's worst dad, but she remained beside Riley, staring in from the outside. Like always.

Five

Freshmen. Sophomores. Juniors. Seniors. Sometimes it felt like high school was nothing more than an experiment to see how kids survived when thrown together. Whether it was a fistfight, shouting match, or popularity contest, drama occurred daily in the hallways at Bradshaw High School. Today was no different.

Emma heard the commotion behind her and turned, expecting to find two girls high on ego fighting over boyfriends or stolen lipstick containers or whatever else girls fought about in school hallways. What she didn't expect to see was a face-off between two of her so-called teammates. Teammates or not, their disputes were none of her business. So why didn't she turn her back on them and head to class? Because she knew what it felt like not to be big enough or strong enough to fight her own battles. And yeah, maybe she was looking for an opportunity to confront Lauren face-to-face.

Ashley hadn't grown any in the past twenty-four hours. Cowering next to Lauren made her look even smaller. Whatever the reason for their argument, half the kids in the hallway had stopped to stare at the mismatched pair. Where were the teachers? Nowhere to be seen. Emma sighed and pushed through the wall of students. Grabbing the kid by the back of the shirt, Emma yanked her out from beneath Lauren's towering body to stand in her place. Maybe now it would be a fair fight.

"Problem?"

Lauren staggered back, no longer able to use her height to intimidate her prey considering Emma had her by an inch. Her eyes flickered between Emma, Ashley, and the witnesses surrounding them, regaining her composure before plunging ahead. "Not anymore. Team voted, and since she's nothing more than a hazard on the court, she's off the team," Lauren said, with a nod in Ashley's direction.

"Really?" Emma glanced toward the kid huddled next to the wall. "Because I don't remember casting a vote."

"Your vote doesn't matter. I know you think you're better than everyone else, but you're not." Lauren crossed her arms and shifted her weight to the side. "You're just a loser looking for handouts."

Bite tongue, breathe deep, and make sure fists remain at sides. Emma could always count on Lauren to make her feel like she never quite measured up. All Emma wanted to do was fulfill her promise to Riley with the least amount of trouble as possible, but Lauren wasn't making it easy. Ever since the whole soccer ball incident in elementary school, Lauren had made her life miserable, ridiculing her about everything from the state of her clothes to her lack of female know-how to her existence on earth. Over the years, she had learned to avoid Lauren, but being on the same team and enduring daily practices with her would take every scrap of control she could muster.

"You'll never be a part of this team." Lauren's voice dropped to a whisper, but it managed to hold onto its cold edge. "I don't care if you're Coach's pet and have all the right moves. This is my team, not yours."

"That's evident." Emma took a step forward, closing the distance between them. Just because she wasn't looking for trouble didn't mean she would remain silent forever.

45

"Because if it *was* my team, we'd actually win a game once in a while."

Lauren's scowl deepened. Did she really think the team was worth staking a claim on?

"If you want to kick the freshman off the team, I go too."

Lauren's shock melted into an evil grin. "Even better."

"Which would leave you with a total of six players, and based on what I've seen in practice, none of you would last through the first quarter of a game without substitutes." She shrugged like she didn't have a care in the world. "But who am I to point out the obvious?"

Despite Lauren's attempt at authority, fear flickered in her eyes. "Sometimes you need to cut the deadweight loose to start fresh."

Emma laughed. "The team's been overloaded with deadweight since you were a freshman, but if that's the approach you want to take, good luck losing every game. Again. I look forward to watching you uphold tradition." For someone who wanted nothing more than to walk away from the girls' team and never look back, Emma sure swayed the conversation in an undesirable direction. Not even Lauren wanted to spend another season as the worst team in the league. Whether she would admit it or not, Lauren needed Emma and the kid if she wanted any chance at winning a game or two this year.

Lauren didn't answer at first. She just glared at Emma, probably trying to decide how big of a hit her reputation would take if she admitted defeat in a hallway full of eager listeners. "Fine, have it your way. But don't think for a second anyone wants you or the disaster on the team."

Like that wasn't obvious enough already. "One more thing." Emma nodded toward the freshman. "Leave the kid alone. If you touch her again, you'll regret it." She really didn't care what happened to the kid with the mammoth feet, but she did care when people like Lauren bullied weaker kids.

Pushing Emma out of the way, Lauren stomped down the hall, her blonde hair swishing in her wake.

"Thanks," the kid said, appearing beside Emma.

Emma watched Lauren retreat down the hall, making sure she wasn't preparing for round two. "Don't mention it." The rest of the students in the hall dispersed, casting backward glances at her like she was the new kid overstepping her bounds.

"I'm not usually so clumsy." Ashley, unable to look Emma in the eye, wrung her hands and shifted her weight from one foot to the other. "I'm just nervous."

"Save it for someone who cares." Emma didn't want to hear excuses or give the kid a reason to continue talking. "Get to class."

Ashley scampered down the hallway, twisting around for one last look at Emma before she turned the corner and disappeared.

Emma spun in the opposite direction to get to her own class before the bell rang, and she collided with a body blocking her path. Strong hands caught and steadied her as she stumbled backward. She looked into a pair of blue eyes she'd know anywhere.

"What was that about?" Riley asked, nodding in the direction of the freshman.

"Nothing," she said, regaining her balance. "Just a little team disgruntlement."

"Who was the kid?"

"No one." It wasn't a complete lie. Ashley didn't register on Emma's radar of importance so she really was no one. No one she needed to be concerned about.

Or so she thought.

◆◆◆

After three days of practice, Emma continued to search in vain for any shred of progress among her teammates. Sure, Coach conducted a daily overview of fundamental skills, but her approach was exactly the same as if an algebra teacher conducted a brief overview of advanced logarithms and expected her students to ace the final exam, keeping a blind eye to their failing grades. The team hopped from one drill to the next as if the fast forward button was jammed in the on position. No progress, just gradual decline into the worst team imaginable.

Emma didn't know anything about coaching, but she knew basketball. The best way to master the sport was to start with the basics and build upward, taking as much time as necessary to master each skill before proceeding, not crossing your fingers and hoping everyone magically developed skills overnight. The more mistakes her teammates made, the harder she played.

On a standard play down the court, she snapped a pass to Madison on the left side. Although Madison's hands were ready for the pass, no defender in sight, the ball sailed through them and smacked her in the face. She froze from the shock of impact, and then whimpered a cry of pain. Were those real tears in her eyes? Seriously? Sure, with the velocity the ball had traveled it probably stung a little and half her face would be numb for a while, but come on. Getting punched in the face with an elbow or a fist hurt way worse, and Emma had endured it a half-dozen times without tears. Did girls really have such a low tolerance for pain?

Coach blew the whistle. The rest of the team huddled around Coach as she inspected Madison's face for any permanent damage.

Lauren didn't waste any time confronting Emma. "Good one, hotshot."

"Get out of my way," Emma said through clenched teeth. Three confrontations in two days. They would never survive the season as teammates.

"Or what?" Lauren challenged her. "Are you going to smack me in the face with a ball too?"

The mere thought put a smile on Emma's face. "I definitely wouldn't be opposed to it."

Lauren's eyes narrowed as she took another step toward Emma, their faces inches apart. "You're a joke," Lauren spit out. "No wonder your mom left you."

The smile fell off Emma's face, and her hands slammed into Lauren's chest. "Stay away from me."

Lauren stumbled backward. When she saw the rest of the girls watching them, her face scrunched up, preparing for tears. Tears she'd probably rehearsed hundreds of times to gain the sympathy vote. Girls! Such the drama queens.

"Hey." Coach stepped between them, her arms spread wide to prevent a full-on attack. "What's going on here?"

"She started it!" Lauren shrieked. "All I did was try and talk to her when she freaked out and pushed me."

Emma rolled her eyes. Great, just what she needed, to be responsible for the imprint of a basketball on the forehead of a girl who couldn't catch a simple pass and for starting a fight with the team bully. And people wondered why she hated girls.

Not a fan of conflict, Coach waved Lauren toward Madison and pulled Emma aside. Here it comes, Emma thought.

"Emma, you're an amazing basketball player, and you're looking great out there," Coach kept her voice down so others wouldn't hear, "but I need you to tone it down a few notches."

Emma's eyes narrowed into slits. "What?" If she toned it down any more she'd be moving in slow motion and lobbing passes to the moon.

"These girls aren't used to your," Coach paused, searching for the right word, "well, let's say, your enthusiasm."

"My enthusiasm?" Emma spit out. Enthusiasm was a

word to describe cheerleaders and little kids on a soccer field. It was not a word to describe basketball talent and an ability to pass the ball to a fellow teammate.

With a slight flinch, Coach nodded.

Emma had never heard of a coach asking a player to dumb down her skills for the betterment of a team. Unbelievable!

"You're kidding me, right?" Emma caught sight of Lauren's smug grin from a few feet away and snapped. "So, instead of having them step it up and actually catch a decent pass, you want me to stoop down to their level and play like a girl?" She didn't care about keeping her voice down. It wasn't like their lack of talent was a secret. "In case you missed it, at the level we're playing, we're going to get slaughtered in every game we play this year."

Coach winced at Emma's bluntness, but Emma didn't care. The woman needed to know the truth. Emma hadn't signed up for this girl-infested team with a goal to carry out the losing tradition. What would be the point?

Coach held up her hands, trying to calm Emma down. "I know. I don't like it any better than you do, but we're in a rebuilding year. What we need to do is take the team where it's at."

"A rebuilding year," Emma repeated. "In other words that will be our excuse for playing bad and losing, is that it?"

Coach didn't respond. Her eyebrows pinched together, and her eyes voiced a wordless apology.

Emma threw her hands in the air and took a step back. Apology not accepted. "Sorry, Coach. I can't play that way. Come find me when you're ready to play some real basketball." She walked out of the gym, feeling the stares on her back as she pushed through the door and slipped into the night without looking back.

◆◆◆

In no mood to go home, Emma found herself at the neighborhood court staring at the hoop from the free-throw line, looking for answers about what to do next. With no ball, and only the moonlight to accompany her, she couldn't even play away her frustrations.

Stupid girls' basketball team. She should've known playing with them wouldn't work. Unqualified coach, stuck-up girls, and a losing mentality—not something she wanted to be a part of. She'd made her decision to sever ties with the girls team as soon as she walked out of the gym—she was set on her decision—so why did it feel like she'd walked out on more than a worthless team?

She could act tough with Riley, she could lie to Coach, she could ignore just about anyone, but now, with no witnesses, Emma couldn't escape the truth. Was it wrong if a small part of her wanted it? To be part of a real team, to wear a real uniform, to play in a real game and feel like she belonged? Riley had said she wouldn't get a scholarship to play on a boys' basketball team, so would it be so horrible to get a scholarship to play on a, *gulp*, girls team? Would she even have a shot at the whole college thing? Was she delusional to think her future could possibly hold something other than living at home and working a dead-end job? She knew better than to let her thoughts drift in alignment with Riley's, knowing it would only set her up for disappointment, but she couldn't help it. A part of her wished and dreamed for the impossible, but it didn't matter. She'd just walked out on any chance she'd have to know.

Emma sighed. The team would be better off without her anyway. Less team conflicts, less injuries. They'd probably throw a party now that she was gone.

She sat cross-legged on the free-throw line, trying not to notice how the darkness crept closer. It always crept closer. Over the years, she had spent too many nights trying to ward off the darkness as she waited in vain for her mom to come home, listened to her dad and brothers fight, and tried to understand why bad things always happened to her. Even now, she couldn't manage to keep the darkness—the guilt, the resentment, the unsettling truth—away. She should have been relieved to finally be done with the girls and the team, so why did her body tense and her teeth clench together at the thought of Coach's this-is-a-rebuilding-year speech?

Before she could formulate an answer, headlights ripped through the darkness and illuminated her before going black. She heard a car engine cut off, a door open and close, and the shuffle of footsteps across the pavement.

"Em? Is that you?"

She should've known Riley would find her. He must have a tracking device on her or something. Was it wrong to prefer loneliness and darkness to her best friend? Riley would want answers—answers she didn't want to defend right now.

"What are you doing here?" he asked, his tone thick with concern. "Did you get out of practice early?"

"Nope."

"You okay?"

"Never better."

"Then what's going on?"

She stood so they'd be at the same level, and he wouldn't tower over her when she broke the news to him. No matter what words she used, he wouldn't like what she had to say. She took a deep breath, her head tilting to the side, feigning indifference. "I quit."

"What do you mean you quit?"

She crossed her arms and held his gaze. "I mean, I quit."

Quitting the team had been the right thing to do, she knew it, but facing Riley and seeing the anger and disappointment twist his face was too much.

He grabbed her arm as she started to turn away from him. "Why?"

She shrugged, determined not to care, determined not to let him make her second-guess her decision. "It wasn't working out for me."

"How about you break it down for me a little more than that?" His fingers tightened around her arm, so she couldn't pull away. Even in the dark she could see his eyes narrow and his face harden. After all the effort it took for him to persuade her to actually join the team, and now he learned it had all been in vain. He hated failure.

"It's a rebuilding year." A death sentence for any team. Riley knew that. Merely saying the words brought a sour taste to her mouth. "No one expects us to win; no one even expects us to play well. Coach Knowles told me to tone it down. She's put training wheels on every single player and refuses to take them off. She's enabling them to be losers, and I refuse to be a part of it." Despite her effort to keep her tone light and uninterested, she heard the harshness in it.

His head tilted to the side and he looked at her through squinted eyes. "Did she actually say that?"

"Pretty much."

He frowned and exhaled through his nostrils. "Well, she's in a tough position, and she's probably trying to figure it all out."

She jerked her arm out of his grasp and stepped away from him. "Why does it not surprise me that you'd defend her?"

"I'm not defending her, I'm just—"

"I just smacked some girl in the face with a ball because she couldn't catch a standard pass!" she shouted, knowing he didn't understand the full extent of her situation. He'd glorified her role on the team and never stopped to gain a clear insight into what she endured every day she played with the stupid, untalented, good-for-nothing group of girls. He could play full-out at practice and not worry about holding back because the guys on his team could actually catch the ball. Emma refused to spend the entire season capping her ability in fear of hurting a girl who couldn't catch the stupid ball. It wasn't worth it. "The team is a joke. None of those girls want to be there. If they did, they wouldn't treat practice like some social event. I promised you I'd join the team to play basketball, not to humiliate myself and waste my time. I'm sorry, Riley," she said coldly. "It's over."

He shook his head and exhaled a laugh of disgust. "You sure this isn't just an excuse for you?"

She jutted out her chin in defiance. "What's that supposed to mean?"

He closed the distance between them and when he spoke, his words came out low and harsh. "The Emma I know isn't a quitter. So the team is worse than you thought." He shrugged. "Big deal. You have so much to offer them, and if you took a step back and stopped being so selfish, you'd see that and wouldn't be trying to run away. They need you, and you know it. You're not mad, you're scared."

"I am *not* scared." Annoyed, yes. Frustrated, absolutely. But scared? Not a chance. Riley didn't believe her. One look at his face, and Emma's temper took over. "What do you know about anything?" She shoved him away from her. "You say I have so much to offer them, but I don't. So what if I can play basketball? Those girls despise me more for it. If anything, the team is better off without me."

"Emma—" he said, reaching for her.

"No." She held up her hand to cut him off and reinforce the invisible barrier between them. "I don't want to hear it. I know you had big dreams for me on this team, but I'm done. You can't make me go back."

He didn't respond. Sometime in the last five minutes the night air had turned cold and chills sprouted on her skin, but she didn't move to dig her sweatshirt out of her bag or suggest they continue their argument indoors. She just stood there, staring at him, staring at her.

What next?

Her answer came when another car pulled into the parking lot beside Riley's jeep. The headlights illuminated the court before shutting off.

Now what? Emma wanted to scream. Since when did people congregate at night on an empty court? Was nowhere private?

They broke their staring contest to focus on the new intruder crossing the court toward them.

"I'm sorry, is this a bad time?"

Emma groaned. Coach Knowles. The last person she wanted to see. "Actually, it is."

"No, it's a fine time." The kindness in Riley's voice cancelled Emma's bitterness. "In fact," he glared at Emma to tell her to behave and play nice, "I was just leaving."

"No," Emma and Coach Knowles said together. Emma grabbed his forearm and pulled him back beside her. He may drive her crazy sometimes, but no way was he going to leave her to face Coach on her own.

Coach held up a hand to stop any further plans of his retreat. "Stay, please." She turned her focus on Emma. "I came to apologize to you, Emma. You were right."

"She was?" Riley asked in surprise.

"I was?" Emma repeated. She had opinions. Lots of opinions. She could voice them all night if she wanted, but no one ever listened to her, and no one ever told her she was right.

"When I took this job, everyone told me I was crazy. They said the team was beyond help, and I was setting myself up for failure, but I didn't care. All I wanted was to make a difference. I thought I could come in here and be this amazing coach and change everything around like you see in the movies." Coach Knowles shook her head and laughed. "The truth is, I'm in way over my head and have no idea what I'm doing."

"I've noticed," Emma mumbled.

"Emma," Riley snapped, elbowing her in the side.

"What?" Coach's confession confirmed Emma's assumption that Jen Knowles had not been hired because of any outstanding qualifications. The woman had probably been the only person to apply for the job. "You'd notice too if you spent an hour at our practices."

"Look, I know I'm not your ideal coach, but I do care about this team." Coach raised her eyebrows knowingly. "Based on how you walked out today, I know you do too, which is why I need your help."

What was this crazy woman talking about? Emma walked out because she *didn't* care about the team. She cared about basketball, and she wasn't about to rejoin the team as Coach's little helper. "You don't need my help. You just want a star player for your team."

Coach nodded. "You're right."

Those words again. Emma wished she'd stop saying them. They just didn't sound…right.

"But," Coach said, her best-friends-forever attitude forgotten, "what you call a star player, I call a leader. If we want any chance to win this season, I need *you* to be the team leader."

Emma remembered Mr. Ledger voicing similar words two weeks ago, but coming from Jen Knowles they sounded more like a cry for help than a rallying of the troops. Regardless, Emma didn't want to be the team leader, she just wanted to play.

Coach Knowles took a deep breath and stood up straighter. "I'm here to ask for your patience and for your trust. You keep doing what you're doing, and I'll do my best to bring the team to your level." She smiled at Emma. "You're ten times the player I ever was, so if there is anything you can do to help the team, I'd appreciate it. And if you gave the girls a chance, I'm sure they'd appreciate it too. It can't be easy on them either, playing with a girl as talented as you."

Emma snorted in protest, causing Riley to elbow her in the side again. She couldn't help it. She was a player, not a coach or a hand holder. No matter how much talent Emma did or didn't have, the girls on the team hated her. Even if she did try to give them pointers, they'd never listen to her anyway.

"Will you come back to the team?" Coach asked, the pleading evident in her tone. "Please?"

"I—"

"Yes," Riley said, cutting her off. He plastered a huge smile on his face, like he'd just been awarded a full-ride scholarship to play collegiate basketball. "She'll come back."

Emma slapped his stomach with the back of her hand. His smile widened, and he wrapped his arm around her shoulders. "I promise she'll behave from now on."

Yeah, right, Emma thought, rolling her eyes as Coach Knowles laughed.

"You do know you have to start with the basics, right?" Emma asked.

Coach nodded.

"And you're going to have to lose your best-friends-forever attitude," Emma said. "We don't need a friend. We need a coach."

Coach raised her eyebrows. "Does that mean I'll see you at practice tomorrow?"

They both waited for her to answer. Knowing she was outnumbered and Riley would never forgive her if she said no, Emma closed her eyes and bit her lip before saying, "Yes, I'll be there."

Riley squeezed her to him and kissed the top of her head. "That's my girl."

Enough with the kissing already!

Sure, Emma had kissed his cheek in a moment of weakness when he'd given her new shoes, but she'd been surrounded by hoards of girls and the air had been poisoned by their irrational emotions. What was Riley's excuse? She tried to inch away from him and put distance between them, but his arm remained firm around her shoulders.

"Okay, then, I'll see you tomorrow." With a wave of relief, Coach Knowles retreated to her car.

Riley, his anger forgotten, smirked at her.

"Stop it," Emma said, not in the mood for him to gloat.

If she thought things would be easier because of her little chat with Coach, she was wrong. They only got worse.

Six

Gone was Coach's let's-just-be-friends smile. Gone were the extended water breaks. Gone was the complacency for tardiness, laziness, and passiveness. The solution for girls who didn't perform to standard during practice? Wind sprints. The punishment for girls who talked out of turn? Wind sprints. The penalty for anything Coach didn't appreciate? Wind sprints. *About time*, Emma thought as her feet thudded on the gym floor along with the rest of the team.

Two short bursts sounded from Coach's whistle, indicating an end to their sprints. Then the fun began. They didn't jump into scrimmaging or learning some complicated play most of the girls wouldn't understand. Instead, they learned to dribble one bounce at a time in the auxiliary gym.

The auxiliary gym was located in the back corner of the school and had been left off the school's renovation plan. Unlike the main gym with its new paint, new wood floor, and new equipment, the auxiliary gym looked the same as it did forty years ago. Instead of the traditional school colors of fire-engine red and white—bold colors inspiring students to seize the day and live up to their potential—the colors of the walls and floor had faded to red-orange and yellow. The lights overhead cast an even duller yellow tinge on the space, and the smell of sweat and old shoes choked the air. At least the gym had hoops. Hoops with nets so old they looked like they would disintegrate with one swishing three-pointer.

The only thing the auxiliary gym was used for was to hide the school's disgraces. In other words, it was the perfect place to exile the girls' basketball team so no one had to see them, hear them, or think about them. They didn't deserve anything better until they won. While the boys' basketball team practiced in the main gym on the opposite side of campus, Emma was stuck with girls in the secondhand gym. No quotes or posters promoted teamwork or inspired students to dream and achieve. It was just aging bricks and mortar. What more did a losing team of eight girls need?

Several times during practice, Emma and Coach Knowles exchanged glances. Coach's look was always part apology for the lack of talent on the team and part fear Emma would bolt from practice again. She shouldn't feel pity for the woman. Jen Knowles had willingly applied for the position, but she had no idea how to coach effectively. She tried hard—too hard—to make practice go smoother, to make the girls learn faster, to make herself coach better. At least Emma wasn't the only one struggling.

Less than twenty-four hours ago, Coach Knowles had stood on Emma's neighborhood court, begging her to come back to the team and do what she could to help. Well, in Emma's opinion, the team was beyond help. Or maybe she didn't want to waste the energy it would take to bring the girls up to par. Either way, she remained silent and let Jen Knowles do the coaching. Sure, there were lots of dropped passes, lots of missed shots, lots of out of control dribbles, but they never moved past basketball basics: ball handling, passing, shooting, and defense. Maybe Jen Knowles did a Google search on proper coaching techniques. Who knew? Whatever she did, Coach Knowles had stopped making excuses and started being a coach.

By the end of practice, the girls actually seemed to know what the game of basketball was all about. Maybe this team of girls was capable of progress after all. Even if it did occur in slow motion.

◆◆◆

Practice finally ended, the weights of restriction lifting. The rest of the team shuffled out of the gym, and Emma sighed in relief. Finally. Peace and quiet. Without girls.

Standing in the middle of the court with a ball under her arm, she took a deep breath and closed her eyes. No feet thudded against the gym floor, no squeals pierced the silence, and no complaining polluted the air. If she listened hard enough, she could almost hear the distant notes of the pep band, the cheers from the crowd, and the yells from Coach creating the soundtrack for Bradshaw's battle for victory against an opposing team. She could only imagine what it would be like to play in a real game against a real team with an actual scorekeeper. In little more than a week, she would know. Until then, she could only dream.

Opening her eyes, she dribbled the ball and listened to it pound against the floor, the sound echoing in the space around her. She had never had a gym to herself before. She could dribble, shoot, and run around like a lunatic and no one would be there to pass judgment on her.

So that's what she did.

Guarded by invisible defenders, she jabbed and spun, guiding the ball from one end of the court to the other. She split the defense and avoided traps, beating her opponents with the double crossover, the two-step, the fake pump, and every other move she knew. No matter where she shot from—from inside the key or from the three-point line—the ball fell through the hoop with nothing but the swish of the net in its wake. Family problems, girl drama, and all tension melted away as basketball allowed her to escape from her world and find peace.

Sweat poured down her face as she played. She loved competing with the guys and feeling the sting on her hand when they high-fived her, standing firm when their bodies slammed into hers, hearing their laughter and shouts when they teased her. But here and now, in the solitude of a secondhand gym, no guy impeded her movements. Here and now, with swift feet and a perfect shot, she felt graceful.

She took one final shot from the three-point line. Her wrist, snapped in follow-through, hung in the air as she watched her shot drop. Nothing but net.

Emma didn't sprint after her ball. She didn't pluck it from the ground and plop it on the rack in haste. Instead, she scooped it from the floor, smoothed the worn leather with her hands and smiled at it like it was an old friend.

Trusting the ball would be there for her tomorrow, she set it on the rack. She turned to walk across the gym and retrieve her bag from the bleachers, hoping to relish in her newfound peace for at least five more minutes, but movement caught her eye. Perched at the top of the bleachers was Ashley, her beady eyes fixated on Emma. Emma's smile vanished. Her peace? Gone.

This is *so* not happening.

The little sneak! She'd been there the entire time, tucked into a corner of the wooden bleachers, watching Emma act like an obsessed basketball loser. So much for privacy. The kid better not be here under the delusion they were friends. Aside from saving the freshman from Lauren's wrath, Emma had given no indication they should be friends, and she wasn't about to start now. Deciding it was best to ignore her unwanted gawker, Emma continued on her path across the gym to the bottom bleacher where she pulled on a sweatshirt with super speed.

The kid scooted down the bleachers one at a time, inching her way toward Emma. Emma's skin crawled as

Ashley continued to gawk at her.

Despite a week of practices and Coach's increased efforts, the freshman was still the worst basketball player Emma had ever seen, but it wasn't due to lack of trying. Some people just had the talent, and some people didn't. Ashley didn't.

"You're an amazing basketball player," Ashley said.

"If you say so."

"How did you get to be so good?"

Unnecessary awe radiated from Ashley's voice, irritating Emma further. "It's called practice." She zipped her bag and slung it over her shoulder. The faster she could escape, the better.

Ashley scurried down the remaining bleachers and hopped onto the floor, where she tripped and fell in front of Emma. Emma shook her head and stepped over Ashley's sprawled body, heading for the door. She didn't make it. The kid jumped in front of her, blocking her exit route.

"Wait," Ashley gasped.

Emma could pulverize the freshman with one swipe of her hand, but she refrained, not wanting to have a mess to clean afterward.

"I know I'm not very good at basketball," Ashley said quickly, brushing strands of hair away from her face. "Compared to you I'm probably the worst player in the world. You make everything look so easy. I would give anything to have an ounce of your talent. I watch you every day at practice and try to copy you, but I always mess everything up. You're way better than Lauren or any of the other girls on the team, but I think we have a good shot at going all the way this year with you on the team, and—"

Emma rolled her eyes to the ceiling. She had a feeling this kid could and would go on for hours. "Do you have a point to all this or are you just wasting my time?"

Ashley looked Emma in the eye, and with as much courage as her little body could muster, she took a deep breath and said, "I want you to coach me."

Well, that was unexpected. Emma laughed. "I don't think so."

"Why not?"

"Because I don't know anything about coaching, that's why."

Ashley plunged ahead, not caring about Emma's lack of coaching credentials. "You don't have to teach me much, just a few things, so I'm not a complete failure in case I ever get to play in a real game. I know, I know, that's not likely going to happen, but what if?" Her eyes glazed over and strayed from Emma's, obviously absorbed in some twisted what-if scenario. "What if for some reason I'm the only one left on the bench and Coach puts me in?"

Then we're doomed, Emma thought.

Ashley snapped out of her trance. "I can't lose the game for everyone."

"Sorry," Emma said, without a shred of sympathy. "I don't give private lessons." She sidestepped around Ashley and headed for the door.

"Please," Ashley begged. "I'll pay you."

Emma whirled around. The mention of money was not a way to entice her. Just because she was poor didn't mean she could be bought. "Is this some kind of joke?" she spit out. To think this freshman would stoop so low sickened her. It was the type of thing Lauren would orchestrate to humiliate her.

"No, no joke." Ashley shook her head, her eyes widening. "I'll do anything. Please."

The sincerity in Ashley's voice was unmistakable, but Emma still wasn't convinced. "Why me? Don't you get enough from practice?"

"Have you seen me play? I need a lot more help than two hours a day."

Emma forced back a smile. She knew more than most how much more help Ashley needed.

"Please," Ashley whined. "I'm begging you."

No one could look as pitiful as Ashley did. It was just plain sad. The kid was all knobby knees, bony arms, and milk-white skin. Her big brown eyes pleaded with Emma. Innocence. When Emma looked into the kid's eyes, all she saw was innocence. Innocence Emma had long forgotten. Add that to the kid's obvious interest in learning Emma's beloved sport, and her heart softened a little around the edges. For some unknown, stupid, sappy girl reason, Emma couldn't find the words to turn the kid down.

She scolded herself silently then took a deep breath and tried to gain a clear perspective of the situation. She didn't know the first thing about coaching, but maybe if she spent a couple hours with Ashley, the kid might be less of a hazard on the court. She certainly couldn't get any worse. Besides, Emma wouldn't be able to stand it if the kid cried because of her. The way her chin wobbled, tears weren't too far away. "Lauren or anyone else hasn't put you up to this, have they?"

Ashley shook her head.

Emma sighed, knowing she was about to make the biggest mistake of her life. "Okay, fine. I'll teach you a few things."

A high-pitched shriek erupted from Ashley as she threw herself at Emma and wrapped her scrawny arms around Emma's waist. "Thank you, thank you, thank you!"

"Okay, okay." Emma tried to wriggle free, noticing there was more strength in this tiny figure than she'd originally thought. "Get off me."

Ashley laughed but released Emma and stumbled backward. She shoved her hand into her bag and pulled out her wallet.

Emma grabbed Ashley's wrist. Not hard enough to leave bruises, but hard enough to relay to the freshman the seriousness of her next statement. "Rule number one, I don't take your money. Rule number two, you do what I say when

I say it. Rule number three, you tell no one about this. Got it?" No way would Emma allow this kid to humiliate her in any way, shape, or form.

"Yes, anything," Ashley said, not threatened at all. "When do we start?"

Emma sighed, wondering how much she'd regret this arrangement later. "When do you want to start?"

"Now?"

Emma laughed, knowing Ashley was completely serious. As tempting as the immediate start time didn't sound, she needed a break from girls and prep time to figure out how to deal with one on an individualized basis for any length of time. "How about tomorrow after practice?"

♦♦♦

Emma didn't know anything about coaching. Everything she'd learned about basketball she'd learned from Riley and his dad. The Ledgers had moved in down the street when Emma was nine. The day after they arrived, Riley appeared in his driveway next to a portable basketball hoop, dribbling a basketball and putting up shots like nothing else in the world mattered. She rode her bike, or rather one of her brother's bikes, back and forth in front of his house, checking out the new kid before her brothers got to him and turned him against her. Her brothers had never been keen on sharing their friends with their little sister, so the only way Emma had a shot at befriending the boy was to reach him first.

As soon as he saw her, Riley gave her the head-to-toe look-over, assessing her assessing him. She could only imagine what he must have seen: a girl with holey jeans, hair askew, and dirt smeared across her face and caked under her chipped fingernails. She expected him to insult her and shoo her away like a stray cat, but he surprised her.

He looked at the basketball in his hands and then

squinted back at her. "You play?"

Did watching her brothers count? Rather than answer verbally, she shrugged.

"Well, do you wanna play?" he asked tentatively.

She shrugged again, not wanting to appear desperate for his friendship. "Sure."

Emma hopped off her bike and joined him in his driveway.

He passed her the ball. "I'm Riley, by the way."

"I'm Emma."

They took turns shooting—Riley making all of his shots and Emma missing all of hers. A few minutes later they heard a deep chuckle behind them.

"I'm gone for five minutes, and you've already found yourself a girlfriend?"

"Dad," Riley groaned. "Emma's not my girlfriend. She's a basketball player."

"Emma, is it?" Mr. Ledger looked into her eyes, like she was a real person, and extended his hand to shake hers. "Nice to meet you."

Riley could have told his dad she was Superman, and it would have had the same effect on her. It made her stand a little taller, raise her chin a little higher, and feel like she could take on the world. For the first time in her life, she wasn't a stupid girl or a little sister or a brat. She was a basketball player; she had a purpose. She liked the way it sounded. Right then and there, Emma decided she would do whatever it took to be a basketball player. It didn't hurt that Riley's dad wanted Riley to be the best, and for him to be the best, he had to play against the best. So that's what Riley and his dad did—they made Emma into the best basketball player they could.

Whether it was their shared love of basketball, an only child's desire for a sibling, or a lonely girl's need for a friend, Riley and Emma had been inseparable ever since.

Now, trying to figure out how to teach the game she

only knew how to play, she tried to remember how Mr. Ledger had taught her. Patience, humor, and the loving touch of a father. He'd shown her how to hold the ball for a shot, how to absorb the ball into her hands to dribble rather than slap at it, how to face an opponent without fear. Mr. Ledger showed her all the things her dad never had time to teach her.

Somehow, during those basketball lessons, Emma learned to trust the Ledgers more than her own family. Maybe it was because the Ledgers gave her cherry popsicles and warm-baked cookies, reassuring smiles and high fives. Maybe it was because Riley made her laugh, and his parents always seemed happy to see her. Sometimes it felt wrong to go to Mr. and Mrs. Ledger when she had a question or problem only a parent could answer rather than to her own dad; sometimes it felt wrong that she felt safer with Riley than her own brothers. After all, families were supposed to stick together. Maybe her parents saw how she sometimes wished she were a Ledger rather than a Wrangton; maybe that's why her mom left and her dad pushed her away.

Emma shook her head. The past was the past. What she needed to do now was figure out a way to teach the freshman how to play basketball.

The school day passed and she still hadn't formulated a plan. Ashley, attaching herself to Emma's side throughout their entire team practice, as if fearing Emma would forget about their deal, didn't help. Talk about suffocation. If the kid could actually dribble without tripping and taking everyone else down with her, it may not have been so bad, but as it was, Emma had tripped over her twice already.

Practice finally ended, but Emma didn't start her individualized instruction with Ashley until everyone left the gym. Ashley was entirely focused. On Emma. Like Emma was a professional basketball player or something. Completely annoyed, Emma hoped she'd survive their one-on-one practice without strangling the kid.

Ashley was small for her age in size and shape, and she was limited in experience. She hadn't figured out how to use her boney elbows to gain respect on the court, so everyone jostled her. It didn't help that Ashley always managed to put her body in the line of action and get run over. The shortest distance between two points was a straight line, but Ashley needed to learn how to take the scenic route to the basket once in a while.

Emma didn't have a clue where to start with the disaster standing in front of her. Taking a deep breath, she held a basketball in front of Ashley's face, hoping words would come if she started talking. "This," she said, "is a basketball." A person couldn't get any more basic than that.

Ashley stared at the ball, her eyebrows arched over wide eyes, her lips slightly parted, and she leaned slightly forward as if smelling a flower.

"You control the basketball." Emma held the ball against Ashley's stomach. "The basketball does not control you. Got it?"

Ashley nodded.

Having seen Ashley's lack of talent in practice, Emma started with the absolute basics to get the kid used to having a ball in her hands without fumbling it. For the next two hours (*two hours!*) Emma taught Ashley how to dribble. Not between the legs or behind the back or some fancy trick move that would end in tragedy, but the basic one dribble at a time. Left hand, right hand, straight line, zigzag, waist high, knee high. In two hours, Ashley became a dribbler.

"How far away from school do you live?" Emma asked as they returned the basketballs to the rack.

Ashley shrugged. "About a mile."

"Do you usually take the bus?"

Ashley nodded. "Except on Friday's when my mom brings me."

"Starting tomorrow you walk to school and dribble a basketball the entire way. Dribble with your right hand half way and then switch to your left. Got it?" Emma expected the kid's jaw to drop in shock or for high-pitched complaints to come spouting out of her mouth, but Ashley just nodded again like Emma's demands made total sense. What would motivate a freshman to sacrifice her leisure bus rides to school in exchange for a one-mile dribble trek without complaint?

"Except on Fridays," Emma threw in. What she wouldn't give to have Friday morning commutes with her own mom. "You can have Friday's off. Okay?"

Another nod. Emma got the distinct feeling she could tell this kid to jump off a bridge into ice cold water every morning, and she'd do it.

"Thank you," Ashley said. "I've learned so much from you. I already feel like a better player."

"Yep."

Ashley may have felt like a better player, but she still had a *long* way to go.

"I mean it," Ashley said, lighting up like a six-year-old at Christmas. "You're an amazing coach."

Emma scowled at the freshman. "I'm not a coach."

Coaches—good coaches—played a significant role in the life of an athlete. They built people into players, guiding them to be better and do better, training them to overcome whatever obstacles tried to take them down. Coaches inspired and motivated a team to unite together and strive for perfection. It took a better person than Emma to be a coach, and just because she taught the kid a few skills didn't mean she was a coach. Not even close.

◆◆◆

Emma didn't live far from school. It wasn't a hop, skip, or jump away, but when she didn't have a car, a bike, or even a skateboard, walking was the next best thing. The darkness never scared her. She knew how to kick and scream and throw a decent punch, and unless someone needed the day's Physics notes, no one would attack a girl who possessed no money or valuables. Her lack of appeal was good considering she'd just endured a full school day, a two-and-a-half-hour team practice, and another two-hour practice with Ashley. Yes, *two hours!* She had only planned to stay for twenty minutes tops, but when she looked at the clock, two hours had passed. Her legs felt like rubber, her arms like dead weights, and her backpack seemed to weigh five hundred pounds. By the time she approached the driveway to her house, her eyes were half closed and her feet shuffled along the ground.

"Hey."

One word, plus the silhouette of a person popping out from behind the bushes in front of her house when the world was pitch black, caused Emma to jump back in alarm. It wasn't an overreacting girly response complete with some high-pitched scream—no way would she sink to that level—but it was the response of any normal person being attacked at night. Her hand curled into a fist and her arm pulled back ready to swing at her attacker, when she recognized Riley's face. "Geez," she gasped, clutching his arm. "Could you not scare me to death next time?"

Moonless night and a boy dressed in black jumping out from the bushes wasn't her idea of an acceptable greeting.

"Wasn't practice over three hours ago?" Riley demanded. "Why are you home so late?"

"What are you, my warden?"

He just stared at her, waiting for an answer.

Riley was the last person she wanted to tell about how her post-practice time was now devoted to babysitting some incompetent freshman girl and teaching her the fundamentals of basketball. It would be like telling him she had to be tutored in remedial math as a senior. He would laugh, he would accuse her of growing soft, or worse, he would actually agree with the whole arrangement. A true confession was not in her best interest. She stifled a yawn. "I had stuff to do."

"What kind of stuff?"

She shrugged. "Stuff. What's with the interrogation?"

"You're not two-timing me, are you?"

Two-timing? Was he serious? She squinted at him, trying to see if he was joking, but it was hard to tell in the dark. "What kind of question is that?"

He shrugged, not in a nonchalant way, but in an I-know-you're-hiding-something kind of way. "Depends on what kind of answer you give."

"My answer hasn't changed," she said flatly, rolling her eyes and pushing past him. She was too tired to play his ridiculous games, especially after spending two hours with a freshman. Riley and Emma were friends. Aside from all the recent kissing action, there'd never been anything more than friendship between them, and two-timing didn't exist with friends.

"So, does that mean you haven't found yourself a boyfriend?" He didn't bother trying to block her way into the house, knowing she would spin around and retrace her steps to face him.

She opened her mouth to speak, but no words came out. How was she supposed to respond to that question? Boyfriend? Where in the world did he get such an absurd idea?

He leaned toward her. "Because if you've found yourself a boyfriend, I need to meet him and put him through the worthy test."

She crossed her arms and raised her eyebrows. This ought to be good. "The worthy test?"

"Yes, the worthy test."

He was completely serious. They'd had a lot of conversations throughout their eight years of friendship and they'd covered a lot of topics, but worthy tests were definitely not among them. Now, as he plunged them into new territory, her curiosity peaked. "Which is?"

"You know, the general Q&A." He started counting on his fingers. "What is his motive for dating you, what are his intentions, and how well *he thinks* he knows you? If he passes, I will guide him through the proper steps on how to court you, and I will personally chaperone all interactions between the two of you for evaluation purposes until he can be trusted."

She laughed. Number one, the thought of a boy liking her in a girlfriend sort of way was crazy. She knew way too much about guys to think of them as potential dating material, and she wasn't exactly girlfriend material herself. Number two, the idea of Riley as the date patrol was hysterical. She could picture it in detail, and knew he would live up to his threats. He'd dress all in black in an attempt to look threatening; he'd have a pen and notebook in hand, which he would continuously scribble in to make her nervous, not to mention his annoying pen clicking habit; he would disagree with whatever her alleged boyfriend said or did; and after his thorough evaluation, Riley would determine the guy could not be trusted, thus fulfilling his role as her protector.

Note to self, in the extremely rare event a boy was interested in her, Riley did not have need-to-know clearance.

All she could do was stare at him. "You are unbelievable."

"So, no boyfriend?"

"No, no boyfriend," she assured him. Was it her imagination or did Riley actually exert a sigh of relief?

He crossed his arms, and his eyes narrowed, studying her. "But you still won't tell me."

She shook her head. "There's nothing to tell."

His shoulders slumped forward, his arms dropping to his sides. "I thought we were friends." He bowed his head and pushed his bottom lip out just enough to look completely crushed. "Best friends."

No way was she going to let him make her feel guilty, no matter how pitiful he looked. "We *are* friends. *Best* friends." Failing to keep a smile off her face, Emma pushed him in the chest.

Laughing, he reached out and grabbed her around the waist to prevent himself from stumbling backward. "No matter what?"

"No matter what," she confirmed, trying to figure out why her heart rate accelerated when he pulled her against him.

"Promise?" He rested his forehead against hers and stared into her eyes, as if daring her to lie to him.

Trapped in his arms, she couldn't do anything except promise. "Yes, I promise." She pulled her face away from his, wanting him to take her seriously. The last thing she wanted was for him to start snooping around. "But that doesn't mean there's anything to tell."

He didn't believe her. Doubt was written all over his face. "Okay." He shrugged in defeat. "I guess you're entitled to your privacy."

"Yes, I am."

She had endured way too much girl time within a twenty-four hour period and still had homework to complete before tomorrow, not to mention strategizing on how to keep a secret from her best friend. "Goodnight, Riley." She broke free from his grasp and headed toward the house.

"I'll find out eventually," he warned. "You know I will."

Not if I can help it, she thought. Without turning back, she raised her arm in farewell.

He waited until she reached the front door before getting in his last words. "And when I do, it better not be a boyfriend."

Seven

Dinner at the Wrangtons' consisted of either fend for yourself, or on the rare occasion her dad bought fast food, like tonight, it was dumped in the middle of the table for a first-come-first-served knockout. Emma's block out skills were perfected around the table as she fought her brothers for food. If all else failed, one quick swipe of her hand through a hole could snatch her at least enough food to ward off hunger pains for the night. She'd learned the hard way about the consequences of missing a meal, but tonight food wasn't her top priority.

"So, Dad." Emma tried to sound as casual as possible, but even she could hear her voice shake. "I made the basketball team at school."

Lance snorted as he shoved a piece of chicken in his mouth. "Big deal. The girls' team sucks." He pushed away from the counter and rammed his shoulder into hers as he passed her on his way to the table for seconds. "What did you have to do, show up?"

The girls' team definitely had its longstanding reputation, and everyone knew it. "They're not that bad," she said to the floor, feeling an urge to stand up for them just to ensure her and Lance didn't agree on something.

Lance shook his head, grabbed another piece of

chicken, and headed for the living room.

Emma's focus returned to her dad. He leaned against the counter, sipping root beer from a can with a plate of untouched food beside him. The last time they'd talked basketball was over two weeks ago when she'd asked him for new shoes.

"Our first game is tomorrow, and I..." She shifted weight from one foot to the other and bit her lip, hating how she knew he would say no, but needing to ask anyway. "I wondered if you'd come see me play."

"Tomorrow?" Her dad scratched his chin like he might be considering the possibility. "I think I have to work."

Idiot, she scolded herself. Of course he had to work. She should have asked him a week ago. Her dad started to walk away, but Emma followed him. "What about next week? Tuesday or Thursday?" She cringed at how her voice sounded on the verge of desperation, begging like some needy child. Why did the small flame of hope inside her never die out, no matter how many times her dad rejected her?

Her dad barely looked at her when he said, "You know I can't guarantee anything. My work schedule changes by the minute sometimes."

Emma nodded. She knew he didn't have control over his work schedule. It was selfish of her to even ask him to take two hours out of his day to watch a stupid basketball game they were sure to lose anyway. Even if he didn't have to work, even if he used to make every attempt to watch Lance play, he deserved a night off from obligations. "Okay," she said. "Maybe another time."

It was a good thing her appetite disappeared—there wasn't any food left to even scrounge for scraps. She retreated to her bedroom to start on homework and divert her thoughts from her family.

Thirty minutes later, enough time for her brothers to finish dinner and for her to finish her Physics homework and half of her English assignment, she heard voices on the other side of the wall. Dad and Lance. She plunged ahead with her homework, knowing if she didn't finish it now, she might not finish it at all.

On the other side of the wall, their voices grew louder and she shuddered. She tossed aside her books and wrapped her arms around her legs, hugging them to her chest. How bad would it be tonight? She closed her eyes, but their words only became clearer. Exhaustion seeped through her as she listened to them fight. Lance needed money. Again. Dad didn't have any to give him. Again. She hated how their voices seeped through the walls and into her bedroom, causing her stomach to twist into knots.

She flinched as something hit the wall and shattered, broken glass cascading to the floor. Lance. Her dad never threw anything, but she could picture him growing still and quiet, his jaw clenching and unclenching as he tried to keep his temper in check. Aside from a few selective instances years ago, her dad never hit any of his kids, but she knew nothing was set in stone. She feared Lance would be on the other end of their dad's fist one day, and she didn't want to be within a ten-mile radius if it ever happened, even if Lance deserved it. She didn't want to witness Lance's reaction or see the rage transform her dad into a stranger.

Not wanting to stick around to find out how tonight's fight ended, she slipped on her shoes, crossed the short distance to her private exit, and escaped into the night. With nowhere to go she walked down the street, catching glimpses of her neighbors through the windows. At one house, she saw a young couple dancing in the middle of their kitchen. The man leaned in and whispered something in the woman's ear. The woman tilted back her head and laughed at the ceiling. Emma paused, watching them twirl in circles, and wondered if her parents had ever acted like that—in love.

Feeling guilty for spying on her neighbors, she retreated

to the Ledgers'. Their house was dark except for the porch light that shone like a beacon in the night. She was glad Riley didn't have to grow up in a house where money limited opportunities and fights erupted on a daily basis. He deserved all he had: great parents, money, love, and laughter. She would sacrifice everything to spare him from a life like hers.

Sitting alone on the Ledgers' front porch dulled her uneasiness. She leaned her head against the high back of the whicker chair and exhaled, her breath floating upward in wisps. She pulled the sleeves of her sweatshirt over her frozen hands and crossed her arms to stay warm. Even freezing on the Ledgers' front porch was better than being at home. She wondered if her family had always been so dysfunctional or if it was just the natural consequence after a wife-slash-mother leaves.

Even today Emma couldn't explain what went wrong and why her mom left. Sure, her parents fought like all parents did, but none of their fights resulted in broken glass and bruises. She still lived inside the house then, sharing a room with Lenny and Lucas. Lance was an all-star basketball player, and Logan was top of his class academically. They hadn't had any more money then than they did now, but they'd been happier. Or so Emma thought. But then one day, she woke up and her mom was…gone. No note, no goodbye. Just gone.

Her mom's desertion splintered the family, changing everything and everyone. Logan retreated into his books, Lance became angry and bitter, Lenny and Lucas stopped obeying rules, and her dad just sort of hardened. Her dad had always been the quiet type, but Emma had difficulty remembering him before everything changed. The more she tried to remember, the fuzzier he became. She had memories of her dad kissing her goodnight, giving her high fives when Riley told him about some move she'd made on the basketball court, and wiping away her tears when she got hurt, but she had no proof these memories were real. How could love for his only daughter vanish overnight? Somewhere, deep within, he still loved her, right?

Emma shook her head, not trusting where her thoughts would go if she forced herself to conjure an answer. She redirected her attention to basketball. Bradshaw's first game was tomorrow against Jefferson High School, and Emma still didn't know if Bradshaw was ready for real competition. Yes, the team had improved, but basketball performed in a nice, controlled, non-threatening environment looked a whole lot different than basketball executed in a full-on competition against players who'd rather knock you to the ground than give you the right of way. The team would look and feel a lot different after their first game.

The only girls Emma had ever seen play basketball were the seven girls on her team. She had no idea what to expect from other teams. Did other teams in the league lack skills, players, and experience too? If so, then Bradshaw may have a shot at winning. After weeks of practice, the team had finally shown signs of improvement. Small signs. They could run and dribble at the same time, shoot and make shots half the time, play defense without tripping, and run a set of wind sprints without collapsing from exhaustion. The only question now was how would they measure up to the competition? Would Bradshaw claim their first victory of the season or would it be the first loss of many? The first game would tell her a lot about girls' basketball and where she fit in. Emma hoped she'd be ready when tip-off came tomorrow.

Sometime between fading out her family's drama and gearing up for tomorrow's game, her eyelids closed and sleep overtook her. Mrs. Ledger was the one to find her.

"Emma? Is that you?"

She jerked awake. It took her a minute to remember where she was and recognize Mrs. Ledger's voice.

Mrs. Ledger took a cautious step forward. "Emma?"

Embarrassed for having fallen asleep, Emma rubbed her eyes and leaned forward. "Hi, Mrs. Ledger. Yeah, it's me. Sorry if I scared you."

Mrs. Ledger breathed a sigh of relief and crossed the porch to sit beside her. "Is everything all right?"

Emma shrugged, remembering her reason for coming over. "It's as good as it ever is."

Mrs. Ledger looked at her with disapproval. She was well aware of Emma's home life since Riley didn't hold back in telling his parents anything. "The boys fighting again?"

Emma nodded.

Mrs. Ledger imitated her nod and sighed. She looked into the darkened neighborhood as if settling her thoughts before continuing. "I hear tomorrow is the big first game."

"Yeah." Emma wished for tomorrow never to come.

"Are you ready?"

She shook her head. "I don't know the first thing about playing basketball with girls."

"I imagine the game is the same whether it's played with boys or girls."

"It's not." Guys could actually catch the ball, girls let it pass through their hands and smack them in the face. Guys could run up and down the court as many times as a Saturday allowed, girls couldn't make it through warm-up laps without stopping to walk. Guys played to win, girls played to socialize.

"You'll be fine." Mrs. Ledger leaned over to pat her arm. "You just have to go out and play your game. Be the beautiful, tough, talented basketball player Riley always tells us you are."

Emma doubted Riley had ever described her with those words. More like a mom's edited version, but she soaked up the smile Mrs. Ledger gave her anyway. Times like these made her yearn for the mom who walked out years earlier without a trace, leaving her to fend for herself among her all-male family.

Footsteps thudded up the porch steps, breaking the closest thing Emma had to a mother-daughter moment. Riley took one look at them, marched across the porch, and plopped himself on Emma's lap. She groaned under his weight and tried to push him off, but he wrapped his arms around her neck and held on, smashing the side of her face against his chest.

Mrs. Ledger shook her head and rose from the chair. "Take care of her," she said, squeezing her son's shoulder.

"I always do." He waited until his mom closed the door into the house before relaxing his hold on Emma's neck. "You okay?"

"I will be when you get off me."

Riley chuckled. He rose from her lap and offered her his hand. "You want to come in for a while?"

One of the best things about Riley was he always knew what she needed. She didn't have to rehearse the latest incident with her family. He always just seemed to know. She slapped his hand away and stood on her own, following him inside.

The Ledgers' house always smelled like fabric softener or fresh-baked cookies or the kind of fresh air that swept through open windows during the first warm days of spring. Sometimes there was a hint of cinnamon or a pinch of lilac underneath it all, but it was always the same—their house smelled like home. It wasn't her home, of course, but sometimes she couldn't help pretending. Pretending she didn't have to go home to the shouting, the work boots caked with mud, or the smell of something rotting in the refrigerator seeping through the rest of the house. She took a deep breath, savoring the moment as she followed Riley into the kitchen.

He threw his keys on the counter, grabbed two bottles of orange juice from the fridge, and headed upstairs to his room, Emma right behind him. She dropped onto his bed. Instead of the springs squeaking with protest, the pillows welcomed her with a hug.

"I have something for you," he said, rummaging through a drawer in his desk.

She sat up. "Let me guess, another old comic book?"

Without answering, he slammed the drawer shut, spun around, and threw something at her. She caught it in her left hand before it hit her in the face. An armband. Red with a white B for Bradshaw sewn into it.

"Don't worry," he said, seeing the look of shock on her face. "It's not my old smelly one. My mom made you one of your own."

She couldn't take her eyes off it. Riley wore one exactly like it for every game he played. His mom made one for him as a symbol to let him know no matter how well he did or didn't play, his parents still loved him. He complained about this to Emma at first, insisting it was some silly mother thing. Yet, she had never seen him play a game without it on. And now Mrs. Ledger was giving one to Emma.

Riley sat beside her. "You okay?"

She nodded, not trusting herself to speak over the lump in her throat.

"You're not going to cry on me or anything, are you?" He nudged her with his shoulder. "Cuz that would be a total girl thing to do."

He was right. Crying was for girls, not for her. She couldn't remember the last time she'd cried. Maybe five or six years ago. The last thing she would do was burst into tears over an armband, especially in front of Riley. She hit him with a pillow instead, and he laughed.

"You're going to be great tomorrow," he said, his tone serious.

Tomorrow. The first game of the season. Would she be ready?

Eight

Braids. Emma didn't do braids. So why were Madison and Christi gripping handfuls of her hair and weaving them together in French-braided pigtails? Because it was game night and this was how girls defined team unity for their first game—by all of them wearing the same hairstyle. Stupid. The worst part was Coach was in total agreement with the insanity. She even threatened to bench Emma for the first quarter if she didn't give in and let them take possession of her hair. Not a way to start the season. Of course, it could have been worse. She could have been Christi whose hair was too short to braid, so in pigtails it looked like the ends of two blown-up firecrackers poking out of her head.

The girls finally tied off the ends of her braids, Coach raced through her this-is-it speech, and it was time to take the court for warm-ups.

Emma had never played basketball in a real gym with fully functioning nets attached to the rims and real-life referees calling fouls. Scrimmaging during practice in the auxiliary gym didn't count since they couldn't form two teams and had difficulty executing a play without Coach blowing the whistle and pushing the rewind button so they could do it all over again. Practice was different. Practicing with girls who had yet to prove themselves in a competitive situation was social hour in comparison. Now, with actual people present to watch their game, everything felt so real.

The Bradshaw girls' team stepped out from the security of the locker room and into the chaos of the gym. Unlike the auxiliary gym with its faded colors, the main gym flashed the school's fire-engine red and white colors. A huge lion roared from the floor at mid-court. From the first day of freshman year, teachers encouraged students to be like Bradshaw's mighty mascot—strong and courageous. So, why, oh why, did weakness prevail in the moment when Emma needed the most strength? It didn't matter that half the bleachers were empty, that no one expected them to win, that despite the pulsing notes of the band echoing around them, she couldn't hear anything except the hammering of her heart.

I don't belong here.

The realization was so strong it knocked the wind out of her. The team ran onto the court, but Emma's feet stopped at the sideline. She didn't belong here on a court full of girls who had dreams for the future and money in the bank. She didn't belong on a court full of girls who had parents in the stands cheering them on. No one had ever expected anything from her. She was just some girl people pitied and passed in the hallways at school. Just because Coach Knowles discovered she was good at basketball and forced her onto the girls' team in the hope she could help them win a game or two, didn't change anything.

A coach, seven girls, and a few dozen fans looked to her to lead a losing team to victory, but she would fail. No doubt about it. She would fail and prove to everyone why poor girls didn't belong on a court full of rich kids.

Coach Knowles stepped beside Emma, clapping her hands and rubbing them together, radiating excitement. She looked at Emma, but she didn't *see* Emma. She didn't see Emma's hands shake or her throat go dry. Coach didn't see the invisible barrier preventing Emma from stepping on the court to join her teammates. All Coach cared about was her first big win.

"I'm sorry," Emma choked out, stumbling backward.

She didn't stay long enough to see fear seep into Coach's eyes or to watch Riley descend the bleachers, knowing at once something was wrong. She sprinted for the exit, no longer able to breathe, hardly able to stand. She burst through the door and into the cold winter night, unaware of the glances people gave her as she pushed past them. Gulping air, she turned a corner and ducked into the shadows of an empty alcove. She leaned against the wall of the school, needing something solid to support her. She would have never thought her first real basketball game would start with her fleeing the scene, fighting to breathe. Bending over, she placed her hands on her knees and tried to find comfort in the fact she was in the dark where she belonged, sheltered from the spotlight.

Invisible.

Almost.

"You okay?" The voice reached out to her, pulling her focus up from the ground.

Riley stood at the edge of the shadows watching her. Only her rapid breathing filled the silence. He stepped from the light into the darkness, slipping out of his coat to drape it around her shoulders.

His coat was warm and Emma pushed her arms through the sleeves and pulled it tighter around her. She looked up at him to say thank you. "I can't do this," she said instead. She hated admitting weakness. Hated the way the words tasted coming out of her mouth, hated the way her body shook in fear of what might happen on a court full of girls, hated how Riley found her hiding in the shadows.

Unable to remain still under his steady gaze, she pushed away from the wall and started pacing. She could dominate in basketball at the park with the guys with no problem, but basketball with girls in a real gym with referees and fans and a scorekeeper and expectations swirling in the air like confetti during a windstorm was entirely different. "I know you and all those people in there expect me to perform some miracle tonight, but I can't do it. I don't belong in there."

He held out his arm to stop her pacing and cocked his head to the side to look at her. "What's this really about, Em?"

Good old Riley. He was the only one who could sense the undercurrent of her hysterics.

Sometimes having a best friend like him was the best thing in the world, and other times it was the worst thing ever because nothing went unnoticed. Lying had never been her forte, and Riley knew it. Telling him the truth— admitting weakness—was her only option. She took a deep breath. "My whole life, people have told me I'm not strong enough or good enough or smart enough to do anything." She looked into his eyes, seeing the closest thing she had to family. She saw his safety and warmth; she saw his desire to help her, comfort her, believe in her, and protect her from the world, but not even he could make her change how she thought of herself. She bowed her head. "Somewhere along the way I started to believe them."

Riley always thought of her as strong and capable, which was probably why she felt guilt well up inside her. She closed her eyes and shook her head, trying to regain a speck of composure. "Just because I can shoot a few baskets and dribble with both hands doesn't mean I belong out there with a bunch of rich girls."

Riley placed his hands on her shoulders and gave her a gentle smile. "Forget about what everyone else has told you. The truth is that you are strong enough and good enough and smart enough to do this or anything else. We've been friends for a long time, and I've seen you do amazing things by just being you. Just go in there and play. You belong out there just as much as any of those other girls."

He believed what he said. She could tell by the way his eyes never wavered from hers and by the way his hands squeezed her shoulders in encouragement. How could he have so much faith in her? She wanted to believe him—to trust him—but she couldn't. Nothing ever turned out right for her. "Even if it were that easy, as soon as I go out there I'm going to forget my own name, fall on my face, and people will blame me for destroying this team."

Riley met her gaze, his smile still intact. "If you forget your name, I'll remind you when you're done. If you fall on your face, I'll pick you up. And if people blame you for destroying the team, well," he shrugged, "you'll probably deserve it."

She exhaled a laugh. Leave it to Riley to find humor at a time like this. He pulled her close and wrapped his arms around her. She rested her head against his shoulder, breathing in the scent of laundry detergent from his shirt and the faint traces of his soap—the smell of safety.

"You'll do great," he said. "Besides, you can't ditch. My parents came to watch you play."

As if things couldn't get any worse. She pulled away from him. "Your parents are here?"

"Well, yeah, they didn't want to miss your high school basketball debut."

She groaned. "Couldn't they have at least waited until my second game?"

"Nope. All the good stuff happens in the first one. I mean look at these adorable braids." He tugged one of them, and she swatted his hand away. "With red ribbons that actually match your uniform. I never thought I'd live to see the day. The guys are going to love them."

Emma swallowed. "The guys?" Riley and his parents were more than enough witnesses. She didn't need the guys too. If she failed, everyone she cared about would witness it. It was all Riley's fault. But did he care? Nope. He just smiled, draped his arm around her shoulders, and guided her back inside.

She was new to the whole official basketball game situation. The announcer, the scoreboard, the opposing team in real uniforms, the team huddle. Needing something to do, Emma gulped water trying not to focus on the two-minute countdown until tip-off. A decade of losing hadn't developed a following of fans to support the team, but the few in attendance were too many for her, especially since she knew half of them. She heard Riley in the stands shouting to her in encouragement. The guys were there too. All of them. So not good. Her eyes scanned the crowd. Mr. and Mrs. Ledger smiled and waved at her. She couldn't believe they'd actually shown up. Riley's family had shown up to support her, whereas, her own couldn't have cared less. She took a deep breath. Now was not the time to dwell on all that her family wasn't.

Coach Knowles herded the five starters to the bench, pushed each of them into a chair, and waited for the announcer to start things off. Emma was too busy staring at her feet, trying to control her shaking hands and remembering how to breathe, to notice Lauren beside her.

"Nervous, Poverty Child?" Lauren spit out.

Emma couldn't even produce an answer. She swallowed, her throat dry again, and remained focused on her feet. Basketball was the only thing she was good at, but what if she choked? What would happen after tip-off when the ball landed in her hands? Would she remember how to dribble and shoot and play the game she'd spent so many years perfecting? She wasn't good in the spotlight. She always froze in the spotlight.

Most people associated the spotlight with fame and glory, but not Emma. The spotlight was more of a full-court press. It was never easy. The spotlight came with unrealistic expectations and pressure to perform to perfection. Sure, Emma could break a full-court press on the basketball court with the guys when there were no witnesses, but it wasn't without difficulty. She had to split the defense, avoid the traps, and work her way up the court without losing the ball to a defender. But when the spotlight slipped off the neighborhood court, followed her to school, and blinded her on a court full of girls, Emma panicked. No, the spotlight was not for her. It was for people like Riley and Lauren who were meant to shine, not for people who dressed in hand-me-downs and lived in a garage. Despite Riley's faith, her own confidence faded.

The announcer's voice boomed over the loudspeaker as he introduced the starting lineup. Emma was the last player introduced for Bradshaw, and when her name ricocheted through the gym, despite the uproar of applause, it took every ounce of strength she had to transfer her weight from the chair to her legs.

Please don't collapse, she told her legs.

She vaguely remembered hearing the guys holler their support, slapping the hand of the opposing team member when they met in the middle of the court, or the actual tip-off. All she knew was the ball was in her hands, and she didn't know what to do with it.

"Don't be a girl," she muttered to herself. A defender stood in front of her. Her form sloppy, her weight on the heels of her feet, her eyes on Emma's face rather than her hips to anticipate her next move. So, this was what it was like playing with girls.

Emma took a deep breath before dribbling downcourt toward her teammates. She passed to Peyton who fumbled the ball before securing it in her hands. Peyton looked like a raccoon caught in the trashcan. She had no idea what to do next. Emma set a screen for Lauren inside the key, and then rolled back to the outside. As soon as Emma cleared her defender, Peyton threw the ball back to her and sprinted to the opposite side of the court where she hid behind her own defender. None of her other teammates worked to get open. Maybe Emma wasn't the only one dealing with fear.

"Okay," she mumbled. *If that's the way it's going to be.* She dribbled once, twice, before sprinting toward the basket. Catching her defender off guard, she executed a quick crossover and cut through the key. No defender collapsed on her, no one shouted a warning about the girl who had a wide-open shot from inside the key. The shot was too easy. Two points.

Bradshaw was on the board.

Emma allowed herself to exhale. Maybe this whole thing wouldn't be as bad as she thought. She looked into the stands and caught Riley's eye. He smiled and waved at her. No, it definitely wouldn't be bad.

Jefferson High School never had a chance to catch up. Game number one final score: Bradshaw 49, Jefferson 37.

◆◆◆

For a rebuilding year, their first game couldn't have gone better. Sure, they still had a long way to go, but beating the second worst team in the league to start off the season had its advantages. So far, they had a winning season.

A certain buzz hovered in the air from their first victory. Even Emma couldn't ignore it. She fought back a smile, not comfortable showing positive emotion among so many girls. She didn't want them to think she actually liked them or anything. They were still the worst basketball players on the planet, but it felt good to win. It felt good to wear a real uniform, play on a real team—even if it was the girls' team—and face an opponent, knowing the score mattered in the end.

Coach tried to congratulate them in the locker room, during what should've been their post-game talk, but she couldn't be heard above the screaming. Emma didn't join her teammates. She covered her ears, half expecting the mirrors to shatter. High-pitched screaming should be outlawed.

Admitting defeat, Coach released them from the locker room. Emma couldn't get out of there fast enough. She fled to the gym, hoping some of the guys stuck around to wait for her. As soon as Riley saw her, he lunged forward and lifted her off the floor in a hug. His arms squeezed tighter around her waist as he twirled her in circles.

"Hey!" she exclaimed, locking her arms around his neck as the gym blurred around her.

"You were amazing," he whispered in her ear before setting her back down.

For the first time since the buzzer announced Bradshaw's win, she let her smile break free as she looked at Riley. "Thanks." The fear and doubt she'd felt before the game seemed like nothing more than a bad dream. Maybe it wasn't so horrible having a cheering section after all.

The rest of the guys encircled her and pulled her from Riley's arms to pat her on the back and congratulate her on the win.

Riley's parents broke through the group of boys, and without pausing, Mrs. Ledger enveloped her in a hug. "You played great."

Mr. Ledger tugged one of her pigtails. "Great job out there, kiddo."

Emma felt her cheeks burn with all the attention. "Thanks."

"Celebration!" Tom called out.

His single word got the rest of the guys going. Waving goodbye to Riley's parents, they herded her out of the gym, across the darkened campus to the parking lot, and smashed her into the backseat of Riley's jeep between Tom and Cy, the biggest guys of the pack. What happened to the star player having front seat status?

Celebrating consisted of scarfing burgers and fries at McDonald's while rehashing the night's highlights. What could be better than being surrounded by guys, eating greasy food, and talking basketball?

For once, she had two dollars in her pocket and could actually order food so the guys knew she wasn't starving herself. At least not on purpose. She approached the counter to order, her eyes scanning the menu. She inhaled the smell of hamburgers, French fries, and apple turnovers, her two dollars clutched in her hand.

Riley appeared beside her, pulling his wallet out of his back pocket. "I got this."

"What?" she asked in confusion. She had money. Two dollars ready to be handed over the counter.

He pushed her arms and her two dollars away from the cashier. "What do you want?"

"Riley, I—"

"I got this," he said firmly. "Now, what do you want?"

The cashier glanced from Riley to Emma and back to Riley again. Emma couldn't help but notice the grease stains on the girl's shirt or how her hair was held in place by a hair net. Emma's future flashed before her eyes. The image consisted of her on the other side of the counter with the grease-stained shirt, witnessing customers fight over food and money. Her breath caught in her throat, and she bowed her head in submission before answering Riley's question. "An ice water."

Riley rolled his eyes and turned to the cashier. "Can I get two number ones and two apple turnovers?"

The cashier rang up his order. Riley pulled a twenty from his wallet and handed it over the counter like it was nothing more than Monopoly money.

Emma felt her cheeks burn, hating the fact Riley had to buy her meal at one of the cheapest restaurants in town because he knew she couldn't afford it.

Riley turned toward her with a smile and handed her their drink cups. "The star player doesn't get to pay for her own food." Before she could protest any further, he said, "You're welcome. Now, will you please go find us a seat?"

She growled at him before spinning around and doing as she was told. Did Riley know how difficult he was? How stubborn and annoying and frustrating? Sure, most people probably thought he was sweet and charming with the way he took care of her and paid for her and never let anything happen to her, but Emma wasn't most people. She hated taking handouts, and the more he did these charitable acts for her, the more she owed him. Their friendship had never been fair; it was completely one-sided with Riley always giving and Emma always taking. She never stopped trying to equal things out and make them fair, but when she had no money and nothing to give him, her options were limited. Riley didn't care. She knew he never expected anything in return, but why? If he went out of his way for her, but expected nothing in return, why did he stick around and want to be her friend at all?

Not wanting to think about her life without Riley, if he would one day wake up and realize the injustice of their friendship, she focused on filling their drink cups with root beer instead. She found the rest of the guys in the back corner of the restaurant, their food scattered over four tables to accommodate all eight of them.

Riley showed up a few minutes later with their food. He set the tray in front of Emma and winked when she glared at him.

"How does it feel to be a superstar?" Jerry asked.

Six heads whipped toward her as she took a huge bite of her hamburger. She nearly choked from the attention. Hoping to evade the question, she chewed slowly, but even after a full minute the guys remained silent, still gawking at her. With no other choice, she swallowed her food. "I'm not a superstar."

"Are you kidding?" Jerry slammed his hands on the table, making them all jump. "The move you pulled in the third quarter when you charged through the key, spun around, and actually made the left-handed hook shot was definitely superstar status."

The rest of the guys nodded and grunted in agreement. She didn't know what the big deal was. They had all seen her play before, and it wasn't like they didn't have superstar moves of their own.

"I can't believe you made that shot," Tom said, the food crammed in his mouth not deterring him from speaking. He crumpled his burger wrapper into a ball and imitated a left-handed hook shot. The wrapper arched through the air and landed on Alex's lap. Alex grabbed the paper and threw it baseball style back at Tom, hitting him in the forehead and making them all laugh.

Emma dunked a fry in ketchup. "It wasn't that big a deal." She was still angry with Riley for paying for her meal, but in her life letting good food go to waste was a crime, and she was starving. What was one more debt to the thousands she already owed him? "You would have done the same thing if you were confronted with a six-foot forward wanting to stuff your face."

"How many points did you have tonight?" Cy asked.

Emma shrugged. She shot, she didn't calculate. She was just grateful to have survived the entire game without having a meltdown.

"Thirty-one," Riley said from beside her.

She looked at him, her jaw dropping. How in the world did he know that?

"What?" he asked innocently.

"Thirty-one." Jerry shook his head. "Amazing."

Tom slurped his soda dry. "So, what's it like playing with girls?"

"Oh, it's a real thrill," she said sarcastically. "They have as much talent as you do."

The guys laughed with her, knowing it wasn't a compliment. Tom grinned and shoved another handful of fries into his mouth.

"So, Emma, heard any good stuff yet?" Cy asked.

"What do you mean?"

Cy looked at her like she was clueless. "You know, which girls think I'm hot?" He flashed his dimples and made his eyebrows dance up and down. Most of the female population thought he was cute with his dimples, chocolate eyes, and face-wide smile, but he already knew that. He didn't need any encouragement.

She snorted. "None."

"Oh, come on, Em. You have to give us something," Tom said. "What do girls talk about?"

"Mostly themselves," she said, rearranging the remaining pickles on her burger. Sometimes she caught bits and pieces of conversations when a teammate mentioned one of the guys, but Emma tried to zone them out. The guys were all like brothers—decent brothers—and she didn't want to hear the context in which girls talked about them. *Gross.*

It was quiet around her, and she glanced up to see all the guys staring at her. Riley, slouched in his seat with one arm resting on the back of her chair, looked amused; the rest of the guys looked expectant. She knew exactly what they wanted. Was this seriously how they were going to spend their time celebrating? By talking about girls? Sure, she'd heard the guys talk about girls before, but never had they used her as their inside source. Could life get any worse?

She dropped her burger and shook her head. "No. Uh-uh. Don't even think about it. I'm not playing spy or messenger girl or cupid. You're on your own." No way was she going to be caught in the middle of some teenage drama that would no doubt blow up in her face. Hooking the guys up with the girls on her team had tragedy written all over it.

The guys groaned.

Cy threw his hands in the air. "What good is it having one of our own on the inside if you're not willing to tell us anything?"

"Trust me," she said, holding up her hand to ward off

further protests. "You're better off not knowing. I wish I was still in the unknown." She sighed, remembering those blissful girl-free days when she could just focus on basketball. "Besides, you wouldn't want me to tell them everything you talk about, would you?"

"You wouldn't sell us out because, unlike them, we're your friends." Jerry's tone was confident, but his eyes flashed fear.

"Not if you force me to do this, you're not." She glanced at Riley, wondering where he stood on this. Was he interested in what girls talked about him and what they said? Did he care? Not that it bothered her one way or another, but she was curious. Unlike the other guys, Riley just sat there, staring at her, listening to them, with the corners of his mouth turned upward like he was enjoying every second. Then he winked at her again like they shared some private joke. She was dying to know what thoughts were swarming in that head of his, but for some reason she was too afraid to ask.

Nine

Sometimes waiting on Riley was worse than waiting on girls. Two seconds actually meant five minutes, and five minutes meant more like thirty. It was Sunday. No school. No girls. No basketball. Spending the entire day waiting on Riley was not exactly what Emma had in mind when he said they should hang out and do something on their free day. He'd asked, but he hadn't warned her he had unfinished chores, incomplete homework assignments from last week, and an angry mom on his tail. Shooting hoops in the Ledgers' driveway was better than waiting for him at her house, but not if thirty minutes actually meant three hours.

She glanced at his house between shots, trying to see him through the windows. He happened to slide into view from his bedroom window on the second floor and caught her looking at him. He raised his hand with a pleading look on his face, indicating he needed five more minutes. She growled and turned away. He'd told her the same thing twenty minutes ago. Pounding the ball against the pavement, she returned her focus to the basketball hoop until she heard the front door open behind her a few minutes later.

"Finally," she muttered. She turned, expecting Riley but it was his dad instead. "Oh, hey, Mr. Ledger."

Over the years, Mr. and Mrs. Ledger had told her multiple times to call them by their first names, but Emma couldn't. Calling them Robert and Kate just didn't feel right. Maybe it was because she still felt like a child in their presence, maybe it was the amount of respect she had for them, or maybe it was a small reminder for Emma not to get too close or too attached because they, too, could leave her.

"You had a pretty good game the other night," Mr. Ledger said from the front porch where he stood watching her. He cleared his throat. "I, uh, noticed you used some of the moves I taught you."

She laughed. Her talent on the basketball court was nothing more than a testament of Mr. Ledger's coaching ability, and he knew it. "What basketball moves haven't I learned from you?"

Mr. Ledger chuckled and joined her in the driveway. "How's the team coming along?" He was dressed in an old pair of cargo pants, ratty old sneakers, and a sweatshirt with paint stains smeared across the front. Even with his messy brown hair and day-old whiskers, Mr. Ledger still looked like the world's number one dad.

She passed him the ball, and he put up a perfect shot, using the same form he'd taught her and Riley.

She shrugged. "Fine, I guess." Yes, they'd won their first game and only lost their second by ten points, but the team didn't flow like Saturday morning games with the guys.

He looked at her from the corner of his eye. "There any more to that?"

It was wrong how Mr. Ledger knew her better than her own dad. He knew the questions to ask and the questions to hold back. He knew what wisdom to share and what lessons she needed to figure out on her own. Thinking back on her childhood, most of her cherished father-daughter moments had taken place with Riley's dad, not her own. She often wondered what made Mr. Ledger so different than her own dad, but she could never figure it out.

She rebounded the ball and twirled it in her hands, trying to put her feelings into words. "Sometimes I feel like the girls just stand around and expect me to do all the work. It's aggravating."

Mr. Ledger barked out a laugh. "Emma, you are an amazing basketball player. Next to you those girls look and probably feel like the worst players in the world. You have to be patient with them."

Patient? Was that even possible with girls? Frustration, annoyance, madness—now those were emotions Emma could relate to in the presence of girls. Not patience. She couldn't sit passively by with a smile on her face and wait for the girls to step it up. It was physically, emotionally, and mentally impossible for her. But feeling Mr. Ledger's eyes watching her, she knew she had to at least try. Besides, her resentment toward the female population wasn't her only problem.

"The most difficult part is not knowing them," she admitted. Even on a court full of screaming, whining girls, Emma couldn't help feeling lonely. Not having Riley and the guys next to her was bad enough, but the game of girls' basketball felt foreign to her. "When I play with the guys I know I have to lead Jerry with the pass, I have to set the screen for Cy on the left because he can't dribble right, and I have to help Tom on defense because he always gets beat on the baseline. The girls can't even catch a pass thrown right to them, much less plow through a couple of defenders for a basket. I refuse to play down to their level, but it's impossible to play at the level I play at with the guys. It's driving me crazy."

Mr. Ledger gave her a compassionate smile.

Emma hoped she wouldn't have to verbally request Mr. Ledger's guidance. She trusted him, respected him, and depended on him to steer her in the right direction, no matter how difficult the path might be. She stood quietly, waiting.

"Let me ask you a question," he said. "When you look at your teammates, do you see how bad they are or do you see how good they could be?"

Ouch. Leave it to Mr. Ledger to know exactly what question to ask to make Emma bite her tongue and bow her head.

He paused, not waiting for an answer but waiting for his words to fully sink in, before he continued. "Sometimes being the best player is not about how good you are fundamentally, but about playing *with* your team. Knowing their strengths and weaknesses, no matter how difficult they are to find. Sweetheart, your purpose is not to make yourself look good and your teammates look bad; it's about making the team look great."

Not exactly the words she wanted to hear, which probably meant he was right. "That doesn't sound easy."

His laughter reminded her of Riley. "Nor is it supposed to, but you're the only one on the team who can do it. If you figure it out, it will all be worth it. I promise."

Why should she care? They were just a bunch of girls. None of it mattered. But when she looked at Mr. Ledger and locked her gaze with his, she knew he had higher expectations for her. He believed in her just like his son. She didn't understand why they made her want to do better and be better, and not be satisfied with anything else.

She longed to have these father-daughter talks with her own dad, not Riley's, but her dad was always so tired or focused on her brothers to take much interest in her. He had yet to ask one question about basketball. Mr. Ledger was different. He cared.

Emma sighed. It was so much easier to complain about her teammates' incompetence and not care. Caring required a change of thought, a change of action, and a change of heart. "It sounds like I have work to do," she muttered, not even trying to feign enthusiasm.

He shrugged and handed her the ball, not wanting to force her into anything. "Only you would know."

Which totally meant yes.

"Will you tell Riley I'll see him later?"

He nodded. "I will."

If there was one thing Emma learned during the next two hours while she conducted her own solo practice at the park, it was that it wasn't about making a perfect pass; it was about making the pass perfect. The difference between the two was vast. She could snap a perfect two-handed chest pass across the court, but if no one was there to catch it, or if someone was there who couldn't catch it, what would be the point? Maybe a perfect pass needed to be low or high or slightly off center depending on who was on the receiving end of it.

Learning the strengths and weaknesses of each girl on her team seemed like an easy task, considering ninety-nine percent of basketball was their weakness, but it was more than learning about their strengths and weaknesses. She needed to learn how to play with them and to them.

During the next week, Emma observed her teammates. Madison couldn't dribble with her left hand, Christi's shooting range didn't extend beyond the key, Shiloh couldn't dribble without looking at the ball, Peyton couldn't play defense to save her life, Steph was all height but no speed, Lauren was foul happy, and Ashley was, well, Ashley. None of this was news to Emma, considering she'd spent every practice cringing over their mistakes, but she couldn't ignore the truth. Madison could hit any moving target with her passes, Christi caused a fair amount of turnovers as a defender, Steph was unstoppable under the basket, Peyton pounced on all the loose balls, Shiloh hammered for every rebound and claimed most of them, Lauren couldn't miss a shot inside the three-point circle, and Ashley had a knack for sneaking through the holes of the defense.

Emma smiled. All she needed to do now was execute a plan to pull the team together. Maybe, just maybe, this team had a shot at something more than a handful of wins. They didn't have to like each other, they didn't have to socialize off the court, and they didn't have to pretend they existed in a utopian society. All they had to do was play basketball. Together. It wouldn't have been so difficult if Emma could get the rest of the girls to focus on basketball long enough to learn something. But girls were girls. They always found a way to distract themselves.

◆◆◆

No matter how much Coach acted like a drill sergeant, stretching and warm-ups never ceased to move beyond social time. Emma stretched in silence, listening to the girls around her chatter about boys. If the guys only knew how they served as the topic of way too many conversations between girls, their heads would explode.

From across the circle, Emma heard a gasp. "We should all go to the dance together!"

No person could fake that much enthusiasm.

Other conversations around the circle broke off as the girls diverted their attention to the unified discussion topic.

"C'mon," Madison said. "It will be so much fun. Just the girls."

Emma didn't even try to hide the disgust on her face. School dance? Just the girls? Seriously? Friday night dances held no purpose other than for teens to congregate and express way too much physical affection toward one another. The idea of attending the dance, especially with a group of girls, terrified her. Girls screaming for attention, guys on the prowl, teachers trying to enforce rules from another century—dances were nothing more than one big drama fest.

No one else shared her animosity. One by one the faces

around her lit up at the idea.

Before she could open her mouth to object, the rest of the girls started squealing their agreement. Emma cringed.

"What about you, Emma?" Christi asked, as if knowing exactly what would put her over the top. "You up for a little dancing?"

Christi's attempt to bust a move in the middle of stretches was not the way to entice Emma to join them. Emma shook her head and held up both hands to ward them off. "I'll pass."

"Great," Madison said with way too much perk. "We'll pick you up at seven, and then meet at Lauren's to carpool together."

Emma's mouth dropped open. "No, I—"

Her protest was lost among the squeals, which lasted throughout the entire practice. A distraction their team didn't need. Basketball Emma could do, no matter what she encountered on the court. But a school dance? With just the girls? She wouldn't survive more than ten minutes. Why did they even want her to come anyway? It wasn't like they'd formed some unbreakable bond during the past week. Okay, so maybe after their first win some of the girls stopped staring at her like she was a solo act in some freak show, but they were still a long way from any sort of friendship.

Emma made it home after her double practices with barely enough time to shower and change before Madison arrived. She knew if she fled, Madison would hunt her down and make a public display of dragging her to the dance. Emma didn't even have time to notify Riley of the hostage situation. She was on her own.

If the girls expected her to dress up in girly clothes and actually care about her appearance, they had another thing coming. Jeans and a sweatshirt. The dance didn't deserve anything more than that.

The bass from Madison's car could be heard from two blocks away. With a screeching halt, the Land Rover stopped in front of her house, and she hopped in before anyone could get a decent look at her one-story rambler. Compared to the rest of the houses in the neighborhood, the Wrangtons' was the black spot, the eyesore, the house everyone turned a blind eye to hoping it would someday disappear. The paint, cracked and peeling, was no match for the summer sun and the winter storms that beat against it every year. Overgrown shrubs concealed half the house from the neighbors' view, and an old truck rusted in the driveway. The grass needed mowing, the weeds needed pulling, and the roof moss needed scraping. Grateful Madison and Christi weren't detail-oriented observers, Emma breathed a sigh of relief as they pulled away from the curb and left her house behind.

The decision to jump into Madison's car proved not to be one of Emma's better judgments. Madison sped down the street, nearly taking out a mailbox and swiping the bumper of a parked car. Despite the restraint of her seatbelt, Emma braced herself against the door and the backseat for additional safety measures against Madison's erratic turns and abrupt stops.

She couldn't help but laugh at Madison and Christi as they sang way off-key to the music blasting from the speakers, knowing every word to every song. Car dancing was another thing Emma didn't understand about girls. What was the point of bouncing while restrained by a seatbelt? They looked like caged monkeys going crazy over a banana. She shook her head and laughed. Knowing what girls did in the privacy of their own cars was one thing, having the visual to prove it was another.

After fifteen minutes of Madison's hazardous driving, they screeched to a stop in front of Lauren's house. Emma unclenched her hands from the edge of the seat and tumbled out onto solid ground, not prepared for the sight in front of her. No wonder Lauren acted like a rich snob; everything in her life screamed it. Even in the dark, the massive two-story house had enough curb appeal to make the rich neighbors jealous. A pristine blanket of grass warned feet to keep off. Brick stairs led to the front porch from the street, bordered on both sides by rose bushes. On the second story, another covered porch wrapped around the house and jutted out on one side beyond the roof. Bay and picture windows took up half the house and welcomed views of Puget Sound and breathtaking sunsets. And pillars. The house had pillars! Huge white columns extending from the ground to the roof like some southern plantation house. Emma's jaw dropped.

Madison knocked on the front double-door and opened it without waiting for a response from the other side. Christi followed. Emma, her eyes drawn upward to the vaulted ceiling of the foyer, tripped over the threshold and stumbled into the house. Madison and Christi didn't pay her any attention. Instead, they climbed the stairs toward the sound of girls, and Emma had no choice but to follow them. She turned a corner in the hallway and found the rest of her teammates zipping back and forth between the bathroom and Lauren's bedroom, putting on the finishing touches of their hair, makeup, and clothes.

They were all dressed in what some would consider cute little girly outfits, ready to impress the wandering eyes of the male population. Too much cleavage, too many bellybuttons, and way too much skin. Emma choked on the smell of hairspray, which hung like a heavy fog in the hallway. The stuff had to be lethal. Some of the girls had on so much makeup they looked like clowns. Emma shook her head. If this was what it took to be a girl, count her out. She would go with the girls to the dance, but she would not succumb to their way of life.

Leaving them to their business, she wandered away and peeked through open doors to catch a glimpse of how the rich half lived. Lauren's house had the look-don't-touch feel. One false step and Emma could do some real damage. Polished floors, glass ornaments encased within glass cabinets, sleek wooden furniture, original artwork. The house wasn't a family residence; it was a magazine photo op. It would take her a lifetime to save enough money to replace anything she broke. She shoved her hands deep in her jean pockets, not trusting them around such expensive stuff, and made her way back to the girls who were still caught up in their self-beautification.

Bored, she crossed her arms and leaned against the wall, staying clear of the high traffic zone. Madison and Christi had jumped right in without even messing up the flow. Emma couldn't wait for the night to be over. The seconds clicked to minutes, which stretched to a way longer waiting time than she would have thought possible. They were going to a Friday night school dance, not the prom. Finally—when Emma was inhaling enough breath to scream at them to hurry it up already—everyone was ready to go.

Until they saw her.

Lauren froze in front of Emma, her face scrunching in horror. "What are you wearing?"

The rest of the girls spun toward Emma and gasped. Like they'd never seen a sweatshirt and jeans before.

"They're called clothes," Emma responded dully.

Lauren spun on Madison. "You actually let her in your car looking like this?"

"I-It was dark," Madison squeaked, scrunching up her face and shoulders in what Emma guessed was part guilt and part fear of being reprimanded. "How was I supposed to know what she looked like?"

Emma saw them all exchange glances. It was wrong how girls could communicate and develop a plan without saying a single word. They swarmed her like flies on fruit. She held up her arms to defend herself, but she didn't stand a chance. Even for her, seven girls against one was a lost battle, especially with all the talking. They pulled, pushed, and prodded her down the hall and into Lauren's room. Emma tried to decipher a few of their words to figure out what they had planned, but the seven girls talked a mile a minute and nothing made sense. Why couldn't these girls show this much initiative and strength in practice?

"Hey, what are you—"

Before Emma knew what was happening, they stripped off her sweatshirt and forced her into some light blue blouse thingy that was way too girly and way too tight for Emma's preferences. They agreed to let her wear her own faded hand-me-down jeans, saying it complimented the look they were going for, but her sneakers were replaced with someone's black loafers. Thank goodness they weren't heels or Emma would've been in serious trouble. From there, they herded her into the bathroom and pushed her onto a stool with her back facing the mirror. Hands clamped down on her when she tried to escape. Not good.

"Hair up or down?" someone asked.

Emma's, "Up," was drowned out by everyone else's, "Down." Did her opinion not count for anything?

They yanked out her hair tie so her untamed blonde waves spilled down her back.

"Wow." Madison let strands of Emma's hair fall through her fingers. "You have beautiful hair. You should stop bunching it up and let it fly free."

Emma blew hair out of her eyes. "It annoys me."

"Then tonight you suffer through it," Lauren said.

Emma glared at her, but Lauren ignored her and focused on applying makeup. Knowing Lauren, Emma would wind up looking like another clown. "Light with the paint," Emma ordered.

"Oh, please." Lauren snatched a brush and some sort of pink powder substance and approached Emma. "You need all the help you can get."

Each time Emma fidgeted or turned her head, five sets of hands grabbed her and secured her again. She sighed. "Is all this really necessary?"

"Yes!" they all answered at once.

Ashley giggled. "Would it kill you to be a girl for, like, five seconds?"

Emma glared at the freshman. "Yes." But no one cared. They were girls on a makeover mission.

Emma stopped fighting and protesting. It was no use. With Lauren painting her face and two or three girls pulling her hair, at least four girls were on standby to apply restraints if Emma decided to move even an inch in the wrong direction. She started following commands.

"Close your eyes."

"Open your eyes."

"Turn your head to the side. Other side."

"Tilt your chin up."

"Don't move."

"Stop wiggling."

She coughed on the intake of hairspray and sneezed at the puffs of powder substances floating in the air. Did girls always use such toxic substances? It took way too much effort to be a girl.

"Done," Lauren finally declared.

Emma breathed a sigh of relief and faced the mirror to see the damage. The only reason she recognized herself was because her reflection cringed when she did. She looked like—dare she say it—a girl. It wasn't as horrible as the clown face she imagined—no bright red lipstick or raccoon eyes or anything—but definitely not the unpainted look she preferred.

"You mess any of this up before the end of the dance," Lauren said with malicious sweetness, snapping the cap back on the lip-gloss tube, "and you die."

Emma seriously believed Lauren would kill her too. Blonde psycho chick with an eyeliner pencil. "Why do you even care what I look like?" Emma asked, baffled by why Lauren had violated her Emma-no-touch policy to give her a makeover for some stupid dance.

Lauren smiled a vicious, twisted smile. "Because

teammate or not, there's no way I'm going to be seen in public with an ugly mutt like you in your white-trash clothes. It would ruin my reputation forever."

A few of the girls gave her sympathetic glances, but aside from Ashley, none of them hesitated to follow Lauren. They filed out of the bathroom and left Emma to sit and stare at her reflection in the mirror. Emma had spent too many years building her defenses to ensure Lauren's verbal slaps didn't hurt her, but once in a while her words slipped through the cracks and shocked Emma into silence. She'd never felt more like the ugly duckling in her life.

Ten

Emma didn't dress in school colors, paint her face, or scream like an idiot to show her school spirit. Aside from the boys' basketball games, she refrained from attending most extracurricular events. Just because the girls dragged her to the stupid dance didn't mean she had to participate. Stationary wallflower, here I come, she thought.

The girls clustered together in the darkened gym, all of them dancing except for Emma. Whatever fun she might've considered having had vanished back at Lauren's house. With Lauren's insults echoing in her head, she felt more out of place than usual. She crossed her arms self-consciously over her chest and fought for balance as the girls bumped into her, trying to get her to dance and show a little enthusiasm. How much longer could she endure this? Surrounded by darkness, music blaring from the speakers, the girls' nonstop squealing, and sure enough, way too much PDA. How could any of the girls think this was a fun way to spend a Friday night?

"Excuse me, ladies," a deep voice sounded beside her. "May I steal Emma for a moment?"

Her heart pounded time-and-a-half at the sound of Riley's voice. What was he doing here? He never came to these dances.

Needing to see him, needing to know he wasn't a figment of her imagination, Emma spun around to face him. Brown spiked hair, sweet smile, blue eyes staring back at her. She breathed a sigh of relief. He was real.

The girls in the circle froze and then nodded in response to Riley's question. He slipped his hand around Emma's, a move which none of the girls missed.

"Shall we?" he asked her.

She would've followed him through the desert with no water if he'd asked. The desert would've been her first choice, but he led her to the dance floor instead. Couples danced around them, spotlights swept through the darkness, and music vibrated the floor, but she could only focus on the boy in front of her.

"What are you doing here?" Her voice reached a pitch higher than she thought herself capable of reaching. Must be a girl thing when overcome with excitement, but she couldn't help it. Riley never came to these dances. He preferred a movie and popcorn or driving around town looking for action.

He shrugged. "Rumor had it a group of girls kidnapped a certain basketball player and brought her here. I thought she could use a wingman."

She threw her arms around his neck and squeezed. Riley almost always initiated the hugging action between them, considering her family wasn't exactly the hugging type, but relief forced her over the edge. "You have no idea how good it is to see you."

He laughed and hugged her back, but when she pulled away, he tightened his hold around her waist to prevent her escape.

"What are you doing?" she asked.

"Do you trust me?"

She could've said no, she could've teased him and made a game out of it, but something in his eyes made her answer seriously. "You know I do."

He smiled, and before she could protest, he grabbed her hand and twirled her around. She was surprised she didn't trip over her feet as he pulled her back to him and wrapped his arms around her waist again, already swaying to the music. This is what he had in mind in terms of trust? Dancing?

"We don't have to dance." She'd never been let loose on a dance floor before; she didn't know what kind of damage she was capable of committing. Thankfully, the DJ put on a slow song, reducing the risk of Emma looking like a complete loser. She had no choice but to wrap her arms around Riley's neck and hold on.

"I know." He leaned his face closer to hers. "But judging by the look of your posse, you won't get far if I release you."

She turned to see all of the girls staring at them. A few of them waved and gave her two thumbs up. Stupid girls. Hadn't they ever seen two friends dance together before? She bowed her head into Riley's shoulder wishing she could disappear forever. "Ever get the feeling you're the center of way too much unwanted attention?"

"Aw, come on. It's not too horrible dancing with me, is it?" he asked.

"Of course not, but you know me. This isn't my scene." She looked at his face, but it didn't seem like he shared her distaste for the situation. "I didn't think it was your scene either."

"It's not so bad," he said, reaching up to sweep her hair over her shoulder, "being here with my girl and watching her get all embarrassed because for once she's being noticed off the basketball court."

Since when did being noticed become a good thing? For Emma, being noticed usually meant people like Lauren laughing and pointing at her, piling on criticisms and insults. Her mom's abandonment and her family's financial status had not escaped anyone's attention over the years.

Her story was well known by pretty much the entire school. Not everyone vocalized their distaste of her like Lauren, but they definitely kept their distance, as if they thought her deficiencies were contagious. All Emma wanted was to spend the evening alone with Riley, not under the prying eyes of a certain group of girls. "I'll do your chores for a week if you can free me from them," she said, nodding in the direction of her teammates, her voice wavering with desperation.

He looked at her in silence for way too long, his eyes studying her face. Times like these made her feel exposed. She never knew what he saw in her, but she could never stay hidden from him.

"You shouldn't always be so afraid of the unknown, Em," he finally said. "You never know if something good will come of it."

The way he said it made her think there was more weight to his words. "Are you just talking about girls and basketball?"

Their swaying slowed to nearly a stop as they looked at each other, neither one breaking eye contact. She felt her cheeks burn and questioned the feeling in her stomach. Almost like nerves, but what did she have to be nervous about? Maybe it was because Riley was close, too close, or maybe it was the dancing making her head spin. Something other than friendship seemed to pass between them. She felt his arms tighten around her waist, felt his breath on her cheek, and was it her imagination or was he leaning closer even still?

Without warning, the slow song erupted into a fast one. The beat vibrated through the floor and pulled them apart. Whatever had passed between them vanished, and Emma exhaled the breath she didn't know she'd been holding. Maybe she'd imagined the entire thing. Stupid school dances always confused things.

Riley didn't seem affected at all as he cleared his throat

and smiled at her. "I might be talking about dancing too."

She matched his smile as he took her hand again and spun her before snapping her back to him. He started wiggling his head and bouncing around, trying and failing to find the beat. Emma couldn't help but laugh.

"What are you doing?" she shouted above the music.

"Dancing," he yelled back.

She shook her head. "That's not dancing."

"It's what everyone else is doing."

Emma looked around her. Sure, Riley's movements sort of resembled those of their peers, but everyone else seemed more competent and graceful at it. Their movements actually looked like dancing. Riley was good at a lot of things, but moving in sync with the rhythm of a song was not one of them. Watching his eyebrows scrunch together in concentration as he tried to mimic everyone else only made Emma laugh harder.

He grabbed her hand. "Dance with me."

"No, way," she said, shaking her head. "You look like a bobblehead on a pogo stick."

His concentrated look gave way to a grin. He shook his head like a dog and stomped around like some kid having a temper tantrum. She bent over, clutching her side, unable to breathe through her laughter.

Stopping abruptly, he grabbed her shoulders to steady himself. "I'm kinda dizzy."

Emma wiped tears from her eyes, choking back more giggles. "It's your own fault."

He slipped his arm around her shoulders. "I think I need to sit down. Maybe the whole dancing thing wasn't such a great idea."

"I told you," she slid her arm around his waist to support his weight, "that wasn't dancing; it was a crime against mankind."

He glared at her. "Very funny."

They found a bench in the commons and sat so Riley

could recoup after his dancing episode. He leaned his head against the wall and closed his eyes, while Emma took a deep breath and relaxed for the first time all night.

Compared to other people, Emma didn't have much in life. She didn't have money, fancy clothes, popularity status, a loving family, or dreams for the future, but maybe having so little helped her appreciate moments like this: her and Riley, side by side, taking it all in—the music drifting up from the gym, the laughter of their peers, the teachers-turned-chaperones attempting to enforce boundaries between couples. Moments like this made the world slow down and helped her breathe a little easier.

She glanced at Riley and smiled. With his eyes closed and his face relaxed, he reminded her of the boy she'd met eight years ago. The one who befriended her over a game of basketball, who protected her from the insults of other kids, who comforted her when life made unexpected turns. She loved how his arm hung loosely around her shoulders, how his hair spiked up in all the right places, how his unexpected presence at the dance calmed her. His eyes flickered open, and she looked away before he caught her staring.

Girls. Three of them walked by, the object of their affections obvious, as they glanced at Riley with smiles intact, hoping he'd look their way. He didn't. He stared past them, his arm draped over Emma's shoulders, like he didn't have a care in the world.

She nodded in the direction of the girls as they gave him a backward glance. "I think I'm cramping your style."

If it had been Tom instead of Riley, he would have abandoned Emma and pursued them like a cat after a mouse, but Riley cast them a quick look and turned his attention back to Emma.

"I could say the same thing," he said.

Emma scrunched her eyebrows together in confusion.

He nodded in the opposite direction, and her attention followed. Two guys she didn't know smiled at her when she made eye contact with them. It wasn't just a friendly you-up-for-a-game-of-basketball smile, but more like a let's-go-find-a-dark-corner-on-the-dance-floor   smile.   Emma shuddered. Scary. She spun her attention back to Riley, not wanting to give the guys any encouragement to pursue her.

Without the darkness to shield her, Riley saw her cheeks burn red, and he laughed. "They've been staring at you since we sat down. Not that I blame them; you do look amazing. Like a real girl."

She pushed away from him in disgust. She hated when he said things like that, especially since Lauren's words were still fresh in her memory. An ugly mutt like Emma wasn't supposed to elicit the attention of any guy or prompt compliments from her male best friend.

"Sorry," Riley said for nothing more than mere formality, "but I did notice."

It must have been the stupid hair and outfit the girls forced her to wear. "It's not my fault I was attacked by a bunch of crazy girls. Seven against one isn't exactly fair odds." She crossed her arms and slouched against the bench. "Trust me; none of this was my idea."

Movement caught her eye, and she glanced up to see Tom and Jerry coming their way from across the commons. Tom gave her a slow head nod and smiled like he was glad to see her. Odd. He usually didn't acknowledge her existence with such friendliness. Looking for a distraction, Emma raised her hand in hello and waved them over.

When Tom got closer, she realized his friendly face looked more like a kid ogling his favorite ice cream. She'd seen this look before. The one he saved for when he saw a pretty girl and was in prey mode. Oh, no.

Tom plopped next to her, way too close for comfort. "Who's your friend, Riley?"

The way Tom's eyes wandered over her made Emma squirm. She scooted closer to Riley. Tom seriously didn't recognize her. He was coming on to her. Gross. Did a girl just have to put on a tight shirt and do something different with her hair for guys like Tom to gawk at her?

Riley patted her leg and laughed. "Oh, you know, just some girl."

"Geez, Em." Jerry grabbed a strand of her wavy hair and pulled it straight. "When did you become a girl?" He let go of her hair and it sprung back into place.

"Oh, man," Tom said, his jaw dropping as recognition hit him. "It *is* you."

"Ya think?" She pushed him away. Dumb jock applied to Tom in too many ways.

The ogling look returned to Tom's face as he slung his arm around Emma's shoulder and pulled her toward him. "I could get used to this."

She shrugged off his arm and stood. "Ew." The idea of Tom thinking of her as an actual girl made her want to punch him. It was just...wrong.

"Why are you dressed like that?" Jerry asked as if it was too weird for him. Good. At least one of the guys was on her side.

"I was attacked by the girls on my team. Their brilliant idea to come to the dance together," she said, rolling her eyes.

"If you're supposed to be with the girls, what are you doing with this loser?" Tom asked, punching Riley on the arm.

"You know how she is," Riley said with a grin. "She just can't get enough of me."

She opened her mouth to respond, but then she heard the familiar voices of her fellow species behind her. She squeezed her eyes shut. Not now. Please, not now. Five more minutes of quality guy time was all she needed.

"There you are," Ashley said, grabbing Emma's arm.

"Hey, kid," Emma muttered. "Do me a favor and come back in ten minutes."

Madison appeared on Emma's other side. "Nice try, but

we're here as a team, and we can't be a team if you're not with us."

Since when did they consider her part of the team? Since when did team spill over the edge of the basketball court and seep into private time? Emma looked to Riley for support, but he just waved at her, smiling his stupid lopsided smile, as hands dragged her away from him. So much for her wingman.

Eleven

Emma had to wash her hair three times to get all the hairspray out, and she'd nearly scrubbed her skin off trying to remove the face paint. After her wingman allowed her to be kidnapped by the girls for the second time, she endured another two hours of giggling, hip bumping, gossiping, and squealing before the dance finally ended and Madison took her home.

Never. Again.

Even though teaching the art of the drive to a freshman who had difficulty not tripping over her own feet proved to be more challenging than Emma expected, returning to one-on-one practices with Ashley was a welcome task after the stupid dance. Sure the kid could dribble, but add a defender and the pressure to score, and the kid froze like an ice cube. The success plan consisted of repetition and slow motion. One dribble, two dribbles, with verbalized instruction every step of the way.

After an hour, and what felt like a thousand repetitions, Emma finally saw progress. Ashley's movements became quicker and more fluid. Her small body, filled with confidence, controlled the ball as she swept around Emma and drove to the basket, pulling up for a shot to complete the play. The kid whooped and hollered after every drive, but

Emma refrained from patting the freshman on the back or giving her any kind of encouragement or praise. That's how egos formed and friendships started.

"Lookin' good, girls."

The voice rang loud and clear in the empty gymnasium. Emma froze. No. No, no, no. This was not happening. Riley was *not* supposed to be here; he wasn't supposed to know about her post-practice sessions with the freshman. She spun around to his all too familiar face smiling back at her.

"What are you doing here?" she hissed, walking quickly toward him to block his attempt at a meet and greet with the freshman.

He strutted forward with a grin plastered on his face. "I told you I'd find out eventually," he whispered in her ear. He looked over Emma's shoulder and nodded at the freshman. "Who's this?"

"Nobody," Emma said through gritted teeth.

"That's not very nice," Riley said like he was some authority figure teaching her manners.

How could she care about good manners or spare the feelings of a freshman when he was two seconds away from finding out her precious secret? She placed her hands on his shoulders and pushed him back toward the door. "Neither are you for showing up here uninvited."

"That's a best friend's right." He spun past her and made a beeline for Ashley, his hand outstretched like he was a boss welcoming a newbie to the job. "I'm Riley, and you are?"

Ashley smiled shyly and slipped her tiny hand in Riley's. "Ashley."

"Nice to meet you, Ashley," he said, his face pinched with mock professionalism. "And what exactly is your relationship to my beloved Emma Wrangton?"

Ashley suppressed a giggle. "Emma's teaching me how to play basketball."

Emma slapped a hand to her forehead. Did freshmen

not know when to keep their mouths shut and not willingly give information just because some guy asked for it?

"Really?" Riley asked in surprise, turning around to look at Emma. It obviously wasn't the response he'd expected.

Ashley nodded. "She's amazing."

"I know," he said genuinely, not taking his eyes off Emma.

"Okay." Emma grabbed him by the arm. "You've figured out my little secret. Now it's time for you to leave."

He winked at Ashley and twisted out of Emma's grasp. "Relax, Em. I'm here to give you a ride home."

"I don't need a ride home."

He ignored her and headed for the bleachers. "I'll sit over here and wait. You won't even know I'm here."

Emma always knew when Riley was around. Even if she couldn't see him, she always sensed his presence. Maybe it was a best friend thing or a girl thing or some twilight zone thing. Whatever it was, she couldn't ignore him, no matter how hard she tried. But what other choice did she have? She turned her back on him and tried to focus on Ashley, knowing her attempts to ban Riley from the premises would only increase his determination to stay.

"Is he your boyfriend?" Ashley whispered.

"No!" Emma snapped. "He's just a friend."

Ashley glanced over at Riley. "He's cute."

Emma rolled her eyes. Typical girl response. "Can we please focus here?"

"Sorry."

Teaching Ashley under Riley's scrutiny was not the easiest thing she had ever done, especially since whenever Emma's eyes wandered toward him, he'd smile and wave like he had every right to watch them. The kid laughed every time. When Emma couldn't take it any longer, she ended practice fifteen minutes earlier than usual.

The three of them walked out together. Riley and

Ashley made small talk. Emma fumed. She hadn't wanted them to meet, knowing Riley would take Ashley under his wing and befriend her, while laughing at Emma for taking on a pity project.

Ashley and her mom gave Emma identical waves, complete with super-duper girly smiles, before driving into the night. Aside from a few side-glances from Riley, their ride home took place in silence. She didn't feel like explaining her actions or listening to him tease her, so she stared out the window at the darkened sky with her mouth closed.

"Why didn't you tell me?" he finally asked. They were sitting outside her house in his jeep. Emma not ready to go in and Riley not ready to let her.

"Tell you what? That I'm teaching some freshman how to put a ball through a hoop?" She continued to scowl out the window, unable to look at his face. Here it comes, she thought. The laughter, the accusation, the ridicule.

"You're amazing, you know that?"

Or not. His sincerity caught her off guard, and she turned to look at him. His eyes were gentle, kind. Like he was watching a stranger with awe. She didn't understand. "For teaching some freshman how to put a ball through a hoop?" she repeated. It seemed pretty basic to her. It's not like basketball was a game for superheroes or anything.

"I'm proud of you."

"Oh, thank you," she said, the sarcasm rich in her voice. "Not only do you play the role of my best friend, but you wear the hat of my dad as well. How fortunate for me. Tell me, what other roles do you play?"

He grabbed her leg just above the knee and squeezed, knowing it was the most ticklish part of her body. It was the only time she squealed like a girl. He laughed as her high-pitched shriek flooded the interior of the jeep, and she struggled to pry his hand from her leg.

"You're not as tough as you think you are." He leaned

back in his seat, watching her. "I think you're actually enjoying this whole basketball thing. Including the girls."

Her jaw dropped. It was the most ridiculous thing ever. She had a strict no-girl-enjoyment policy. It was ironclad, as in unbreakable, nonnegotiable, nontransferable. "You're delusional."

"Why else would you spend time teaching a freshman girl how to play?" he challenged her. "It doesn't exactly fit your profile."

"I didn't have a choice," she protested, remembering only too well how the entire mess started in the first place. "The kid cornered me after practice, begging and pleading, two seconds away from drowning me in her waterworks."

He chuckled. "I'm just glad it wasn't a boyfriend. A freshman I can handle, but a boyfriend? Too much drama."

She shook her head, his comment not worthy of a response. To him, a boyfriend would cause more trouble, but she'd prefer the boyfriend to a team full of girls any day.

He smiled, amused. "It'd be okay, you know."

"What?"

"If you liked them."

"I don't," she said firmly.

"I know," he said, "but if you did, some day, it'd be okay."

Lauren's sneer popped into her head, along with Madison's tears after the ball smacked her in the face, and Ashley's wide, beady eyes every time she saw Emma execute a move on the court. Liking them was not an option.

◆◆◆

Emma and Riley walked to the neighborhood court together. The air was cold and crisp and tasted like freedom. After a week of practicing with the girls, plus the extra hours with Ashley, Emma relished in the opportunity to play with the guys again. To play without holding back and

123

worrying about whether her passes would knock some girl down. All she wanted was one girl-free Saturday with the guys, which was why the sight of Ashley huddled next to the fence stopped her in her tracks.

"What are you doing here?" Emma demanded of the freshman.

It was Riley who answered. "I invited her."

She spun on him. "You what?"

"You heard me."

"What, five days a week plus overtime with her isn't enough? She has to encroach on my weekends too?" Emma took a deep breath and held it to prevent from screaming.

"Relax," Riley said. "I figured the kid would like to see how real basketball is played. What better people to watch than you and me, huh?" He nudged Emma with his elbow, but she wasn't flattered by his compliment.

"Hi, Ash." He smiled at Ashley, causing Emma to scowl. The last thing the freshman needed was encouragement to stick around.

Ashley looked at Emma with innocent eyes. "I don't want to impose."

"You're not," Riley said before Emma could respond. "Stick around and learn a thing or two."

Why did he always get his way? Even if she called in an army full of people whose sole mission was to take her side, Riley would still get his way. Life wasn't fair, it was infuriating. She remained silent, but it wasn't a secret that she was two seconds away from going lethal, and Riley knew it.

"Excuse us." Riley grabbed Emma's arm and pulled her away from Ashley.

Emma twisted out of his grasp. "You could have at least warned me she'd be here."

"What for? It's not like she has the plague or something." He looked at Ashley as she stared at the guys on the court, her mouth open and eyes shining. "Besides, she kind of reminds me of you as a freshman."

"Is that supposed to make me feel better?"

He laughed and passed her the ball, trying to distract her. He seriously didn't understand the issues she had with girls. This entire time she'd thought they were on the same page of the same book governed by the same set of rules. Riley had never been interested in girls until they became the central point of her madness, and now he wanted them as allies.

Emma scowled at Ashley, wondering why Riley had taken an interest in her and why Ashley was so intent on invading every part of Emma's life. Her one day of real basketball with people she liked? Corrupted. Taking a deep breath, she found comfort in the fact Ashley would be watching from the sidelines. Her feet would not step onto the court to foul up the game or trip someone or give the guys a reason to tease her. Today, Ashley was a spectator, not a player.

Emma joined Tom, Jerry, Riley, and Cy to shoot around until the rest of the guys showed up. No duck and cover method here. All shots, if not going through the net, at least hit off the rim. No girly shots. No air balls. No whining or crying. Saturday was a great day, even with the annoying freshman in tow.

"Who's your little friend?" Tom asked, approaching Emma and nodding toward Ashley.

Her lips curled in disgust. "No one. Just some girl from my team."

"She's cute."

Emma shot the ball. "Don't even think about it." She recognized the prey-mode look in Tom's eyes and was well aware of his habits toward the female population. He earned his bragging rights through demonstration, not by sitting on the sidelines and dreaming. "She's too innocent for you."

Tom looked at Ashley and smiled as impure thoughts formed in his head. "I can fix that."

125

Emma spun toward him, yanked his arm behind his back and slammed him face-first against the chain-link fence, causing Tom to grunt in pain. A move she should thank her brothers for some day.

"Hey," Tom growled.

She tightened her grip on his arm, vaguely aware of Ashley and the guys watching her. "If you touch her, I swear I will break both your arms and make you cry like a baby in front of the entire school so no girl would ever think about giving you the time of day ever again." She felt Tom's arm in her hand, heard her voice threaten him, and felt her stomach sicken over his comment about the freshman, but why in the world should she care? Girls were the enemy, not Tom, but she couldn't help her reaction.

He held up his free hand, showing mercy. "Relax, Emma. I was just messing around."

"Go mess around with someone else," she said through clenched teeth, releasing her hold on him and shoving him away. Her friendship with Tom, although better than her relationship with any of her brothers, wasn't built entirely on conflict-free resolutions. Regardless, she would take his side over any girl's. At least she thought she would. Until now.

She whirled around, unable to look in Tom's direction, and found herself face-to-face with Riley. "Impressive," he said, his face unreadable. "If I didn't know better, I would think the freshman is starting to grow on you."

"That's ridiculous," she seethed. A momentary lapse of control didn't mean anything. "I just don't want his filthy thoughts distracting my players. We've got enough to worry about without him creating drama."

He shrugged. "If you say so."

She hated when he did that. Saying he believed her when he totally didn't, everything about him gearing up for the I-told-you-so moment.

They finally had enough guys to make the game fun,

and Emma soon left the drama of the day behind and just played basketball. The fast breaks down the court, the all-out defense, the passes firing from one set of hands to another. Surrounded by guys. No girls. Basketball at its best.

Ashley was their own little cheerleader, cheering and clapping from the bleachers any time someone made a shot or executed a good move, no matter what team they were on. At first the guys looked at Ashley like she was crazy, but as the game wore on they smiled at her, took breaks to give her high fives, and just like that it happened: Ashley became their own little mascot. Emma found the whole scene annoying, but when they took a break an hour later, not even Ashley's presence cast a shadow on her mood.

She joined Ashley on the sidelines and snatched her water bottle from the ground.

"Riley is so cool." Ashley watched him goof around with some of the guys. Of all the guys out there, Riley had given Ashley the biggest smiles and the most attention. Why wouldn't Ashley love him?

Emma gulped water and swiped the back of her hand across her mouth to catch any loose drops, her eyes on Riley. "Yep. He's the best."

Ashley peered up at Emma, her eyes curious. "Do you like him?"

"Of course I like him," Emma said. "He's my best friend."

"No," Ashley said. "I mean do you *like* him?"

Emma looked at the freshman wondering if the kid was hard of hearing. "Didn't I just say yes?"

Ashley laughed and shook her head.

"What?" Emma's mood soured the longer their conversation stretched out.

"You're completely clueless," Ashley said, not a bit shy at stating her opinion. "What I'm asking is, do you like Riley as more than a friend? Like as a boyfriend?"

127

"What?" Emma screeched. Where in the world did the kid get such a stupid idea? "Of course not. Do I look like the kind of girl who spends her days swooning over some sleazy guy?"

The freshman laughed again. "Number one, it doesn't matter what you look like, you're not immune to love, and number two, we're not talking about some sleazy guy." She looked across the court at the boy in question. "We're talking about Riley."

Emma couldn't prevent her eyes from wandering in Riley's direction. Riley and Jerry launched balls from half-court, seeing who could make the first shot. Before he took the ball to shoot, Emma knew Riley would take a two-dribble head start, shoot the ball from his hip, and bounce on his toes, waiting for the ball to drop. She also knew the way he clicked his pen when doing homework, the way he hummed when everything felt right in his world, and the way his thoughtful eyes rested on her and the corner of his mouth lifted into a smile whenever he saw her. She knew everything about Riley. It was called friendship.

"I've seen the way he looks at you and believe me, there's more there than friendship."

Emma clenched her teeth, her hands balling into fists. "No. There's not."

As if to prove Ashley's point, Riley glanced over and caught Emma looking at him. He gave her an up nod and a smile, his gaze lingering longer than necessary before his demeanor became more lighthearted, and he waved at Ashley. Ashley didn't have to say anything. Her raised eyebrows and I-told-you-so smile said it all. Emma ignored her. Riley had looked at her like that a thousand times. What was the big deal? But then Emma's thoughts snapped back to the night of the dance. The way his arms wrapped around her waist and pulled her close, the way he held her gaze, the way she'd felt something other than friendship pass between them.

His words echoed in her head, *It's not so bad, being here with my girl.* Did he really consider her his girl? Did he see her as more than just one of the guys? She remembered the connection between them at the dance and how, near the end of their slow dance, he leaned in as if to...*no!* It couldn't be. Riley would not have kissed her in the middle of the dance floor with all those people. Would he?

Emma's heart pounded in her chest. Her mouth suddenly dry, she gulped down water, spilling half of it on her shirt and nearly choking. She gripped the edge of the bleachers to steady herself as the court started spinning, vaguely aware of the freshman watching her.

"You really didn't know?" Ashley asked gently.

Emma heard the sympathy in her tone. Like Ashley considered herself an adult mentoring some child. Emma squeezed her eyes shut. This whole thing was ridiculous. Ashley was the kid. She didn't know anything, especially about Emma's relationship with Riley. It was probably just some psycho girl trick to derail her, to cause tension between her and the boy she couldn't live without. The last thing she needed was to second-guess every smile, every word, and every touch her and Riley had ever exchanged. She wasn't about to let some girl corrupt the only good thing in her life.

Emma threw her water bottle on the ground. "Look, Riley and I are *just* friends. Nothing more. So keep your thoughts to yourself or I'll call it quits with our one-on-one practice sessions. You got it?"

Fear flashed in Ashley's eyes. She clamped her mouth shut and nodded.

"Hey, girls," Riley said, coming up behind Emma. He settled his arm around her shoulders like usual, sending a sense of protection and friendship through Emma, which only aggravated her more. Now was not the time for his friendliness. She shrugged off his arm, threw Ashley a glare, and stalked across the court, needing a basketball and a few guys who wouldn't play easy on her.

She and Riley were friends. Nothing more. So, why, when she glanced over at Riley and he smiled at her, did her stomach turn over like the engine of a car? And why did the sight of him with Ashley aggravate her? Must be a stupid girl thing. Hanging out with girls made her crazy. It made everyone crazy. Riley would never like Emma as anything more than a friend...would he? She shook her head to clear it and focused on basketball.

She would've preferred to be guarded by Tom. If she pushed, he would have pushed back, not caring if she was a girl or not. If she fouled him, Tom would seek revenge until it was a full-out challenge of who would win, especially after their little incident a while ago. Emma got Riley instead. He knew her too well to react. When she pushed him, he'd give her a step or two. If she fouled him, he'd tickle her ribs. But he always knew when something was wrong. Just like best friends do. The key word being *friends*.

"You okay?" Riley asked.

She held the ball at the top of the key, crouched in triple threat position. "I'm fine," she said coldly.

"Why don't I believe you?"

"I don't know. That's your problem." Okay, so that was a little harsh, but it was for the best to ward off any weird feelings between them, especially with the freshman watching. "You going to guard me like a girl all day or are you going to give me something to work with?"

He frowned. "Em, what's wrong?"

Like she was going to rehash Ashley's ridiculous assessment for him. "Nothing. Let's play." She resisted the urge to apologize to him. Ashley and everyone else needed to know nothing more than friendship existed between them.

She wouldn't let it.

Twelve

Emma glanced at Riley's profile. It was best to observe him when he was distracted by driving and wasn't aware of her staring. The thought of Riley and her being anything more than friends was absurd. Sure, his gaze lingered on her longer than any other guy she knew, and he was more affectionate with her than the other guys were, especially after the kissing on the cheek incident, and her stomach fluttered at the prospect of seeing him sometimes, and her heart ached when they were apart. But so what? This behavior was typical for friends. Best friends. Nothing else existed between them. Nothing else could exist.

Rain poured from the sky. Even with the windshield wipers thumping back and forth on full speed, the road to school was barely visible. Leaves and debris clogged the street drains, causing water to partially cover the roadway. Not ideal weather to travel in for an away game.

Riley hunched over the steering wheel, as if being six inches closer to the road would allow him to actually see the lane.

"Stop breathing so hard." He adjusted the vents. "You're fogging all the windows."

She took a deep breath, opened her mouth, and exhaled, adding an extra layer of fog to the interior of the car.

"Do you want to walk to school from here?"

"Only a crazy person would walk to school in these torrential rains," she said. "Besides, you're too nice to cast me out of the car without an umbrella or a decent rain coat."

He laughed at her. "Yeah, you're right. I am nice. Unlike some people I know." Despite the road conditions, he risked a glare in her direction to emphasize his point.

See? Nothing but healthy best friend bantering.

They pulled into the school parking lot where dozens of kids darted from their cars to the school building. Riley parked the car and switched off the engine. They watched the downpour, hoping it would let up for a minute or two so they wouldn't get drenched on their dash into school, but the black clouds overhead weren't going anywhere. Rain pelted the roof of the car like bullets, causing them to shout above the noise.

"You ready?" he yelled at her.

"Ready as I'll ever be!" she yelled back.

"One." They grabbed their backpacks from the backseat and secured them over their shoulders.

"Two." Hands on the door latches for a quick evacuation.

"Three." They hopped out of the jeep, slamming the doors behind them, and raced to the school building. Days like these didn't make the parking lot's distance from the school convenient. Sure, it would have been smart to bring umbrellas or raincoats, but wet stuff was a pain to store in lockers. Their feet sloshed through the puddles, the rain soaking them by the time they took refuge inside the school.

"Well, that was fun." Riley shook his head so drops of water splattered Emma's face.

She pushed him against the lockers in retaliation and he laughed.

"I'll see you in second period." She left him to stare after her. Her shoes squeaked against the linoleum floor as she weaved her way through the hall. She spun the numbers on her locker, shook water from her backpack, and transferred books from her locker into her bag for her morning classes. Everything was wet. The thirty-second sprint from the parking lot into school was enough time to dampen everything in her bag. Hopefully, teachers took into account the current weather conditions when they asked for homework.

"Hi, Emma."

The voice didn't hold the deep tone of Riley or one of the guys. Emma turned toward the girl's voice and froze. "What happened to you?"

Yes, Emma was wet, but Ashley was soaked from head to toe like she'd been dunked in a swimming pool with her clothes on, the basketball in her hand glistening with water. She had a silly grin on her face. "Nothing."

"Why are you so wet?"

Confusion registered on Ashley's face. "What do you mean? It's Tuesday. I walked to school like you told me to. I'm not good enough to dribble and hold an umbrella at the same time."

Did freshmen not have a shred of common sense? "I didn't mean you had to walk in the torrential downpour," Emma said, keeping her distance from the waterlogged kid. Water continued to drip from Ashley's clothes, creating a puddle on the floor around her.

Ashley shrugged. "It's not so bad. It's just a little water. Besides, I think my dribbling is awesome." Her face lit up, and she spun the ball in her hands. "I dribbled the entire way and only lost control of the ball three times. Pretty good, don't you think? I even tried some of your fancy dribbling moves to avoid the puddles. They didn't work out so well, but I'll get there. I think I'm ready for the game tonight. Do you think I'll get to play so I can show you? I have a good feeling. We're definitely going to win tonight."

"That's great." For once Emma wasn't interested in talking basketball. Ashley stood dripping water all over the floor with a basketball clutched in her hands like she hadn't just walked a mile in the pouring rain. What was with this kid? "Do you have a change of clothes?"

Ashley shook her head. "I'm fine. Really."

"You're fine until you have to sit through six hours of classes. Trust me." Emma knew from experience what it was like to sit through school in sopping clothes, which is why she was always prepared. She dug into her locker and pulled out a pair of sweats and a t-shirt. They didn't smell fabric-softener fresh, but they didn't smell like mildew either. "Here," she said, offering them to Ashley. Despite her lingering irritation from her last conversation with Ashley, she couldn't let the kid suffer. "They'll be huge on you, but at least you won't freeze."

Ashley grabbed the clothes with her free hand. "Thanks."

Emma gave her one more look-over and shook her head. "And from now on, no more walking to school in the rain, got it?"

Ashley smiled. "Got it, Coach."

"I'm not your coach," Emma said with an edge to her voice. "Don't ever call me that again."

Ashley giggled. "Whatever you say."

The kid weaved through the bodies towering above her as she made her way to the bathroom to change. Emma shook her head again. It was the only thing she could do when she watched Ashley. Even as a freshman, Ashley was the most pitiful kid she'd ever seen, but Emma couldn't help but smile at the image of her dribbling down the street, dodging raindrops and puddles to improve her basketball skills. No, she didn't like Ashley—it went against her no-girl policy—but something about the kid was difficult to ignore.

She hoped the freshman was right about them winning tonight. They'd won their first game of the season, but they'd lost their two games since then. More than anything,

Bradshaw needed a victory, especially against their cross-town rival.

♦♦♦

Bodies slammed against each other, elbows hammered to find a way to the basket, fingernails drew blood. The battle between Bradshaw and Evergreen High School gave new meaning to the concept of cross-town rivalry. Even Emma, with no history on the girls' team, could feel how the game against the number one team in the league was about so much more than basketball. The snide remarks, the unnecessary fouling, the smug grins. Evergreen didn't want to beat Bradshaw; they wanted to humiliate them.

Having figured out Emma was the star player, Evergreen attacked her from all sides. She couldn't just shoot or drive, she had to jab, fake, spin, and fight her way between two and three defenders for every shot. No matter how good of a player she was, Emma couldn't play this game alone. Her teammates, focused more on avenging fouls than winning, threw up random shots, forced their way through two or three defenders only to lose the ball, and lagged behind on defense. Despite how much Bradshaw needed a victory, this game wouldn't be the one for them.

Halfway through the second quarter, Bradshaw down by twenty, Ashley subbed in to give Emma a rest. From the second the freshman stepped onto the court, the Evergreen players targeted her, knowing she was the weakest player on the team. She couldn't take two steps without being bumped or fouled. Ashley spent more time on the floor than upright, but she was a fighter. The kid pushed her bruised body off the floor every time and resumed the game at a sprint. Whatever she did during her mile walks to school every day, the kid was right, she could dribble. She kept the ball low, close to her body, weaving through defenders, and dribbling down the court to set up each play just like Emma had taught her. When fouls resulted in shooting a one-and-one shot, Ashley stepped to the line, spun the ball in her hands, and sunk two shots like a pro. Emma couldn't help but smile.

"Emma."

She heard Coach call her name, but she held up a finger, indicating she needed another minute, and snatched a water bottle off the floor to give the kid some extra playing time. No matter how much the freshman improved, Coach didn't let her play longer than a minute or two before plucking her out and sentencing her to the bench. Emma felt Coach's eyes on her for the signal to sub her back in, but she kept her eyes on Ashley.

"Emma."

Coach's impatience escalated as the freshman got smashed between two defenders and fell to the floor, so Emma finally nodded and trotted down to the sub-in table. The buzzer sounded and Emma intercepted Ashley coming off the court. She placed her hand on the kid's head and said into her ear, "Plant your feet and don't let them push you around. Use your speed and agility to fight back, all right?"

Ashley nodded and Emma smacked her on the back and rejoined her team on the court. By the time the second quarter ended, half the team was on the verge of fouling out and Bradshaw trailed by over thirty points.

Coach held the door open and ushered the girls inside the locker room for their halftime pep talk. Some of the girls found a seat on the one wooden bench in front of the chalkboard, while the rest of them leaned against the lockers. The place smelled like stale perfume and body odor.

Coach Knowles took her place in front of them. They waited for her to dissect the first half and draw the plan for the remainder of the game, to give some awe-inspiring speech and tell them to fight back, but her eyes only scanned the clipboard in her hands. Did the woman know half time was only ten minutes long? The silence stretched way too long before Coach cleared her throat. "You girls are doing great out there. We just need to...refocus a bit."

Seriously? After the extended silence, Coach's only advice was to refocus a bit? They needed to focus period. Too many of Evergreen's points were earned from the free-throw line. Wide-open shots with no defenders? Who could miss them? If Lauren and her groupies didn't foul them every five seconds, maybe Evergreen wouldn't get so many free shots.

"Let's watch the fouls. Lauren. Shiloh. Madison. You each have three. Two more and you'll foul out. And we can't afford that." Coach's demeanor wasn't one of strictness or authority. She had resorted back to her old let's-just-be-friends self.

"It would help if the refs didn't make such lousy calls," Lauren muttered.

"Or maybe they could try calling fair for both teams," Shiloh added.

Emma almost choked. "Are you kidding me?" She couldn't help it. The words popped out before she could swallow them. If Coach was going to act like a wallflower, someone needed to speak up. Did they even understand what constituted a foul? "From what I've seen, I'm surprised you all haven't fouled out already."

"Oh, here we go," Lauren said, rolling her eyes. "Didn't your mom ever teach you to speak only when spoken to? Oh, wait. I guess she wasn't around long enough for that."

No one spoke as Emma's hands clenched into fists. She took a deep breath, trying to remain calm. As much as she would've loved to teach Lauren a thing or two, Emma let her comment slide and plunged ahead with the real issue. "Newsflash! Your strategy of fouling every chance you get isn't working. Evergreen is shooting ninety percent from the line, which means for every ten shots they take, they make nine. As in nine points." Emma looked at each of her teammates. "You guys want to win? Play smart. Stop fouling. Let them run into you and draw the foul for a change. Make them send you to the line and then sink two shots like it's the easiest thing you've done all day."

Madison and a couple others exchanged glances before looking at Emma, their brows creased in doubt. Coach Knowles stood in the front of the room, arms crossed, watching the team, but not intervening. Big surprise there. How had a woman who hated conflict ever get signed on to coach a girls' basketball team?

"In other words, we need to be like Ashley and let them clobber us," Lauren said, unconvinced Emma knew what she was talking about.

Emma looked at Ashley who bowed her head, her cheeks flushing. "Yes, like Ashley," Emma said. "They may be fouling her, but at least she's not handing them the ball and giving them wide open shots. If you haven't noticed, Ashley's had a few opportunities to score from the free-throw line and six of our points are from her."

"Lucky shots," Shiloh muttered.

Emma saw Lauren and Madison nod in agreement.

"Lucky shots?" Emma crossed the room to confront Shiloh. "And how many points do you have? Maybe four? And, unlike Ashley who's only played for two minutes, you've played almost the entire time. Interesting."

Shiloh diverted her eyes, and Emma looked around the room at her so-called teammates. Not even when they were losing by thirty points did they show any interest in playing as a team.

Before anyone else said anything, Emma continued. "Unless we want to lose this game by fifty points, we'd better step it up and start playing basketball. Stop fouling, start scoring, and start playing like a team. Let's take control of this game." She stood like an idiot with her hand outstretched for the team huddle, waiting for her teammates to join her. No one moved. Emma's one attempt to initiate a team action was denied. The seconds ticked by, feeling like an eternity, until Ashley stood from the bench in front of her and placed her hand on Emma's. She gave Emma a smile. Emma winked in return. One by one each of the other girls finally stepped forward.

Coach extended her hand into the circle. "Team on three."

Emma bolted for the door, flung it open, and emerged from the locker room. The gym didn't feel as claustrophobic as the locker room, at least not at first, but then Emma caught sight of her defender from Evergreen, Valerie Hockus. Valerie was Evergreen's shining star and the girl knew it. Sure, she was a decent player, but nothing Emma couldn't handle.

With an arrogant grin, Valerie looked at the scoreboard and then at Emma. A silent slap in the face.

"I don't want to lose by fifty points." Shiloh, her brown skin still glistening with sweat from the first half, stepped beside Emma. "Tell me what I have to do."

"Block out and get the rebounds," Emma said, more as a challenge than an encouragement. "When they miss their first shot, we can't let them get the rebound and go up for a second or third attempt."

Shiloh cracked her knuckles, her scowl firmly in place as she stared at the other team. "Done."

Shiloh usually looked like nothing more than a six-foot-one stick figure, but standing beside Emma on the sideline, something about her changed. Maybe her tentativeness morphed into confidence or maybe her energy channeled into a purpose, but Emma felt herself smile, knowing the second half would be an entirely different ballgame.

Shiloh stopped fouling. She didn't reach in, she didn't swipe at the ball when someone went up for a shot, and she didn't ram into people to make a statement. Instead, she planted her feet, held her hands straight up in the air, and drew the offensive fouls. As she stepped up to the free-throw line, she met Emma's eye, and then put two shots through the basket without hesitation. Her four points increased to six, then ten, then twelve, but the most impressive part wasn't her scoring, it was her rebounding. Everyone heard Shiloh's grunts as she pushed off the floor, her hands extending above everyone else's, to snatch the ball from the air and bring it back down to playing level.

She was unstoppable.

Each time, she'd look for the outlet pass and snap the ball to Emma, like they'd been playing together for years. And just like that, Bradshaw reclaimed possession of the ball and the game. Evergreen's lead started to dwindle.

By the start of the fourth quarter, Bradshaw only trailed by twenty. Shiloh and Madison had avoided adding additional fouls to their record, but Lauren, who'd fouled out near the end of the third quarter, watched the fourth from the bench. With eight minutes on the clock, Evergreen tried to maintain control of the game and not let Bradshaw score any more points, but Bradshaw refused to give up, knowing if they couldn't win the game they'd at least turn a few heads and not go down without a fight. The intensity and viciousness of the game hadn't relented in three quarters and, if anything, it only escalated in the fourth. Bradshaw wasn't the same team as last year, and every player on the Evergreen team knew it. Evergreen may have held their lead, but it wasn't easy.

With two minutes left on the clock, Evergreen raced down the court on a fast break. Three-on-one. With a teammate on either side of her, Valerie brought the ball up the court with only one defender to face, Emma. Two points should have been a piece of cake, but the girl went one-on-one with Emma instead of taking a team approach. Sure, she had some fancy foot moves and fluid basketball skills, but Emma had played enough with the guys to read body language.

Valerie jabbed right, then left, faked a crossover and

then pulled up for a shot.

Smack!

The sound of Emma's hand blocking the ball ricocheted through the gym, and the ball soared out of bounds.

Boos and claps erupted from the crowd in an uproar of sound. Despite Evergreen's protests, the ref announced it a clean block.

Evergreen set up on the sideline to inbound the ball, and Bradshaw matched up with them. With a minute and a half left on the clock, the score no longer mattered to either team. Evergreen would win, no doubt about it, but Bradshaw wasn't done turning heads. On back-to-back plays, Christi stole the ball and raced downcourt to add four points to Bradshaw's score, Madison and Steph attacked the basket on a breakaway, and Steph scored with an easy jump shot. Everyone waited for Emma to make her move.

The seconds on the clock clicked backward giving just enough time for Emma to set up for the final play. She could have passed, maybe she should have, but she knew her teammates weren't ready for this moment yet—being in possession of the ball with ten seconds left on the clock against their cross-town rival. Being fifteen points down with less than ten seconds on the clock left time for only one thing—give the crowd something to remember them by.

Emma held the ball at the top of the key, face-to-face with Valerie. Sweat poured off her face, her heart beat time and a half, and her hands dribbled the ball between them. Waiting. Emma smiled; she loved these kinds of moments. Five seconds on the clock, five seconds to make her final move. Emma dribbled between her legs, once, twice, jabbed right, spun left, and plowed her way through the key. Two defenders collapsed on her, their hands raised to block her shot, but they were a second too late. Emma slipped between them, secured the ball between her hands and pushed off the floor. Suspended in the air, she looped the ball down and around before flipping it up over the rim of the basket as the final buzzer sounded.

Bradshaw lost by thirteen points, but it didn't matter. The roar from the Evergreen fans cheering for Bradshaw, the looks of hope in her teammates' eyes, and the anger and fear filling Valerie's face made Emma think of only one thing: rematch.

Thirteen

Highlights of their game against Evergreen swept through school the following day like the gusty winds of December. None of the guys had witnessed the game, but they could all retell the story of Emma's block and her final drive to the basket in detail to any eager listener. Courtesy of the freshman.

"I wish I could have been there," Riley repeated for the millionth time as he leaned against the wall of lockers while Emma swapped books out of her bag.

"It wasn't a big deal," she reassured him. Given the option, Emma always preferred to talk about basketball, but ever since last night's game against Evergreen, she grew restless whenever the subject came up. For the first time since entering high school, people actually started to look *at* her rather than *through* her. She felt exposed.

Riley's jaw dropped to the floor. "Not a big deal? Ashley can't stop talking about it. She said you dominated the game."

"I can't imagine the freshman using the word dominated to describe me."

He rolled his eyes. "So I condensed all of her Wonder Woman stories about you into one word. It still doesn't change the fact Jerry's right. You are a superstar."

This time Emma rolled her eyes. The whole basketball business was out of control. Since when did Riley and the guys take a freshman's word over hers? Did their years of friendship mean nothing? It was bad enough the guys treated her like some celebrity, but did the rest of the school have to suddenly acknowledge her existence simply because of her performance on the court? Kids who had spent the majority of their lives ignoring her nodded hello, congratulated her on a game well played, and stopped talking when she entered a room to stare at her. She even saw a few guys she didn't know reenact her shot block with wadded pieces of paper. Unbelievable! Emma wasn't interested in popularity or being liked because of some stupid trend.

Despite everyone's sudden interest in her, she did her best to ignore them and focus her efforts on planning for her one-on-one practice with Ashley. Even though the kid was starting to look like a real basketball player, she still had a lot to learn. As practice ended and their teammates filed out the door, Emma positioned Ashley at the top of the free-throw line with her back to the basket. The kid needed to learn how to catch a pass, spin to the basket, and make a split decision of whether to drive or shoot.

When Ashley's attention flickered to the sideline behind Emma, Emma didn't think much of it; when the kid nudged her arm and nodded toward the sideline, Emma spun around to scold Riley for making another one of his surprise appearances. Words froze on the end of her tongue when she saw, not Riley, but Shiloh and Peyton. With arms crossed and eyebrows raised, the two girls looked at Emma expectantly.

Recovering from the presence of two additional girls, Emma didn't try to keep her tone soft and welcoming. "What are you doing here?"

Shiloh nodded toward Ashley. "The freshman said you give private lessons."

Emma glared at Ashley. Rule number three of their little one-on-one practice arrangement: tell no one. So much for trusting Ashley to keep a secret.

Ashley's eyes bounced between Emma and the unwelcome visitors before throwing her arms up in innocence. "What? Shiloh asked why I stay after practice every day, so I told her you were teaching me a few things. I couldn't *lie*."

Emma closed her eyes and shook her head, trying her best not to reprimand Ashley. She turned back to Shiloh and Peyton. "The freshman was wrong. I don't give private lessons."

Shiloh shrugged. "Whatever you want to call them, we're in."

"In what?" Emma asked.

Shiloh rolled her eyes. "We're here to learn."

"Learn what?" Yeah, they had to spell it out for her. The last thing she wanted was to jump to conclusions only to give them ideas that were sure to drive her insane.

"You've seen us play. You know our strengths and weaknesses. We'll learn anything you want to teach us."

"I don't want to teach you anything. That's what Coach is for."

Peyton laughed. "We all know Coach is a flake. She has no clue how to coach, so it's up to you."

Emma opened her mouth to protest, but Shiloh held up her hand. "Look, I want to up my game to the next level, and to do that I need someone who knows what they're talking about to help me out. I've seen how you helped Ashley. I'll do whatever you tell me," Shiloh brushed by Emma, retrieved a ball from the rack, and joined Ashley on the court, "but I'm not taking no for an answer."

Peyton shadowed Shiloh, and as she passed Emma she whispered, "Same goes for me."

Were seventeen-year-olds too old to throw volcanic temper tantrums? Because Emma wanted to. Badly. Why did girls continuously invade her life? Did they know or care if their presence was unwanted? Emma looked to Ashley, hoping for backup, but the freshman just smiled, welcoming her new friends like sisters.

Outnumbered three to one.

Emma's head fell backward, looking to some higher power for strength and a whole lot of patience. "Fine," she exhaled in defeat. What other choice did she have? "But one strike, and we're done."

Emma scowled at their three identical grins, wondering how in the world her one-on-one practices with Ashley became three-on-one lessons with half the team.

◆◆◆

Emma didn't need to worry about Shiloh and Peyton saying anything about their private lessons to the rest of the girls. The next day at practice, aside from a few glances in her direction, they ignored her like usual. They laughed and joked around with Lauren and Madison and left Emma outside their clique, thank goodness. Truth be told, she preferred it that way. Sure she could teach them a few things about basketball, but she wasn't ready for friendship. It was best to keep it less personal and more basketball.

Five free throws. That's all each of them needed to make before they could escape from the gym for the evening. For Emma, free throws were like breathing. She could nail five free throws in less than ten seconds. For the rest of them it took anywhere from two minutes to half a day. Emma cringed at Madison's form. No wonder she couldn't make a shot to save her life. Evidently, Madison knew she lacked in the shooting department. How could she not? For every one free throw she made, she missed twenty.

"What am I doing wrong?" Madison whined to no one in particular.

Were these cries for help contagious? First Ashley, then

Shiloh and Peyton, and now Madison. Emma told herself to remain silent, to bow her head and not care about Madison bursting into tears. Emma wasn't a coach, she wasn't a friend, and she wasn't Santa's little helper. So why did she step in front of Madison, kick her feet shoulder-width apart, square her shoulders to the basket, straighten her shooting arm, and adjust her hands on the ball?

It was all Ashley's fault. If Emma had never started coaching Ashley, she wouldn't have thought twice about letting girls work out their own salvation. Despite Coach's increased efforts, some of the girls still had a long way to go in developing their basketball skills. Madison looked at Emma with admiration. Or maybe it was disgust. Emma couldn't quite tell from her scrunched up face. At least Madison didn't freak out when Emma touched her. She just stared at Emma, not sure what to do next.

Emma pointed to the basket. "Shoot."

Madison did as instructed. Her eyes nearly popped out of her head as the ball swished through the net.

Thank goodness, Emma thought. She rebounded the ball and passed it back to Madison. At least Madison had enough sense to try and copy Emma's changes to her form. Emma only had to adjust the position of her shooting arm and her hand placement on the ball.

Two in a row. A smile crept onto Madison's face when she looked at Emma. An actual smile. Emma was impressed it wasn't a sneer. Maybe there were differences between Lauren and her groupies.

Rather than acknowledge Madison's smile with one of her own, Emma ignored it and turned away. Another smile was plastered on Ashley's face, like she'd known all along how great Emma could be. Emma dropped her gaze to the floor.

Six attempts later, Madison sunk her final free throw. The girl screamed and flung herself at Emma before Emma could defend against an attack. Way to go Madison for overcoming her Emma-has-cooties mentality, but a little personal space would be appreciated. What was with girls and all the hugging?

When the psycho girl's arms didn't budge after five seconds, Emma couldn't take it anymore. "Okay, okay. Off."

Madison released her, but the girl's grinning face and hysterical giggles didn't retreat far enough away. Emma took initiative to put five feet of distance between them, deterring any thought of additional hugging action.

The team gathered at mid-court for their end-of-practice huddle, an action devised to promote team unity. Smashed into a huddle to shout a meaningless word at the top of her lungs with a bunch of girls didn't feel like team closeness to Emma. If guys surrounded her, she'd smell the sweat from their bodies and traces of food on their breath. Girls coated themselves with so much deodorant and perfume it was hard to breathe without choking.

Before the team could disperse, Lauren's high-pitched shriek ricocheted off the gym walls. "Wait, wait, wait." She ran to the sidelines and returned carrying a stack of papers. "I just wanted to remind everyone about our annual team-building event this Friday."

Team-building event? No one had ever said anything about a team-building event. Wasn't there enough team building going on during practice? Too much could be detrimental.

Lauren shoved a flyer in her hand.

Emma looked at the pink and blue flyer and her mouth dropped open in horror.

Fourteen

"**R**iley Aaron Ledger, get out here!" Emma screamed. "Now!" She pounded on the Ledgers' front door, ignoring the pain in her fist each time it struck the wood. If the door hadn't been locked, she would have burst into the house and forced Riley to show himself. He had to be home. His jeep was in the driveway. He couldn't evade her. Not this time. Of all the dirty, rotten moments in her life, the team-building event would definitely take spot number one. She pounded harder.

The door finally swung open and Riley appeared in front of her.

"Geez, Em. You're going to—" One full look at her face made his eyes widen with concern, and he grabbed her shoulders. "What's wrong?"

Her hands made fists at her sides, crumpling the flyer still clutched in her fingers. "You got me into this, now you have to get me out." Her whole body shook, and it took all of her self-control not to scream.

"What are you—"

"I've done everything expected of me and more." The words tumbled out of her mouth. "I've attended every practice and busted my butt in every game. I'm teaching Basketball 101 to some annoying freshman and her two

149

sidekicks. I attended the stupid school dance to build team unity." She held up the flyer. "But I am *not* doing this."

"Em," he said, holding up his hands to prevent her from attacking him. "You're seriously freaking me out right now. Slow down and tell me what you're talking about."

"I'm talking about this stupid team-building event," she said through clenched teeth.

"Okay." He shook his head, his forehead scrunching in confusion. "I think I'm missing something."

She slammed the flyer against his chest. "This is all your fault."

He pulled the crumpled paper from her fist and straightened it. She watched as his mouth upturned into a smile; his laughter started seconds later.

Her eyes narrowed into slits. "This is so not funny."

He bent over in hysterics.

Shaking her head in disgust, Emma spun around to leave. Help would obviously not come from him. He caught her around the waist before she got to the edge of the porch, and he positioned his body in front of her. "I'm sorry," he said, the traces of laughter still radiating from him. "I just can't imagine you at a—"

"Slumber party!" she finished for him, throwing her hands in the air. "I can't do it. I won't do it. I won't spend an entire night surrounded by girls. I'd rather be bitten by ten rattlesnakes and left to die in the desert."

"That's a little extreme, don't you think?"

"No! It's not extreme," she yelled at him. "Do you have any idea what girls do at slumber parties?"

He shook his head.

"Neither do I, but it can't be good." Images of mud masks and cucumber eyes formed in her head and she cringed. Giggling and gossiping, squealing and screaming. Emma gagged. She wouldn't go, she couldn't. Not if she had any dignity and self-respect. But what choice did she have when Coach threatened to bench anyone who didn't attend? Did Coach actually think some stupid slumber party would miraculously unite the team and help them win?

For the next eight days all the girls talked about was the slumber party. What to wear, what to bring, what to do. But the worst part, for once, wasn't the girls. It was the guys.

"Think about it Emma, you're going where no guy has gone before."

"You'll be our inside guy."

"You go in, get the dirt, get out, and reveal all."

Riley didn't help either. Sure, he stood beside her, but he couldn't keep the smile off his face. Emma was alone. Before she knew it, eight days had passed, and she hadn't managed to convince Coach to spare her sanity and let her off the hook. Instead, Emma found herself packing a bag and preparing for the worst night of her life.

♦♦♦

Riley stopped his jeep at the curb across the street from Lauren's southern plantation house and shut off the engine. Emma should've gotten out of the car, but she remained frozen in the passenger's seat, staring at the house. Lights shone from the windows and silhouettes of girls danced on the other side of the blinds. The sound of music drifted to her in the night.

"Would it be wrong of me to admit I'm afraid?" she asked quietly.

He turned toward her. "Afraid of what?"

"Of not fitting in." She didn't know how to be a girl. She didn't know how to relate with people who despised her. Sure, they expressed signs of gratitude when she gave them pointers on the court, but they had yet to form a sense of camaraderie. She didn't know how to survive an all-girls slumber party.

As if to demonstrate her point, Madison and Christi walked up the driveway to the front door, each carrying two bags, a sleeping bag, and a pillow. Emma and Riley watched as they rang the doorbell. A few seconds later, Lauren threw open the door and they all started screaming. High-pitched, glass-shattering screams.

Emma covered her face with her hands. "Kill me now."

"It can't be that bad." Riley squeezed her shoulder. "I mean, they are just girls."

She glared at him. He didn't understand. No matter how much he tried, he couldn't understand. Yes, these were girls. Girls who barely tolerated her existence at practice and at school where authority figures maintained peace between them. Lauren's house was dangerous territory. Sure, her parents may be home, but no way were they going to maintain visual on them during all hours of the night. This was bad. This was very, very bad.

"Okay, maybe it will be that bad," Riley said, seeing the look on her face, "but you can do this."

She could've stayed in the car with him all night, assessing the situation and imagining how bad the slumber party would be, but life had other plans.

A knock on the window caused Emma and Riley to jump. From the other side of the glass, Ashley waved frantically, a huge smile on her face.

Riley nodded at Ashley. "At least the freshman is excited."

"And that's supposed to comfort me how?"

He reached over and squeezed her hand. "You'll be fine."

Ashley, unable to wait another second, yanked open the passenger door and practically dragged Emma out. "Hi, Riley."

"Hey, kid," he said, raising his hand in greeting. "Go easy on our girl, will ya?"

Ashley giggled. Emma grabbed her stuff from the backseat and followed Ashley around the front of the jeep. She took one look at the house and returned to the car. Her hands clutched the window frame of Riley's door. "Keep your cell phone on and with you in case I need to be extracted. I expect you to come in full armor."

Ashley yelled to her from across the street, telling her to hurry.

"And bring back up," she added.

"You got it," Riley said. "And Em?"

"Yeah?"

"Try to have fun."

The screaming started as soon as the door opened. Fun was not an option.

For some girls, spending an entire night dressed in cotton candy colors, dancing around like Spiderman on jetpacks, and stocking up on gossip may have been a dream come true, but for Emma it was cruel and unusual punishment. She didn't know where she fit among the giggling clusters of girls, so she lingered in doorways and observed from the shadows, not wanting to draw attention to her oversized sweat pants and faded t-shirt. On the basketball court with her teammates, she could at least pretend to fit in, but no matter how many pointers she gave the girls, they would never accept her. Not that she wanted to be friends with them or anything, but maybe it wouldn't be horrible to not feel like such an outcast. Maybe.

When the energy level began to fizzle and pizza arrived, the girls couldn't resist a nice and quiet game of Truth or Dare. Evidently it was a popular game at the female watering hole. To make it more interesting, Lauren stripped it to just Truth.

Madison, not shy about revealing her secrets to anyone willing to listen, volunteered to go first. Sitting in a circle, all the girls focused their attention on Madison as she revealed her latest crush victim. Alex. Poor guy. What did he ever do?

"Last week in Physics when I dropped my pen and it rolled under Alex's desk, he bent over to pick it up, and when he gave it back to me," Madison's eyes widened in excitement, "he smiled."

Emma snorted. One smile from a guy was all it took to get girls to swoon? Note to self, tell the guys never to smile at a girl unless they wanted to be marked and targeted for marriage.

"What?" Madison asked innocently. "We definitely had a moment."

"Must have been a short-lived moment," Emma muttered, unable to bite her tongue and remain silent.

Madison's face retracted in hurt. More hurt than Emma would have thought possible by a comment coming from her mouth.

"Is hurting me your favorite thing to do?" Madison whimpered.

Six heads swiveled in Emma's direction to see if she'd admit to being the heartless and cruel person she portrayed. It didn't help when Madison's chin started to wobble. Tears would soon follow, and Emma didn't want to go down that road again.

"I—" Emma started, but she was cut off by Madison's outburst.

"What do you know anyway?"

Six pairs of eyes snapped back to Emma, and she froze. She knew Alex was a nice guy with a sweet smile he used on everyone. Consider it one of his bad habits, but Emma doubted Alex could get through an entire hour without smiling at someone. He was the type of guy who cut out early on Saturdays to spend time with his little sister, rescued kittens from trees, and would rather be picked last for a team to spare someone else the embarrassment. To sum him up, Alex was the smiling type of guy. Based on the unpredictability of girls, Emma figured the truth probably wasn't something she should vocalize amid a half-dozen boy-crazed girls.

"I know I need more pizza." Emma jumped up from the floor with plate in hand and practically sprinted to the kitchen. She cringed when she heard footsteps. Madison and the rest of the girls surrounded Emma, trapping her with the pizza. Not such a bad predicament considering there were still two pizzas left and she was hungry.

"Tell me what you know. Please." Madison's face had never looked so pitiful. Was this what guys had to deal with? One word and a girl broke down in tears. No wonder guys were weak. It was better to give in than to be the cause of a girl's waterworks.

Emma looked around at everyone watching her and knew she wouldn't be able to escape, so she caved. "Last weekend at the basketball court, Alex mentioned that he asked a girl from another school to the winter formal."

"Mentioned how?" Madison raised her chin to appear stronger than she felt. "Mentioned it like his parents forced him to ask her or like he really wanted to go with her?"

"I don't know." Did she have to dissect every word and body movement to satisfy these girls? He'd asked out another girl. Obviously, he hadn't felt the same connection as Madison. "He just said he asked her and she said yes." He was so excited about it, he could hardly concentrate on the game, but no way was she going to be that honest.

Christi raised her eyebrows. "And you just happened to be in on the conversation?"

Emma sighed. "I've been friends with these guys since elementary school. They talk about everything around me, especially on the basketball court."

Steph leaned forward, like this was the best news she'd heard all year. "Like what girls they like and stuff?"

Emma shrugged. "Sometimes."

Madison shook her head and slammed her hands on the counter. "I don't get it! Why do all the guys love you so much? I mean, you're not *that* pretty, you break every code of fashion with your boy clothes, and you spend most of your time scowling at everyone. Not to mention your financially challenged situation. You're a total nobody!"

"Thanks for that," Emma muttered.

"I'm sorry," Madison practically yelled at her, not sounding sorry at all. "But do you know what it's like not to be good at anything? Or to have guys look right past you when you try so hard to get their attention? Do you know what it's like to watch from the sidelines when everyone cheers for you like the rest of us don't exist? How are we supposed to compete with all your fancy dribbling moves and three pointers? It's not fair that you have it all."

"Is that what you think?" Emma asked in disbelief. She looked into the eyes of each of her teammates and noticed most of them nod in agreement. All this time Emma thought the girls hated her because she was poor, not because all her friends were guys. She shook her head in irritation. "You're the ones with the rich parents and the fancy cars and the paid college tuitions, and you think *I'm* the one who has everything?" Girls!

Emma tried to remain calm, but she couldn't stop her fingers from gripping the edge of the counter or prevent her voice from rising in volume. "Basketball is what I do, it's all I've ever done. I've been friends with these guys since elementary school. I can't help it if they would rather play basketball with me than be alone with you. If you spent half as much time practicing basketball as you do complaining, you might actually be a decent player, and guys might actually like you if you didn't have such a whiny voice or an ego the size of Mt. Everest."

Silence screamed back at Emma as the girls stared at her. She waited for them to shriek their protests or rise in rebellion against her. When they didn't, she grabbed a couple pieces of Hawaiian pizza and squeezed through the herd to reposition herself on the floor. In twos and threes the rest of the girls joined her.

"Emma's turn," Lauren said with false sweetness, as if the kitchen scene had never happened.

Emma knew better. Nothing about this scenario could be good. "I'll pass." The last thing she wanted was to engage in another girl fight. Payback. Revenge. Hatred. Emma didn't want any part of it.

"Everyone plays." Lauren cocked an eyebrow. "Unless you're afraid of a little…truth."

Emma grasped the concept of the game. Tell the truth and nothing but the truth. But for Emma, trust was earned not forced, and when the motive for a game was to extract dirt and gossip to take back to school on Monday, Emma wasn't in the mood to be a target. She'd been around girls enough to know they could chew you up and spit you out without breaking a nail or messing up their hair, especially after being provoked. But Emma knew she didn't have a choice—no way would she let Lauren intimidate her.

As she watched Lauren exchange looks with half the girls sitting in the circle, one thought came to mind: ambush.

Stay calm, she told herself. She had already endured seventeen years of ridicule, so one night couldn't be much worse. Her life wasn't exciting enough to entice much interest.

With a smug grin held in place, Lauren cleared her throat to begin the interrogation. "What's the *truth* behind your relationship with Riley?"

That's it? Her friendship with Riley was what Lauren wanted to know? Riley would get a kick out of that.

"We're just friends." It sounded more like a question, but Emma couldn't help thinking it was too easy.

"Of course you are," Lauren said, totally not believing her.

"Have you kissed him yet?" Peyton squeaked from across the circle.

"What?" Emma shrieked. "No."

"Has he kissed you yet?"

"No," Emma said firmly. "We're *just* friends."

"How do you explain the dance?" Madison raised her eyes, expecting to catch Emma off guard.

"What about the dance?" Emma asked. "You mean because he saved me from you clowns?"

Everyone had an answer for her.

"He held your hand."

"He slow danced with you."

"He couldn't take his eyes off you."

They fired their observations at Emma, causing the room to spin. So much for a dance between friends. She clutched her head with both hands. "Stop." Emma waited for silence. "We. Are. Just. Friends. Nothing more."

Lauren snatched her cell phone from the coffee table and flipped it open. "I wonder if Riley would say the same thing."

Under normal conditions, Emma would protect Riley from being dragged into this situation, but considering the night kept getting worse, she'd give anything to hear his voice. "Go ahead. Call him up."

Without hesitation, Lauren started dialing. Whether she had always known Riley's number or memorized it for the occasion, Emma didn't know, but Lauren punched speakerphone and all eight girls leaned forward when they heard the phone ring.

"Hello?" The voice on the other end was unmistakably Riley's, and Emma breathed a sigh of relief.

"Hi, Riley. This is Lauren." She tucked a strand of hair behind her ear like she thought he could see her, like she thought he cared about her appearance. If Riley ever showed interest in Lauren, Emma would personally beat him up.

Riley chuckled like he was either expecting her call or picturing Emma at the slumber party with her sworn enemies. "How's the party?" he asked.

"Great," a few girls said through their laughter.

I can think of another name for it, Emma thought.

"So," Lauren said. "We have a question for you."

"Okaaay." Emma could hear the hesitation in his voice.

"How would you define your relationship with Emma?"

Silence rang from Riley's end of the line. For a minute Emma thought he'd been disconnected. "Em, you there?" he finally asked.

"Having the time of my life like I told you I would," Emma responded, knowing he'd hear the sarcasm.

"You're not tied and gagged or anything, are you?"

She smiled. If only he knew. "Not yet, but the night's still young."

Emma relaxed a bit at the sound of Riley's laughter, until Lauren cleared her throat and regained control. "So, back to the question."

"Yeah, about that," he said, stretching the words out. "I'm gonna pass."

"Don't tell me a guy like you is afraid of one simple question." What was with Lauren's manipulative approach?

"What can I say?" Despite his relaxed tone, Emma heard the hardness to it. Even he wasn't fooled by Lauren's attempt at innocence. "I was never a fan of Q&A."

With a sly smile playing on her lips, Lauren clasped her hands together. "Sounds to me like you've got something to hide."

This time when Riley spoke, the hardness won out. "Nothing to hide, just nothing to share."

"Okay, then how about an easier question." Lauren's eyes wandered around the circle of girls until they landed on Emma. Emma froze, knowing she wouldn't like what came next. "Did you know Emma's in love with you?"

"What!" Riley and Emma exclaimed together. The whole idea was absurd. Emma should have known Lauren would go for the kill. She'd probably been planning this moment for weeks.

"Oh, please," Lauren said with a roll of her eyes. "Like it's not totally obvious with the way she's always drooling over you. It's sad. I mean, how can a guy like you even be *friends* with a girl like her? It doesn't make sense to me unless, of course, you're receiving some sort of," Lauren paused for effect, "benefit."

Emma should've laughed. She should've crushed Lauren's whole friends-with-benefits accusation and not given it another thought, but it wasn't about the words. It was the implication. The only reason Riley would slum so low to be friends with Emma—the picture of poverty, disgrace, and repulsion—would be if she made it worth his time. How could Lauren taint the only good, pure thing in Emma's life?

Emma's body tensed, her hands clenching into fists, her insides boiling with hatred.

Riley, however, laughed. At least he hadn't lost his sense of humor during her life crisis. "It sounds to me like some people underestimate the power of true friendship."

"Friendship." Lauren laughed a vicious laugh. "Helping the less fortunate must make you feel pretty good about yourself, Riley. You couldn't have picked a better charity case. Emma's so pathetic you had to buy her basketball shoes so she could play on the team, she wears her brothers' recycled clothes, and she doesn't have a mom around to teach her how to be a real girl." Lauren paused, her upper lip curling in disgust as she met Emma's glare. "She's the most pitiful person I've ever met."

Hundreds of comebacks fought on Emma's tongue to be flung like daggers at Lauren. Emma knew once they started they wouldn't stop, and she was afraid of what might happen if she lost control. Ordinarily, she would have shrugged off Lauren's comments without a second thought, so why was it so hard this time? Because as much as she wanted to deny it, it hurt seeing herself through someone else's eyes.

She felt the girls watching her, their eyes wide in fear. Not even Riley had a response.

With her body shaking, her hands still clenched, Emma forced her words to remain steady. "I need some air."

"Emma?" She could hear the concern in Riley's voice, but not even he could stop her from exiting the room in search of solitude. If she stayed a minute longer, she couldn't guarantee anyone's safety.

♦♦♦

Sitting on the back patio, surrounded in darkness, Emma searched the stars for answers. She knew she shouldn't have come to this stupid slumber party. Girls like her didn't mesh with girls like Lauren, no matter how much time passed or how many games they played together. She wanted nothing more than to leave, but she refused to give Lauren the satisfaction. She looked at the pool, the manicured lawn, and the basketball hoop, never feeling more out of place. What would it be like to live in a world where you could buy everything you needed and still have enough left over to buy what you wanted?

She pulled her knees to her chest and wrapped her arms around her legs. Nothing Lauren had said was a lie, but maybe the truth was supposed to hurt worse than lies. Emma tried to imagine what her life would be like if her mom was still around. Would her family be scraping by just to survive each day? Would everyone hate her? Would she be more girl and less Emma? Would the garage double as her bedroom? Maybe not having answers was for the best. Maybe she wasn't supposed to have it all.

Maybe she didn't deserve it.

"Hey."

Emma looked up to find Ashley plop down beside her. The kid handed her a bowl of ice cream smothered with chocolate sauce, marshmallows, and peanuts. "I figured dessert was in order."

"Thanks." Emma graciously accepted the dessert. Free food was always a plus.

They ate their sundaes in silence, staring at the pool and listening to the shrieks of laughter from inside the house. For a team-building event, the slumber party fell way below expectations. None of the girls inside cared whether or not two of their teammates sat outside their little clique; no one cared if the team splintered.

"You okay?" Ashley asked, breaking the silence.

"Peachy."

They caught each other's eye and laughed.

"At least now I know why you hate us so much."

Emma looked at the freshman, her forehead scrunched in confusion. Even if she wanted to scream at her teammates ninety-nine percent of the time and tell them to get it together, Ashley would be excluded from her extreme distaste of the female population. "Who said I hated you?"

Ashley shrugged. "I've seen you play with the guys, and I've seen you play with the girls. With the guys, you look like you're enjoying yourself. With the girls, you always look so mad. I've never seen anyone scowl and shake her head so much."

The guys and the girls were two different worlds. If Ashley or anyone else took a step back to look at the girls, they would glare and shake their heads too. Emma sighed. "I don't hate the team. I just don't relate well to girls."

"You don't relate well to girls," Ashley repeated. She looked at Emma, questioning her confession. "That is the lamest excuse I've ever heard."

Emma couldn't help but laugh. "What do you expect? I have four brothers, my mom left when I was a kid, so my dad raised me, and all my friends are guys. Girls are just too weird for me. Besides, if anything, they're the ones who hate me."

Ashley shook her head. "They don't hate you."

"They don't?" Emma knew hate when she saw it. A month full of glares, rude comments, and degrading confrontations spoke volumes of hatred, especially from one particular individual. "Not even Lauren?"

"Nope." Ashley stabbed her spoon into her remaining clump of ice cream. She stirred the contents of her bowl, the chocolate syrup swirling like a ribbon in the vanilla ice cream. "She's just jealous of you."

Rolling her head toward Ashley, Emma had a hard time accepting the whole jealousy angle. "And why would the girl who has everything be jealous of the girl who has nothing?"

Ashley kept her head bowed over her bowl and her spoon stirring. "Riley, for one."

"We're just friends," Emma clarified for the umpteenth time.

Ashley continued without acknowledging Emma's response. "You're the most awesome basketball player in the world, and for the first time in her miserable life, Lauren is outshone by someone, for two."

"That's ridiculous."

"And the fact most guys would rather hang out with you than be with her."

"But I already told you, we're just—"

"Friends?" Ashley finished for her, raising her head from her ice cream swirl to meet Emma's gaze.

Emma nodded slowly, questioning the look in Ashley's eyes.

"You may be just friends," Ashley said, "but any one of those guys would take a bullet for you."

She searched the kid's face for a hint of humor, but found none. Emma shook her head, determined not to let the kid's comment catch her off guard. Sure, she would sacrifice anything to help the guys, but to them she was just a basketball buddy. "No they wouldn't. The only reason they tolerate me is because I'm a decent basketball player and they find it amusing that a girl can beat them on the court."

Emma meant it as a joke, but Ashley didn't laugh, and Emma felt the smile slide off her face. Ashley's eyes filled with sadness or sympathy or maybe a mixture of both as she watched Emma. When the kid spoke, her voice was soft, bruised. "You really don't know how awesome you are, do you?"

Something in the way Ashley looked at her made Emma's throat tighten and her eyes burn. It took her a second to realize that Ashley looked the way Emma felt whenever she saw her dad after a fight with Lance. The way her heart split when her dad's face fell into his hands, and how she longed to comfort him and tell him he wasn't the world's worst father, but knowing, no matter what she said, he wouldn't believe her.

When Emma didn't respond, Ashley continued. "Why else would the team come to you for basketball advice? Why would the guys' faces light up whenever they see you?" Ashley set her bowl aside and turned her body to face Emma more directly. "Why else would Riley look at you like you're the most beautiful, strong, and wonderful person he's ever met?"

There was no mistaking the sincerity behind Ashley's words. The kid meant everything she said, but why? How could the freshman have so much faith in someone who didn't deserve it? Emma scolded the tears pooling in her eyes and was powerless over the one that set itself free to slide down her cheek. Turning away, she quickly swiped it away with the back of her hand, hoping the kid hadn't noticed. "Yeah, well, I guess there's more to my story than what you see."

"Maybe," Ashley said simply.

Emma looked to the sky, willing her stupid tears to retreat and find some other victim. The words of a freshman should not have this kind of an effect on her. As a freshman,

Ashley was young and naïve and had no concept of truth when it came to reading people. Otherwise, she would see Emma in the same way everyone else did, as a poor worthless girl people pitied.

Neither one of them spoke as Emma fought to regain control of her emotions. A dog barked and two more answered. One girl screamed inside and a few more laughed. The words of one song gave way to the bass of another and then another. Through it all Ashley remained at Emma's side. Emma wondered why. Maybe it was because she, too, was an outsider, cast away by the other girls on the team. Or maybe she knew when someone needed a friend. Whatever the kid's reason, Emma realized it wasn't horrible having the freshman beside her. For a girl, Ashley wasn't so bad.

Ashley caught Emma staring at her and a competitive smile played on her lips. "Considering body size isn't important, I bet I could beat you on Wii basketball."

The thought of the freshman beating Emma at anything was impossible, especially when it came to anything basketball related. "Not a chance."

"Care to bet on it?" Ashley held out her hand to seal the deal. "I win, you teach me one of your fancy basketball moves, no matter how difficult you think it is, and if you win, you get a day off from me."

"You're on." Emma shook Ashley's hand even though part of her wanted to renegotiate the terms. Maybe she didn't want a day off from the freshman.

They stood to return to the house, to the suffocation that only came with the riches, but they never made it to their game.

Fifteen

A black hooded figure stepped onto the porch in front of Emma and Ashley at the same time an arm snaked around Emma's waist and a hand clamped down on her mouth to prevent her from screaming. Beside her, Ashley didn't have a chance against her attacker. The guy picked her up like a newspaper, tucked her under his arm, and covered her mouth with a hand of his own. Emma saw the fear in Ashley's eyes, and knew she had to protect the kid from any harm. She fought against the arms holding her and they tightened.

"For a girl in need of an extraction, you sure do put up a fight," a strained voice said in her ear.

Riley. She should have known. Her body went slack in his arms, and he removed his hand from her mouth.

She turned around as he pulled his facemask off, a playful grin on his face. "Do you always have to go to such extremes?" she asked.

Emma reached over to pull the facemask off Ashley's attacker and revealed Tom. Jerry hopped off the porch to join them.

"It sounded like I needed to crash the party, so I followed orders and brought back up." Riley nodded toward the guys.

Emma raised her eyebrows in question. Leave it to Riley to take her orders seriously and act on them. "The cat and mouse, huh?"

Riley shrugged. "They were the only losers available on a Friday night."

Emma laughed. "Figures."

"Hey." Tom set Ashley on the ground and secured Emma in a loose headlock. "We had plans, big plans, but when a brother needs back up," Tom and Riley bumped fists, "plans change."

No matter what the girls put her through, Emma could always count on the guys. Why did brotherhood consist of loyalty and trust and sisterhood consist of backstabbing and betrayal?

"So, what's the plan?" Jerry rubbed his hands together. His wide eyes jumped back and forth between Riley and Emma, ready to fulfill his mission.

"Yeah," Tom said, tightening his arm around her neck. "We rescuing you and holding the little one hostage?"

Ashley giggled. She probably would have loved being held hostage by them.

Jerry made a fist with one hand and punched the palm of his other hand. "Or we can take on the entire group of snobby girls for you. Teach them a thing or two about respecting the awesome Emma Wrangton."

He may act tough, but if push came to shove and the girls attacked, Jerry would be the first one defeated. Emma wanted to remind him of his limited ability in the whole courage department, but a girl's voice snipped their reunion short.

"Hello, boys."

The group of them turned at the sound of Lauren's voice to see the rest of the girls in V formation behind their leader, craning their necks to get a better look at the male intruders.

"Hello, ladies." Tom released Emma and straightened

his shirt, no longer interested in pursuing the hostage situation. Traitor.

Tom looked from the girls to the backyard court to the basketball resting at the base of the hoop, and his mouth twisted into a sly smile. "You ladies up for a friendly competition?"

It took two seconds for Madison and Peyton to jump off the porch and join Tom underneath the basket. Talk about motivation. Emma would have thought those two girls would do a better job at keeping their desperation for male attention in check for their reputations' sake. Guess not.

Tom turned to Riley, his arms spread wide like the world was under his control. "You two take all the time you need, the ladies await." Turning his attention back to the girls, Tom whisked Jerry away with him, leaving Riley and Emma alone. Riley grabbed Emma's hand and led her away from the commotion. They sat cross-legged on the opposite side of the pool, watching Tom and Jerry play two-on-five against the girls.

Riley looked at her from the corner of his eye. "You okay?"

Right smack dab in the middle of one of the worst nights of her life, and Riley wanted to know if she was okay? She sighed. "I'm fine."

"Don't lie to me." He nudged her with his shoulder. "If you were fine your eyebrows wouldn't be scrunched together like you're trying to compress all those thoughts in your head so they wouldn't be so heavy." He studied her profile as she watched her fingers play with a loose thread from her sweatshirt. "Don't let what Lauren said get to you. The girl's crazy."

She kept her head bowed, unable to look at him, unable to respond. It was bad enough he had listened to Lauren's words over the phone, but now that he was here in person, her embarrassment escalated.

"Em." He reached over and took hold of her hand,

taking her focus away from the thread. "Talk to me."

She took a deep breath and exhaled slowly, knowing he'd force it out of her sooner or later. She'd always been able to talk to him about anything. He knew about the void left over after her mom left, how her body trembled after witnessing a fight between her dad and brothers, and how she relied on him when her own strength failed. He knew everything about her, but not even he realized the depth of her fears, especially when they revolved around him. Fears she kept inside because she was too afraid of them becoming a reality. But maybe now was the time to clue him in.

Not completely recovered from her conversation with Ashley, Emma closed her eyes, hoping tears didn't resurface. "Maybe Lauren's right," she whispered.

"About what?"

"A guy like you being friends with a girl like me." She couldn't resist looking at him to gauge his reaction.

"She's not." He responded without hesitation, his gaze on her steady and confident.

Emma wished she could be so sure. Wished she could erase the doubt and fear she felt and just trust in their friendship. "But what if she is? I have nothing to offer you. All I am is a huge burden. You should be friends with people who can pay their own way at the cheapest fast food restaurant in town, who don't rely on you to be chauffeured, and who you don't feel obligated to protect all the time." Words surged from her mouth and they couldn't be stopped. "I don't know why you've stayed my friend all these years, and words can't even come close to expressing how grateful I am for you, but I can't help thinking you'd be better off without me." What was wrong with her? She could definitely blame girls for this entire stream of babble. They always wanted to express their feelings. They were slaves to their irrational emotions. The complaining, whining, high-pitched voices like fingernails scraping on a chalkboard or the haunting sound of a cat's growl. Ridiculous behavior must be contagious.

He squeezed her hand. "And what if I don't see things like you do? What if I like how things are between us?" The calmness in his voice balanced the anxiety in hers.

"Then I'd say you're wasting your time."

Riley bowed his head to hide his smile. "Why don't you let me worry about that?" She opened her mouth to respond, but he brought a finger to her lips, silencing her. "I understand what you're saying, Em, but I'm not going anywhere. For better or worse, you're stuck with me." An amused smile appeared on his face. "Besides, considering you're in love with me, do you really want me to leave you alone?"

She groaned and covered her face with her hands, Lauren's words echoing way too clearly in her thoughts. "I am *not* in love with you."

"Sure you are," he said in Tom-like fashion as he leaned back on his hands and stretched his legs out in front of him. "I'm a lovable kind of guy." The lights from the pool made his skin look milky white and cast shadows in all the wrong places, making it difficult for her to read his facial expression. She couldn't tell whether or not he was joking.

He winked at her. "Don't worry, the feeling's mutual."

She laughed and pushed him away. Leave it to Riley to tease her at a time like this.

A high-pitched squeal from the court tore her focus away from Riley. Christi and Steph tried to steal the ball from Tom, but even he proved to be a better ball handler than them. Emma grimaced as the girls fouled him miserably. Had they learned nothing in the past month? "Ugh. They drive me crazy."

"Hey," Riley said. "Forget about them. All you have to do is get through the night, and then you're home free. You'll only have to deal with them at practice. What's one night?"

She met his eyes. Believing him. Trusting him. But not even Riley could predict the future. His statement only proved to be the infamous words of a guy who had no idea what kind of impact one night at an all-girls slumber party could have.

◆◆◆

Emma didn't get much sleep. Considering she was at the mercy of seven girls who majored in slumber party sabotage, the idea of falling asleep haunted her. She spent most of the night staring at the ceiling, listening to the deep breathing of girls around her, waiting for the sun to creep above the horizon and shed light on a new day. As soon as it did, she packed her things and fled to the park, the freshman in tow.

The cure for post-girl-slumber-party madness was a few hours with the guys, kickin' back and shootin' hoops. Riley. Jerry. Cy. Carson. Alex. Ben. Even Tom. No sight was more refreshing than the guys on a basketball court. No girls—with the exception of Ashley—allowed. Emma exhaled, half convinced last night was just a nightmare. But then she saw Jerry nod to Tom, and Tom smiled like an idiot to Carson, and Carson missed the easiest shot in the world, which caused Cy to stop talking and stare at a spot behind Emma. Something was wrong. Slowly, Emma turned.

No! This was *not* happening. No girls—especially not *those* girls—were going to invade her Saturday basketball game with the guys. Emma stomped across the court to where four girls from the team stood. "What are you doing here?" she demanded.

Madison held up her hand, declaring peace. "Relax, Emma. We're just here to watch."

Emma didn't care. She didn't want to be anywhere near girls right now. One night was bad enough. "Sorry, but this is a closed game." Emma's eyes narrowed. "No gawkers allowed."

"It's a free country and a public park." Christi sat on the bleachers, declaring her unwillingness to leave. "We can do anything we want."

"What's the matter, Poverty Child?" Lauren strutted past Emma and sat next to Christi. "Afraid of a little...competition?"

Madison put a restraining hand on Emma's shoulder before Emma could step forward and smack the grin off Lauren's face.

"Stop it, Lauren." The high-pitched whining was gone from Madison's voice, and the warning look she threw Lauren was enough to silence even Emma. What had happened in the past hour since Emma fled from the slumber party? Madison had never stood up to Lauren before, so why now?

Madison refocused on Emma. "We're just here to watch. We promise not to interfere."

Yeah, right. Their mere presence was interfering, especially when Emma so desperately needed guy time. The girls had spent the last eighteen hours together. Didn't that warrant at least a forty-eight-hour break to ensure Emma's sanity remained intact?

Everything clicked into place then, and Emma took a step back to examine the girls in front of her. "This is because of what I said at the stupid slumber party, isn't it?" She shook her head and laughed. "Do you honestly think the guys are going to talk about anything with all of you here?"

The girls exchanged looks with a couple of shrugs. Unbelievable!

"They're going to be too busy showing off for you to even play a decent game of basketball, much less reveal their innermost secrets." Emma tried to put it all into perspective for them—tried to get them to leave—but they stood their ground and stared back at her.

"Look, if the squirt can watch," Lauren motioned toward Ashley, "we can too."

Were these four girls that desperate to gain attention from the male population?

"Sorry we're late."

Emma turned at the sound of another girl's voice to see Peyton and Steph join the herd. Emma shook her head. Her teeth clenched so tightly she couldn't speak.

"Hey, Em," Tom said, stepping beside her and resting his arm on her shoulder. "Your friends come to play?"

Emma watched as Tom flashed one of his I'm-too-cute-to-resist smiles, and the girls laughed like they were actually flattered by him. Gross. "No," Emma said coldly, glaring at her teammates. "They were just *leaving*." She shrugged off Tom's arm and spun around to join the guys on the court, ending her conversation with the girls and not giving them time to contest her decision. So what if they hated her more? She refused to let her two worlds collide.

Distracted by the anger coursing through her body, Emma almost smacked into Shiloh who appeared out of nowhere to block her path.

"What?" Emma barked.

Unaffected by Emma's outburst, Shiloh glanced over her shoulder at the other girls like all she had was time. She cocked a hip and an eyebrow in the manner of someone with a bad idea. "You know, if we plan to beat Evergreen, it might not be a bad idea to let us stay and watch." She shrugged. "Who knows? We might learn a thing or two from you and your friends."

Seriously? Had Emma not made herself completely clear? "I don't think so."

Emma turned to go, but Shiloh grabbed her arm to prevent her from leaving. "Emma, wait."

Shiloh's whole demeanor changed. Bowing her head, her confidence gone, Shiloh cleared her throat as if trying to gather courage. "What I really came to say was...I'm sorry.

About what happened last night. Lauren was way out of line with what she said about you and Riley."

Okay, that was…different. Emma didn't know what to say. She narrowed her eyes at Shiloh, questioning the girl's motives. Emma waited for the catch, something to indicate she was being set up for more humiliation, but she couldn't detect anything amiss.

"I should've said something or done something." Shiloh raised her eyes to Emma. "You didn't deserve that." Unlike most girls, Shiloh didn't do the longwinded babbling thing to get her point across or defend her actions. She said what she had to say and then left it up to Emma to respond. Emma liked that about her, but she still didn't understand why, in the past five minutes, two girls had broken free from Lauren's authority to actually be civilized toward her. Could a stupid slumber party make that much difference?

"Don't worry about it," Emma muttered.

"So, we good?" She held out a fist, a peace offering.

Emma sighed and tapped her knuckles against Shiloh's. The last thing she wanted was more drama. "Yeah, we're good." What else could she say?

Despite how much she didn't want the girls invading her Saturday morning with the guys, Emma softened as Shiloh gave her a sincere smile. She looked at her teammates, then back at Shiloh. She bit her tongue and shook her head, knowing she was going to regret this. "And I suppose you can all, you know, stay."

Shiloh's eyes widened with surprise and hope.

Emma stepped closer, her finger pointed at Shiloh so the girl would take her seriously. "Just make sure they don't act stupid, and keep them out of my way. One strike and you're all out of here."

Shiloh smiled and tapped Emma's shoulder with her fist. "You got it."

So much for only having to put up with them at practice. Shiloh jogged over to tell the girls the good news, and Emma went to find Riley.

He stood a few feet away, watching the whole situation. "Looks like you've got groupies," he said, staring over her shoulder at the intruders.

"Don't start."

Riley laughed.

"Will there ever be a time when my two worlds don't collide?" she asked. Guys were guys except when girls were around. She endured five days a week with the girls. All she wanted was some guy time. One day. Was that wrong?

The girls spread across the aluminum bleachers, and Emma forced herself to look away before nausea overpowered her. Why did girls always ruin everything?

Sixteen

How a team as dysfunctional as Bradshaw could hop onboard a winning streak and not be bucked off was a mystery to most people. News spread like wildfire after each of their wins. They weren't the best in the league—that title still belonged to Evergreen—but they were known as a team to beat. Some called it luck and some said the competition lacked, but for the girls at Bradshaw who'd come from a history of losing, winning was winning. After their loss against Evergreen, the Bradshaw team stopped making excuses and started getting good. The school couldn't believe the girls' basketball team had actually won a game much less five in a row. The crowd grew at each of their games, people wanting to witness their success directly to ensure the rumor wasn't fictional.

Teachers kept Emma after class to talk about the latest game, goals for the season and, believe it or not, strategy, like coaching suddenly became part of their credentials. Kids who'd ignored her for the better part of seventeen years learned her name overnight and would nod or slap her on the back like friends to congratulate her on the latest win. It all freaked Emma out, especially when it escalated to the point of school-wide recognition via an assembly.

The only thing good about school assemblies was the

shortened class periods. When a student had no school spirit and no popularity status, assemblies held no importance. Emma usually sat in the bleachers next to Riley and the guys, one face among a thousand. She'd never actually been front and center during an assembly with everyone's eyes on her.

Emma hated crowds, especially ones high on school spirit. Now, as she stood on the gym floor with the rest of her team under the scrutiny of the entire student body, she was anything but invisible. Jerry, also known as the student body president, revved the crowd with stats about their winning season. The rest of the team surrounded Emma, smiling and waving to their friends in the bleachers. It was all part of the plan—the reason she agreed to join her teammates in the spotlight. Wave and smile for a minute or two to give people something to cheer for and then exit stage left. Time had to be running out.

No sooner had she looked at the exit door closest to her than she heard Jerry speak her name—right into the microphone. The crowd applauded and she cringed. This was so not part of the plan.

"How does it feel to be part of a winning team?" Jerry shoved the microphone in her face. All she could do was stare back at him, feeling a thousand pairs of eyes burning through her. Jerry knew she wasn't into this whole look-at-me moment. He was the one who'd promised her she wouldn't be singled out, just wave and smile.

"You told me I wouldn't have to talk." Even though she spoke quietly to Jerry, the microphone took her words and amplified them for the entire school to hear.

Jerry and everyone else laughed. Great.

"Sounds to me like our star player has a bit of stage fright." Again, Jerry spoke into the microphone, addressing all those in attendance and giving them something else to laugh at her about. "Emma Wrangton," he said loud and clear with the biggest grin on his face. "Tell us what it's like to be a superstar!"

Shouts erupted around her. Again, so not part of the plan. Shaking her head, Emma's eyes narrowed into slits, hoping Jerry got the message that he better cut it out. No, he just grinned at her and shoved the microphone in her face again.

"I'm not a superstar," she mumbled into the microphone, her face burning in humiliation.

Lauren stepped beside her, grabbed the microphone without hesitation, and slung her arm around Emma's shoulders like they were lifelong friends. So not true and not even headed in that direction. "I think what our fearless captain is trying to say," Lauren said, squeezing Emma's shoulder, "is that we're a team. We win and lose together and, come Friday, we're going to win!"

Her speech ended with a thunder of noise from the bleachers. Were a few words yelled into a microphone all it took to get a thousand high school students to act like groupies at a rock concert? It didn't matter. Emma was grateful to exit stage left and hide in the shadows while the assembly droned to an end.

Once they were safely out of the spotlight, Emma inched toward Lauren. As much as she hated the thought of approaching her archenemy, Emma knew she owed Lauren a thank you. Taking a deep breath, she tapped Lauren on the shoulder. "Thanks for saving me out there."

Lauren scowled at her. "Someone had to. You were making us all look bad, *captain*." She spit out the last word with contempt on her tongue.

As students flooded onto the gymnasium floor toward the exits, Lauren rammed her shoulder into Emma's and vanished into the crowd. How Lauren could turn on and off her emotions for the public eye, Emma didn't know. Must be a girl thing.

Emma watched as kids exited the gym, talking and laughing. A few of them acknowledged her with words and head nods, but she ignored them, knowing it wasn't her, but the prospect of winning they appreciated.

Hands clamped down on her shoulders from behind. "Nice job out there, Em," Jerry said not even trying to hold back his laughter. "You really have a way with words."

She spun around and punched him.

He rubbed his arm, trying to gain sympathy by scrunching his face in pain. It didn't work.

"Thanks for throwing me under the bus out there," she snarled. "What was that? You know I don't talk in front of people."

"You're famous now," he said, as if that explained it all. "You better get used to it."

No sympathy! Unable to take another second of his superstar nonsense, she pinned him against the wall, her eyes blazing into his. Jerry was one guy she knew she could overpower in a heartbeat. He stood a couple inches taller than her, but muscles had yet to find him. Besides, he didn't have the impulse to hit a guy, much less a girl. She would never intentionally hurt him, but he didn't need to know that. "Listen, Jerry, I appreciate your support and all, but I'm *not* a superstar. I'm just a basketball player. So unless you want to explain to the world how a girl gave you a black eye, you'd better stop with the whole superstar business, you got it?"

Maybe she expected him to cower under her rage or readily agree to call it quits with casting the spotlight on her. What she didn't expect was for him to smile like an idiot and act like her threat held no power.

"There's my superstar," Riley said, coming up behind her and wrapping his arms around her waist before she could protest. He picked her up off the floor and spun her around, setting her down a safe distance away from Jerry. When she turned around to face them, Riley and Jerry shared identical grins. Did they not understand how none of this was funny?

Riley put his hand on her waist, no doubt to tell her to relax, but Emma pushed away from him. "Don't."

Riley, along with everyone else, had enjoyed every second of her humiliation, stuttering like an idiot in front of the entire school. And people wondered why she hated the whole school sports thing. She didn't want special treatment, she didn't want to be recognized at school assemblies, she didn't want her friends to treat her differently. She just wanted uninterrupted Saturday basketball games with the guys and some good one-on-one friend time with Riley before he packed for college and left her behind. Was that too much to ask?

Yes. Yes, it was. Because if she'd known what her wish would result in she never would've asked for anything.

♦♦♦

Riley held Emma's hand as he led them down their trail to the waters of Puget Sound. Beneath the trees, the night seemed darker than usual. Clouds hovered overhead, obscuring the moon and threatening rain. Emma loved the rain at night. She loved sitting with Riley by the water, listening to the raindrops splatter the rocks and sharing stories about what life would be like when they grew older. Now, with graduation less than seven months away, the transition from childhood to adulthood had come too fast and not without its price. Tonight, she preferred to listen to their feet squishing in the mud than swap what ifs and maybes about their futures. Riley proved to be in the mood to chat.

"Em?" The word came out soft, cautious. "Do you ever think about…us?"

In the dark, she could only make out his black silhouette as he walked beside her, her hand clutched in his. She couldn't see his face, didn't know what kind of answer he wanted, but she stiffened. Thinking about the restrictions of time and the inevitability of change, she felt the weight of his question and tripped over a tree root she normally would have avoided. Somehow, Riley caught her, saving her from a face-plant.

He secured her against him. "You okay?"

"I'm fine."

A cloud shifted, spilling moonlight through the tree branches and illuminating Riley's face. She looked into the eyes of the only person who really knew her, and her heart ached. How many more times would they sneak out of their houses to walk the beach and sit on their favorite piece of driftwood? How many more times would he take her hand and lead her through the dark? The year was only so long. In so many ways, the basketball season was flying by, which meant the rest of the school year would arrive not far behind. Then what?

She bowed her head so he couldn't see her face. "Yes, I think about us," she said. "I think about how next year you're heading off to college, destined for greatness, while I'm—"

His hand guided her face back to his. "Destined for greatness right alongside me."

She gave a weak smile, slipped out of his embrace, and continued down the path. He fell into step beside her, his hand slipping around hers again.

The tree branches stretched out, ushering them to the beach. She looked across the water. Beneath the calm surface, the current swirled and twisted, forcing debris in different directions, showing no mercy. Kind of like how, at the end of the school year, life would force Riley and her apart.

"I know you only want what's best for me, Riley, but no one in my family has ever gone to college. My brothers barely made it out of high school, and my mom dropped out as a senior. My dad works two jobs to support the family and it still isn't enough. Based on that, my chances for college are pretty much nonexistent."

"Don't say that," he said firmly, dropping her hand and spinning her to face him. "You haven't even tried." He let out an exasperated sigh. "Em, you're not stuck in the life your family chose for themselves. You're better than that. You deserve to go to college and be happy just as much as me or anyone else."

"Why?" she shouted. "Because you want me to?" She would never be one of those people who packed up after graduation and set out on a new adventure; she was trapped. "I'm sorry, Riley, but life doesn't work that way. Next year you'll be at some fancy college surrounded by new people and new opportunities, and I just...I don't see how I'll fit into all that."

His eyes softened. "Listen, Em." He placed his hands on her hips and pulled her closer. "You are my best friend and that's never going to change. I don't care if you're so poor you live in a cardboard box, if you fail to graduate high school, or if thousands of miles try to separate us. I'll always love you just as much as I do now."

It was the 'L' word that tripped her up and caused her breath to catch in her throat. She couldn't remember anyone ever telling her she was loved. Not her mom, not her dad, and certainly not her brothers.

Love.

Emma couldn't define it based on her mom fleeing in the middle of the night never to be heard from again, by her dad's inability to make eye contact with her, or by the collective feelings from her brothers that she should disappear and never return. What did the word *love* even mean? But then she saw Riley standing in front of her and thought about all the times he'd draped his protective arm around her shoulders, brought her food when he knew she hadn't eaten, and supported her every second since the day they'd met.

Emma waited for him to take the word back, to admit

he'd made a mistake in saying it, but he didn't. She tried to look away, tried to break the connection between them, but she couldn't.

He reached up to brush a strand of hair away from her face, his fingers lingering longer than necessary on her cheek. "If you don't believe anything I say," he whispered, "believe this." He leaned in and pressed his lips against hers.

She probably shouldn't have kissed him back. There was no probably about it, she should *not* have kissed him back. They were friends. *Best* friends. Non-kissing friends! But maybe Ashley was right. Maybe Emma wasn't immune to love, especially not when Riley was concerned. And that scared her more than anything.

Sometime after their lips met, but before incoherent thought kicked in completely, Emma pushed him away and stumbled backwards, rocks clattering beneath her feet.

"Em," Riley said, reaching for her.

She held up her hands to ward him off. "I have to go." The more distance she put between them the better.

"Emma, don't leave," he begged. "Please."

Only the pain in his last word stopped Emma from fleeing into the night and finding solace among the shadows.

"I'm sorry," he said. "I just thought—"

His words ended there, like he expected everything to automatically make sense. "You just thought what?" she choked out, backing away. "You and I both know this would never work between us."

"Do we?"

"Yes."

"How?" His eyes searched her face. "How do we know? Because the way I see it, there's no reason it wouldn't work. We've been best friends since fourth grade, and you've always been the one for me."

She shook her head, refusing to get caught up in the

moment. She wouldn't hold him back or drag him down into a life he wasn't supposed to live. There were so many other girls out there, so many other girls better for him. Why couldn't he see that?

He took advantage of her hesitation to close the distance between them and place his hands on her cheeks, willing her to look at him. "Tell me you don't have the same feelings for me that I do for you."

She opened her mouth to speak, trying to form the words, but she couldn't lie to him. Not now. Not ever. The desire to be near him, the fear of losing him, the way her stomach reacted when he touched her. He made her feel safe, happy…loved. Maybe her feelings for him did extend beyond friendship.

A smile of relief appeared on his face when she didn't answer. "That's what I thought."

She may not have been able to lie to him or explain exactly how she felt about him, but it didn't mean anything had changed between them. "We can't," she whispered.

"Why not?"

"Because you deserve better."

"Better than what?"

She looked up at him, tears blurring her eyes. "Better than me."

Seventeen

Emma scrambled up the path, falling a few times in her haste, but each time rising again to pursue her course.

She heard Riley calling her name and running after her, but she didn't turn back. With her head start, he would have difficulty catching her before she reached her house. Branches lashed at her face, tree roots and mud tried to trip her, but she didn't slow down. She charged ahead, fighting her way back to safety.

The trail opened to the street, and she burst from the trees and mud, pushing her arms and legs faster now that no obstacles stood in her way. Raindrops fell from the sky and splattered on her face, mixing with the tears sliding down her cheeks. Her feet thudded against the pavement, her chest burned from forcing back sobs, and still she ran. Ran until her feet crunched the gravel driveway. Ran until the shadows surrounding her house enveloped her.

She threw open the outside door to her garage-slash-bedroom, stumbled over the threshold, and slammed the door behind her. Leaning against the door, she tried to catch her breath. This isn't happening, she thought as her eyes frantically scanned the garage. For what, she didn't know. Maybe a hiding place. Maybe a sign for what to do next. It was only a matter of time before Riley burst through the door looking for her. She didn't know the answers to a lot of questions, but she knew she wasn't ready to face him yet.

She snatched a blanket and pillow from her bed and, for the first time in five years, snuck into the house to sleep on the couch, knowing Riley wouldn't follow her inside. The rest of her family was asleep, or at least locked behind their bedroom doors for the night, so she didn't have to formulate a reason for her actions. She stretched out on the couch and stared up at the darkened ceiling, her heart racing.

Riley had kissed her.

She'd kissed him back!

She covered her face with her hands trying to settle her thoughts, but it didn't work. She kept seeing his face lean closer and closer; she kept feeling his lips on hers. Now what? They couldn't just go back to the way things were yesterday. A kiss was a serious breach on their friendship.

It wouldn't have been so bad if they'd kissed and then realized there wasn't anything between them, but the girl in her—no matter how underdeveloped that part of her was— didn't need a second opinion to know there was way too much in their kiss to forget.

Emma refused to let her eyes close. The morning would come soon enough; she didn't need to encourage it with sleep. She didn't know what tomorrow would bring, or if she even wanted to know. Nothing about this year had gone as planned. Nothing about her life had gone as planned. Riley was her friend. He wasn't supposed to kiss her and send her life into a tailspin, especially not now when they only had so much time together before he left her for good.

Riley.

She wouldn't survive without him. Sure, he'd come home from college for holidays and to visit, but it wouldn't be the same. She knew they wouldn't survive as devoted pen pals or phone buddies, and the last thing they needed was a kiss looming over them. He deserved to live his life without feeling obligated to remain her friend—without feeling pity for the poor girl he left behind.

Her chest tightened, her eyes burned, and as hard as she fought to keep her tears in check, they came anyway. Big, fat, stupid girl tears spilled down her cheeks, and she cursed every one of them. The more she tried to wipe them away the faster they came. With no other choice, she buried her head in her pillow, and for the first time in years cried herself to sleep.

◆◆◆

The short snippet of sleep Emma got was plagued with visions of Riley and the kiss, but all of it disappeared when she was jolted awake by Lance kicking her. Hard.

She bolted upright, disoriented. Why was she sleeping on the couch?

"Move," Lance growled.

She looked up at her brother and last night's events came flooding back to her.

"Go away," she said groggily, flopping down on her pillow and covering her head with her blanket. Returning to sleep had no appeal but neither did moving and giving Lance the satisfaction of stealing the couch from her. All she wanted was to curl into a ball and let the next ten years pass by her.

Emma heard a grunt and felt the couch slant forward. The next thing she knew, she landed with a thud on the floor. Lance jumped over the back of the couch and took her place, stretching the length of the couch so there was no room for her. He propped a box of donuts on his stomach and turned on the TV.

There were a lot of things she wanted to say to him, but she bit her tongue and hauled herself off the floor, not in the mood for a confrontation. Snatching her blanket and pillow, she retreated to her bedroom, hoping Riley wasn't there waiting for her. She meandered through the path of boxes and broken equipment until she saw her corner and breathed a sigh of relief. All was clear.

Then she saw the note on her bed:

CALL ME - R

She dropped onto her bed, picked up the scrap of paper, and crumpled it. This was one request she couldn't fulfill. At least not now. Riley had kissed her. She'd kissed him back. She covered her face with her hands, not knowing what to do. The world was flipped, turned upside-down, and Emma had no idea how to right it.

She didn't need this. She needed to prepare for next week's games, she needed to hang out with the guys, and she needed her best friend.

◆◆◆

It was difficult to avoid Riley when he was such an intricate part of her life. Aside from his family's annual two-week vacation in the summer, Emma couldn't remember the last time they'd gone twenty-four hours without talking to one another. Now, on hour sixty-six, Emma started to think maybe she'd made too much of things. So, he'd kissed her. Big deal. Sometimes friends kissed, didn't they?

No. They didn't. Not like that. How could this have happened?

"You okay?" Shiloh asked, breaking through Emma's internal panic. "You seem distracted."

Emma rolled her eyes. "I'm fine."

Daily practices with Shiloh, Ashley, and Peyton meant giving them a few basketball pointers, not dishing out her life story. She knew enough about girls to know how their gossip thread worked. Fast and inaccurate.

Unable to concentrate, Emma led the girls through one drill after another to keep them busy. For all she knew, they could've missed every shot they took and dribbled the ball off their feet a million times. Emma hadn't noticed. It was only a matter of time before her and Riley came face-to-face again. What would she say? What would he say? What would they do? She'd avoided him all weekend, not returning his calls and hiding out in random places so he couldn't track her down. She'd even skipped her Saturday basketball game with the guys, which had never happened before. At school their paths had only crossed once, but the bell cut their greeting short. It was only a matter of time. She knew Riley wouldn't let her avoid him forever.

Emma paced the sideline as the girls practiced, eyes staring unseeing at the floor, teeth gnawing her fingernails. A pause in Ashley's dribbling caused Emma to glance up. The kid stared past Emma, her face lighting up with a smile.

"Hi, Riley," she said.

Emma spun around, and sure enough, Riley was making his way across the gym toward her. Her heart fluttered, and then sped up. Not now, not now, not now. Their post-kiss reunion should not happen in front of three female witnesses.

"Hey, Ash," Riley said, his eyes never leaving Emma's. No more than ten feet separated them, but it felt more like a thousand miles. He was mad. Mad at her. She hated it when he was mad at her.

He closed the distance between them and she bowed her head, unable to look at him. He probably thought she was stupid for running away and avoiding him all weekend.

"Can we talk?" he asked quietly. He stood only inches away from her. Too close. Way too close.

She was only too aware of Shiloh, Ashley, and Peyton listening to them.

"I'm kind of busy." How much longer could she keep this up?

He placed his hand under her chin and raised her face to look at him. "Then I'll wait."

His blue eyes held hers in a steady gaze, indicating there was no negotiation and no evading him this time. He would wait, no matter how long it took.

Considering her practice with the girls had barely started, it would be a long hour and a half with his eyes boring into her back. She tried not to look at him, tried to ignore his presence and concentrate on teaching the art of reading the defense, but her eyes kept wandering over to him, sitting against the far wall, watching her.

Rather than continue practicing, the three girls surrounded Emma, shielding her from Riley's view.

"Is everything okay between you and Riley?" Ashley whispered, her eyebrows creased with worry.

"It's fine, why?"

They all looked at Riley, then back at Emma. Talk about obvious. Shiloh was the one to speak. "Because you both look like you've lost your best friend."

Note to self, never ask why again. Emma's eyes wandered over to Riley. Again. He looked how she felt all right and exactly how Shiloh described. "We may be experiencing a little..." Emma paused searching for the right word, "turbulence."

"Should we leave?" Peyton asked.

"No," Emma said quickly. The last thing she wanted was to be left alone with Riley. One kiss was bad enough, but who knew what would happen now? Would he kiss her again? Would he yell? Would he tell her their friendship was over? She couldn't lose him.

Ashley giggled. "Tell me you're not using us as an excuse to avoid him."

"Of course not," Emma said, rolling her eyes.

Peyton raised her eyebrows, challenging Emma's lie.

"I'm not," Emma emphasized. "I'm just...not ready to talk to him yet."

"What happened?"

Emma peered at Ashley, hoping her height still held some sort of authority. "None of your business, freshman."

Shiloh looked at Riley and shook her head. "Well, it's

not going to get easier the longer you put it off, and he doesn't look like he's going anywhere without you, so I'm leaving." Shiloh looked at Peyton and Ashley. "You two coming?"

Peyton didn't hesitate. She followed Shiloh across the gym and with one quick glance over her shoulder, they slipped through the door and disappeared. Emma knew she should be grateful they didn't insist on sticking around to watch, but fear flickered within her at the prospect of facing Riley alone.

Ashley, eyes filled with compassion, gave a one-shoulder shrug before turning to follow the girls. Emma grabbed her arm as she turned to leave, thinking quickly for a reason to make her stay. "Practice isn't over yet, and if you leave early, I can't guarantee I'll stay to help you tomorrow."

Ashley squinted up at her. "Are you threatening me?"

"No." Emma wasn't the threatening type. "I'm just encouraging you to make the right decision."

"Otherwise known as threatening."

Emma clamped her mouth shut. Getting her way with a freshman should not be so difficult. "Fine, we play one-on-one to ten. If you win, you can leave. If I win, you stay for the next hour with no complaint."

"I'll play you one-on-one," Ashley said carefully, weighing each word. "First basket wins. If I win, I leave. If you win, you get five minutes, and then I leave." She crossed her arms, sealing the deal.

"What kind of a compromise is that? I lose either way."

Ashley smiled. "That's kinda the point."

Since when did freshmen possess negotiation skills? Freshmen were supposed to fear seniors. They were supposed to follow the rules set by their elders, not make up their own. Emma may have been older, she may have had the height advantage, she may have been smarter and wiser and better at basketball, but one look at the kid made her realize she was not the one in charge.

"Fine," Emma growled. At least she'd get five minutes.

With a glance in Riley's direction, Emma passed Ashley the ball. It was the least she could do—give Ashley a chance before she claimed her victory. Emma anticipated Ashley's first move to the right, her strongest side. Ashley didn't disappoint. She dribbled once to the right, spun the quickest spin move Emma had ever seen, and headed for the basket. Not bad for a freshman, but didn't she know not to drive through the center of the key against someone twice her size? Emma readied herself for the block, but the kid was good. Securing the ball between her hands, Ashley lunged toward the basket with her right foot, selling the shot. Emma bent her legs, ready to jump, but instead of continuing to the basket, the kid changed direction. Ashley took a huge step sideways, brushing past Emma, before pushing off the floor with her left foot. Caught off guard, Emma's feet never left the ground. All she could do was put a hand in Ashley's face as a distraction. It didn't work. Free from her defender, the freshman extended her arm toward the basket and flipped the ball off the backboard. The ball fell through the net, completing Ashley's look-at-me-I'm-brilliant move.

The freshman beat her with the infamous two-step. Emma knew the move well. She used it all the time against the guys, and they could never stop her. But how in the world did the freshman execute it to perfection against Emma?

Emma's jaw dropped. "Where did that come from?" It definitely wasn't something they'd covered or something Ashley had ever attempted during team practices. It was a move common in basketball, and hundreds of people could execute it, but not the freshman standing before her.

Ashley shrugged. "You pulled the same move on the guys at the park a while back, and it was the coolest thing I've ever seen. I've been practicing."

"Obviously," Emma said, unable to hide the astonishment in her voice. Until then, Ashley had never surprised anyone with her basketball ability.

The smile had yet to leave Ashley's face as she tossed Emma the ball. "Have fun."

All Emma could do was watch as the kid walked out of the gym with a bounce to her step, like she knew Emma was still trying to figure out how in the world she lost to a freshman.

"It looks like your hard work is paying off," Riley said, appearing beside her.

"Yeah," she grumbled as they watched the kid disappear out the door, her scrawny arm raised in farewell. "Too much."

Riley turned to face her. "Can we talk now?"

"Actually, I—" Her words faltered when he grabbed her hand and led her to the wall where he dropped to the floor and pulled her down beside him. She tried to reclaim her hand, but he tightened his grip so she couldn't slip away.

They stared at the basketball court in silence. It was the kind of silence friends shared when waiting for words to come and dissolve the tension. Usually, she'd have been able to predict what Riley would say, how he would act, how much she'd have to grovel to get out of trouble, but in the current situation, she had no idea about anything. Their friendship had crossed over into something else, something foreign to Emma both as a friend and as a girl. So she remained still and quiet, waiting for him to start speaking. He didn't like to let things simmer until they faded or were buried and lurking in the shadows of time passing. But what would a conversation about the breach in their friendship entail exactly? There could be yelling or arguing or—

"I've missed you."

Or the simple confession of a guy who missed his best friend. And just like that, Emma's defenses crumbled. "Me, too," she whispered. She felt the weight of her admission, and it scared her. Scared her because she realized how much she relied on him to be at her side. What would she do when he left for college?

She glanced at their hands, still clasped in Riley's lap, and knew she couldn't avoid him any longer.

He took a deep breath before continuing. "I'm not sorry for kissing you, Em. My only regret is not doing it sooner."

So much for thinking he spent the weekend regretting the kiss. "Riley, I—" she started, not knowing exactly how the sentence would end. Before she could add words to what would surely be a string of babble, Riley spoke.

"I'm scared, Em."

His voice was low and anxious as words tumbled out of his mouth, dragging her along beside them. "Next year I'll be leaving everything I've ever known and heading off to some college. Call me crazy, but I like high school, I like my friends, and yes, I love my parents. Next year at this time everything will be different. I mean, what if college basketball isn't all it's cracked up to be? What if I'm not good enough to make the basketball team? What if I fail all of my classes? What if I'm stuck in college forever because I don't declare a major? I don't have any idea what I want to be when I grow up."

She could only imagine what it would be like to leave everything she knew and start fresh without everyone knowing her entire history and punishing her for it. She supposed things were different for Riley since his life was perfect already, but everything would work out for him. It always did.

Emma squeezed his hand. "You'll be fine, wherever you end up. You'll have basketball and new friends and—"

He fixed his eyes on her. "But I won't have you."

Her breath caught in her throat. How in the world was she supposed to respond to that?

He shook his head and laughed a helpless laugh. "I feel

like time is slipping away from us, and I don't want to lose you after graduation. I know you think our friendship is one-sided, but you're wrong. Em, you mean more to me than anything. I can't do this without you. Ever since the day I met you, I've dreamed of us going off to college to play ball and meeting up with the guys during holiday breaks to swap stories and seeing where life takes us. Together." His eyes never wavered from hers. "I won't leave you behind. I can't."

She didn't know what to do. Should she throw her arms around him and never let him go, or should she walk away and force him to embrace a life without her? No matter what they said now, neither one of them could guarantee the future. Taking a deep breath, she forced a smile. "Riley, I'll be fine."

He shook his head. "No, you won't. You'll slip into the same lifestyle your family did. I'd hate myself if I left you here, went off to college, and came back to discover you're wasting your life away. You deserve so much more." His voice was frantic, pleading. She'd never seen him like this before. "I know this thing with the girls' team is hard, but it'll be worth it. As soon as college scouts see you, they'll be knocking down your door to sign with them."

Sure, in theory it all sounded great. College scholarship. Leaving home. Not being left behind when everyone else started the next chapter of their lives. But in reality nothing ever went as planned, and Emma refused to get her hopes up, knowing she'd only get hurt in the end. "And what if I don't want all that?"

He raised his eyebrows in question. "Don't want it or don't think it's possible?"

She looked away. "What difference does it make?"

"It makes a huge difference." His emphasis on the word huge and the way he crushed her hand confirmed his frustration. "Em, sooner or later, you're going to have to figure out what you want. Not what you think you do or don't deserve, but what you truly want."

"I—" But her words ended there. Truth be told, she wanted the life he envisioned for her. She wanted to go to college and play basketball and learn about the world and what it had to offer. She wanted to spend holidays with Riley and the guys laughing over what it felt like to be freshmen all over again. What she didn't want was to set herself up for failure, abandon her family, or give her dad another reason to hate her. For her, the cons way outweighed the pros. Riley wouldn't understand, so she told him the next true thing. "I don't want to hold you back. I don't want you constantly worrying about me. You deserve to go to college and become rich and famous without me weighing you down."

She expected him to protest and tell her she had it all wrong, but he didn't. He grew quiet and still, hardly breathing. She figured silence would engulf them again, but Riley wasn't finished. He threw a quick glance in her direction before dropping his gaze to their interlaced fingers. "I think about you," he confessed. "I lie awake at night and wonder if you're warm enough or if you had enough to eat for the day or if your brothers are giving you a rough time. I'm afraid a time will come when something will happen to you and I won't be there to protect you."

It should have been the role of a mother or father to protect their daughter from the harms of the world, so why was Riley filling the void in her life?

Because she didn't have anyone else.

"You can't save me from everything," she said, her tone more serious than she'd intended.

He nodded. "I know, but everyone needs a wingman, right?"

Thinking back on how the last time he'd claimed to be her wingman he'd allowed her to be kidnapped by the girls, she couldn't help but laugh. "Yeah, well, I think your wingman skills need some work."

He laughed with her, and for a moment it was as if nothing had happened between them. She didn't care how much time they had left. As long as they got to spend it together, maybe things wouldn't be so bad.

"Can I ask you a question?" he asked when their laughter faded.

"Of course," she said, hoping it was a question she could handle.

He looked at her with worried eyes. "Kissing me. It wasn't like kissing one of your brothers, was it?"

"Ew. Gross." Her laughter resumed. Of all the questions in the world to ask. "No, kissing you was definitely not like kissing any of my brothers. Far from it."

His smile stretched across his face. He released her hand and crushed her into a hug. "Good."

Hopefully her comment hadn't given him false hope that they had a future together as anything more than friends.

◆◆◆

Two days later, the doorbell rang during breakfast. Lenny got up to answer it. The Wrangtons weren't exactly the kind of people who had visitors, so any time the doorbell announced one, it was usually a friend of Lance's or Logan's or someone trying to sell something. Emma wasn't prepared for Riley's voice to cut into her morning meal.

Whatever his reason for showing up unannounced so early in the morning, Riley couldn't wait to greet her or her family properly. After saying hi to Lenny and stepping over the threshold into her house, he shouted to Emma from the living room. "Have you seen it yet?"

"Riley?" she asked, scooting her chair back from the table and standing to intercept him. "What are you doing here?"

A newspaper was folded under his arm. He whipped it

out and slapped it on the kitchen table. "It's an awesome article all about you and the team. Well, mostly about you."

"What?" she asked tentatively. She was vaguely aware of how everything in the kitchen froze: the coffee cup halfway to her dad's mouth, Logan's mouthful of food, Lance's scowl, Lenny's fist mid-flight to hitting Lucas on the head. She grabbed the paper with shaking hands and gazed at the black and white face staring up at her.

Her face. Her picture.

The photo captured Emma in full uniform smiling into the camera, which must have been strategically placed in the stands near Riley during one of her home games. Another photo featured her suspended in midair, surrounded by defenders, with her arm extended toward the hoop and the ball on her fingertips. No doubt her final shot against Evergreen. Words couldn't describe how Emma felt. Her face, her name in the caption beneath the photos. Spelled right and everything. It was a mistake. It had to be. She'd never been in the paper before. The headline stood out in bold black letters:

HS Senior Gives Losing Team Hope

Emma scanned the black print. It described Bradshaw's losing history, coaching changes, and the team's struggle to find players. They introduced her as the basketball powerhouse of the league and made her out to be some sort of basketball superhero who saved Bradshaw from another year of shame. Talk about pressure. Coach talked about her being the thread holding the team together and how privileged she felt coaching such a talented athlete.

She continued to scan the article, her head shaking in shock. During her interview with the reporter, never once had she mentioned the guys or growing up with Mr. Ledger as her coach, so she couldn't figure out why she was reading the details of her life in black and white. At least not until her eyes settled on the quote from the one and only Riley Ledger. "When it comes to basketball, Emma's a superstar."

"How did this happen?" she groaned. Didn't people understand basketball was a team sport? Emma didn't want, nor did she deserve, the spotlight.

Riley laughed. "When a newspaper reporter asks you a bunch of questions, it usually means they're writing an article about you."

"Emma got interviewed by the paper?" Lenny asked. It was the first time he'd ever shown interest in her.

Her dad leaned over her shoulder to look at the article. "When did this happen?"

Her mouth opened, but no words came out. What could she say? Two weeks ago, after one of their games, Coach had asked her if she would mind answering a few questions for some reporter. Two weeks. It was long enough to answer the questions and forget about it. Until now.

"Why didn't you tell us?" Lenny asked.

"I—I don't know," she stuttered, still in shock. Since when did her family want her to tell them anything? "I mean, I knew they were doing an article, but I thought it was about the team. I didn't think they'd do an exclusive on me."

"Why not?" Riley exclaimed, slapping her on the back. "You're the star of the team and the league, and from the sound of it, you underestimated the impact you had during the game against Evergreen. Man, I wish I would've been there."

Emma didn't want to talk about the Evergreen game. She wanted to know why a reporter singled her out, printed a photo that would surely take the cross-town rivalry thing with Evergreen to a whole new level, and used quotes from people she trusted to aid in her destruction. "I see you got yourself a quote in here too," she said, glaring at him.

"What?" Riley's hands, palms up, shrugged along with his shoulders to portray innocence. "They asked me what I thought about my best friend tearing up the court, so I had to be honest."

"Uh-huh," she said. No way was she going to let him off the hook for not telling her about his part in this whole conspiracy. She was just glad she hadn't said anything she'd regret when they asked her about the team. Thank goodness they didn't twist her words to sound awful.

Lance threw his own paper onto the table. His chair groaned when he scooted away from the table and stood. Casting Emma and Riley a scowl, he exited the room, breaking whatever bond her family had shared.

Emma glanced at the clock, knowing if she didn't leave now there would be another tardy on her record. She snatched the paper, grabbed Riley by the arm, and said goodbye to her family.

During the ride to school, Riley tried to convince her how great publicity was for her future. How college scouts looked for this sort of thing, how other teams feared this sort of thing, and how best friends loved this sort of thing. Emma didn't say much. She let Riley ramble while she stared out the window. Sure, part of her was ecstatic about seeing her face in print, but the other part of her dreaded what it meant. Would people expect more from her? Would her image of greatness shatter when people realized she didn't come from a family of money? Couldn't she just play basketball without having to worry about fame and publicity distorting the season?

Unable to look at the article anymore, she threw the paper in the back seat. Hopefully, no one at school had seen it. Seriously, how many high school students actually woke up early enough on a school day to read the paper? She sighed. Two more blocks and she'd know. At least the kiss with Riley seemed a thing of the past and hadn't left them with awkward moments of silence. With Riley by her side, she could endure anything.

Or so she thought.

Riley's appearance at her breakfast table was bad enough, but then she caught Tom and Jerry posting copies of the article all over her locker with a handful of gawkers reading over their shoulders. So much for thinking no one read the paper.

She pushed between them and ripped the papers from the wall. "What do you think you're doing?" she snapped.

Tom nonchalantly leaned against the wall and crossed his arms, while Jerry grinned at her. "Now do you believe me?"

"About what?"

He grabbed her shoulders and shook her. "About you being a superstar."

She closed her eyes, forcing herself to count to five before she erupted. "I'll give you ten seconds to get out of my sight."

Jerry released her shoulders and gave her a one-two punch on the arm before flashing his grin and disappearing with Tom, a stack of newspapers secured under their arms.

"Don't be too mad at them," Riley said, pleading their case. "This is one of the best moments of the year. Seeing our Emma in the paper."

"Best moments of the year?" she asked. Was he crazy? She may not have been an expert on best moments, but she knew all about worst moments, and a newspaper article with her face in it was nothing to celebrate. It put her front and center in the spotlight she so desperately tried to avoid. Brick by brick, she felt the pressure of expectations piling up on her, weighing her down, and she wasn't the type of person who could carry the load. Sooner or later, she knew the blocks would fall and she'd be left worse off than when she started.

"Emma, did you see it?"

One second Riley's face was in her field of vision and the next she was nose to paper with her black and white photos again. Emma would know Ashley's voice anywhere.

She ripped the paper from Ashley's hands and glared at the kid standing beside her.

"Isn't it great?" Ashley asked.

No longer did Emma's anger and irritation faze Ashley. The kid just stared up at her all wide-eyed and beaming, rejoicing in Emma's fame. "No, it's not great," Emma snapped.

Riley put his hands on Ashley's shoulders in a big brother sort of way to protect her from Emma's wrath. "Don't mind her, she's not used to being a celebrity."

Ashley giggled. Between the freshman and the guys Emma was ready to punch something.

The first bell rang, causing kids to scurry to class. Ashley waved goodbye and was swept away by the current of students going in the opposite direction. Riley walked with Emma to first period, his arm secured around her shoulders. Kids she barely knew waved to her as they passed, complimenting her on the article. She cringed every time.

"Since when do high school students even read the paper?" She knew for a fact ninety percent of the kids in her sophomore World Issues class had failed every weekly quiz because none of them watched the news or read the paper to catch up on current events. High school couldn't have changed that dramatically in the past two years.

"It's the sports section." Riley shrugged. "Everyone reads the sports section."

They approached her classroom and saw Tom and Jerry posting another article outside the door. Spotting Emma, both guys took off before she could reprimand them, giving each other high fives as they ran.

Ripping the article off the wall, she focused her energy on Riley. Her clenched fist held the crumpled article up to his face. "Did you put them up to this?"

"Of course not," he said, his hands held up in innocence. "But I'm with them. It's about time something good happened to you." He grabbed her shoulders and, with a smile, shook her. "Em, you're in the paper. Relax and enjoy it. Jerry's right. You're a superstar, and there's nothing you can do to change it, so deal with it." He squeezed her into a hug, pressed his lips to her forehead, and then walked backward toward his class. Looping his thumbs through the straps of his backpack, he gave her a smile. "Later."

She watched him go, the feel of his kiss still on her forehead. This whole kissing thing was getting way out of control. What happened to the days when they would say goodbye with playful punches and shoves?

She sighed and entered her classroom. Most people would be thrilled to see themselves featured in a newspaper article, but Emma couldn't muster anything more than irritation. Why? Because the definition of something good was all a matter of opinion. If it was like Riley said, and the article was something good happening to her, she knew it wouldn't last long. She knew it would only be a matter of time before the world crashed down on her...again.

Eighteen

One week later, Riley trailed behind Emma as she led the way through her house to the kitchen, seeking water. Lots and lots of water. Sometimes Saturday basketball games required more than one water bottle. Logan, sitting on the couch reading yet another book, barely glanced up as they passed.

"Wouldn't it be awesome if you guys made it to the playoffs?" Riley leaned against the counter and watched her retrieve two glasses from the cupboard. Since the girls' team had jumped on a winning streak, putting them in the top half of the league with only four losses, Riley was on a kick for them to go all the way.

She held up her hands, a glass grasped in each. "Whoa. Let's just focus on the rest of the season, shall we?" It was premature to get excited about the possibility of what might happen when they still had a handful of games left, including another face-off with Evergreen High School. Even though Bradshaw had beat some of the other tough teams in the league, she knew their second game against Evergreen wouldn't be like the first.

"Without you, none of this would be possible, you know." He crossed his arms and smirked at her, like he expected a thank you for forcing her on the team in the first place.

"That is not true." She turned on the faucet and filled a glass with water. He may want a thank you, but he would never get one.

"It is true," he said. "How else would you explain how the girls' basketball team went from ten years of losing to one year of winning with the only major change being you? You play ninety-five percent of every game with an average of twenty-five points. Players don't get any better than you."

She set the glasses on the counter and opened her mouth to respond, to tell him she was only a piece of the whole, but someone else spoke first.

"And what are you, Emma's private cheerleader?" Lance said as he entered the kitchen, heading straight for the refrigerator. "Where are your skirt and pom-poms?"

It wasn't so much what her brother said, but the way he said it. The way his eyes narrowed, the way his tone dripped with loathing, the way his lip curled into a sneer as he spoke to Riley. Riley didn't deserve that.

Emma's cheeks burned, her hands balling into fists at her sides. She knew she shouldn't react to Lance's arrogance, but she'd had enough. "What is your problem?"

Riley pushed away from the counter and grabbed her arm to hold her back, but she twisted free and stepped toward Lance.

"Nothing." Lance scanned the shelves for food. "I just think it's funny how everyone thinks you're God's gift to the world when you're nothing but a loser. You're wasting your time playing that stupid game."

Maybe he was right, maybe she was wasting her time with basketball and nothing would come out of it, but who was he to make such a statement? "And how would you know? You've never even seen me play."

"I don't need to see you play," he tossed over his shoulder. "I've been there, remember?"

Yes, she did remember. She remembered him being the

one with his face plastered all over the paper with headlines shouting about how great he was and how far he would go in basketball. He'd jeopardized it all when he let his grades slip and stopped showing up for practice. "Yeah," she said, "I remember. I remember how you could have been great, but you chose to pursue the big dumb jock route instead."

Lance slammed the cupboard door and spun around to face her. "You don't get it, do you?" he roared. "No matter what you tell yourself, you're no better than I am. You're on a long road to nowhere."

Riley stepped closer to her, but remained quiet. He knew not to interfere, but he wasn't stupid. If Lance got mad enough to hit her, Riley wouldn't stay on the sidelines to watch.

Emma looked at her brother, saw the depth of his hatred for her and the world in his eyes. She didn't want to believe the only road unfolding before her led to the same place Lance stood. Maybe she was a loser and maybe basketball wouldn't take her to college, but maybe Riley was right. Maybe there was something more in store for her than living in the garage and being consumed by years of regret and anger like the rest of her family. "Just because that's your story doesn't mean it has to be mine."

Lance laughed a malicious laugh. "Don't tell me you've been listening to your rich boyfriend." He pointed at Riley. "The only reason he's your friend is because he feels sorry for you. Why else would a guy like him waste time on a loser like you? Do you think you'll go to college, get some high-paying job, and live happily ever after?" Lance shook his head. "You're pitiful with all your hopes and dreams. Riley may not admit it, but he knows it just as well as I do."

She'd heard Lauren say similar things, but it was different coming from her own brother. Different because it felt more real—more true. As much as she wanted to look at Riley to see if Lance's accusations held any truth, she couldn't. She would die if she saw guilt in his eyes.

"You're just like her," Lance spit out.

"Just like who?" The question was out of her mouth before she could decide whether or not she wanted to ask it.

"Who do you think?" Lance yelled. "You're just like her. You're just like Mom. She was always talking about how much more to life there was, and how she had all these dreams of going to college and getting some fancy job. She left because she wanted something more, something better. Better than Dad, better than us."

His words hung in the air like fog that numbed the senses and disoriented thought. In the last five years, their mom had never been the topic of family conversation. They didn't rehash old memories of her or voice inquiries into what she was doing now. She was a phantom. Yet Lance shouted her back into existence in a way that clawed at Emma's insides.

"That's not true," she said quietly, her words barely breaking through the fog. She didn't know why she felt obligated to defend the woman who'd walked out on them, but she refused to believe her mom would abandon her family to pursue a better life without them.

"It is true," Lance shouted at her. "Haven't you ever wondered why Dad can hardly stand to look at you or why you sleep in the stinking garage?"

Yes, she'd wondered, but she'd always figured it was because, as the only girl, her dad wanted her to have the privacy she needed. But, as she listened to her brother, everything clicked into place.

"It's because you remind Dad too much of Mom, and he knows you're going to crush him like Mom did with all of your childish dreams and hopes for a better life!" Lance's face grew red as he yelled, but with every stinging truth he flung at her, she sensed his satisfaction. Like he'd been waiting for years to break her. "Dad hates you. He hates having you around as a constant reminder of her. Just because you can dribble a stupid ball and make a few shots, doesn't make you special."

Emma didn't want to hear more. She didn't want to look into Lance's eyes and know how much he meant the words he spoke, but her feet and eyes remained transfixed as they were. It was like reliving a nightmare. Her mom's abandonment. Her dad's indifference. Her brothers' resentment.

Lance leaned in, his eyes narrowing. The next words out of his mouth, said just above a whisper, hit her the hardest because of the sincerity and loathing behind them. "You're worthless."

A hand wrapped around her wrist and pulled her backward, and then Riley stepped in front of her, shielding her from her brother. "That's enough," Riley said threateningly, matching Lance's tone and sneer. They stood inches apart, neither one backing down. Emma knew she should separate them and drag Riley out of her brother's firing zone, but she couldn't move. Riley's eyes remained locked on Lance's for what seemed like an eternity before he slid his fingers down Emma's wrist and grabbed her hand.

"Let's go," he said.

She didn't have strength for anything except to let Riley guide her out of the kitchen, away from Lance, but her feet stopped when they entered the living room. Logan still sat on the couch, his book cast aside, evidently listening to her fight with Lance. He'd heard, but he'd done nothing to come to her defense or shut Lance up before he'd said too much. But it wasn't Logan meeting her gaze that made her stop.

It was her dad.

He stood ten feet away from her, leaning against the wall with his head bowed. How long had he been there? What all had he heard?

Without raising his head, her dad glanced up and met her eyes for the first time in years. It was then she knew he'd heard it all. She stood there, needing him to provide her with answers, to debunk Lance's accusations and tell her not to overreact, to tell her he loved her like a father was supposed to.

She waited.

Waited for something more than guilt to be reflected in the way he looked at her. Waited for him to close the distance between them and be the dad she needed him to be. Just when she didn't think she could stand it any longer, her dad diverted his gaze from her to the floor. Maybe he needed a minute to collect his thoughts, to transfer the truth into words and tell her this was all just a big misunderstanding. Emma waited with a scrap of hope, but she felt Riley's hand tense in hers. Her dad's silence held a different meaning for him. As much as she wanted to deny it, she knew Riley's assessment was right. Her heart split, and she held back a sob as she felt the weight of Lance's words crash down on her, knowing they were true by the way her dad remained silent.

Her dad hated her.

She didn't resist as Riley pulled her through the front door, away from her so-called family. Her eyes stared unseeing at the ground as Lance's words and her dad's face burned in her memory. She couldn't think. She couldn't breathe.

"Em?" Riley glanced her way as their feet hit the sidewalk. "You okay?" His voice was tense, controlled, like he didn't trust himself to speak.

"I'm fine," she said automatically, not able to tear her eyes away from the ground. She felt numb. Broken. Empty.

Nothing felt right. Not even Riley's hand in hers as he led her down the street to his house. His grip was too tight, his arm too stiff. She didn't know whether to be comforted or afraid by Riley's loyalty to her. What if Lance's accusations about him were true? What if the last eight years of friendship boiled down to eight years of pity?

Emma knew their friendship didn't make any sense—that a boy like him shouldn't care about a girl like her—but did that mean it was all a lie?

She felt Riley continuously look her way as they walked to his house, as if trying to sense how close she was from breaking, but she kept her eyes fixated on the street, hearing her brother's words repeat over and over in her head.

Dad hates you... You'll never amount to anything... You're worthless.

The safety of the Ledgers' driveway caused Riley to stop and face her. He didn't look into her eyes, and it took Emma a second to realize it was because he couldn't. The muscle in his jaw twitched, his nostrils flared. He looked like he wanted to say something but couldn't find the words. It didn't matter. She knew there was nothing left to say. Her brother had said it all.

She felt sorry for Riley. Over the years, he had witnessed a few selective instances when she'd caught one of her brothers' fists, and in one instance her dad's backhand, but he'd only seen the bruises, never the actual fight. He'd only heard her edited version of the truth, never listened to the live commentary.

Riley placed his hands on the sides of her face and finally raised his eyes to meet hers. She didn't know what he saw when he looked at her. Maybe shock over what had happened or grief over what it meant. Or maybe he saw the emptiness left over after all hope of gaining her dad's love vanished. Whatever he saw made his scowl give way to pain and his shoulders slump forward in defeat. He rested his forehead against hers and closed his eyes. "I'm sorry," he whispered. "I'm so sorry."

She didn't know if he was apologizing for her brother, her dad, or for himself, but the pain in his words made her eyes blur with tears she desperately tried to smother. Her eyelids slid closed, and she tried to regain her composure so

Riley didn't see her weakness. When he pulled away a moment later, he smoothed hair away from her face, kissed her forehead, and reclaimed her hand to lead her inside the house.

Both of his parents were in the living room, and they looked up when Emma and Riley entered. They rose from the couch when they saw Riley and Emma's faces.

"Can Emma sleep here tonight?" Riley asked before they could bombard him with questions.

Emma was aware of how his voice was distant, cold. She glanced at Riley's profile and saw his tense jaw, his rigid stance.

He exchanged a look with his dad before Mr. Ledger nodded. "Of course."

"Maybe for a few days?" Riley asked looking at Emma.

"Anything," his dad said, knowing enough not to ask details.

Mrs. Ledger put her arm around Emma and turned her toward the kitchen. Riley held onto her hand until the distance pulled them apart. Emma wished he'd stay with her, but his mom had taken initiative and guided her toward the back of the house, waving Riley toward his dad.

Mrs. Ledger patted Emma's shoulder. "I don't know about you, but warm cookies and milk sound good right now."

Warm cookies and milk—the gift of a mother. Emma sat at the kitchen table, staring at the grains of wood. She wanted to ask Mrs. Ledger, Riley's mom, the only mom she knew, what would cause a woman to walk away from her family, from her children, without looking back. But Emma couldn't formulate the words on her tongue. Besides, Mrs. Ledger wasn't the kind of mom who could answer that type of question.

Mrs. Ledger opened and closed cupboards, trying to make small talk, but Emma didn't raise her head from the table. She kept her head bowed and her mouth closed, trying not to cry, trying not to draw attention to herself, but she'd never been invisible in the Ledgers' house. Not even now.

Sensing her small talk strategy wasn't working, Mrs. Ledger sat beside Emma and reached over to cover Emma's hand with her own. "Sweetheart," she said, "you're like a daughter to us. You can stay here as long as you need. If you need anything it's yours. Okay?"

Emma nodded, still not trusting herself to meet Mrs. Ledger's eyes in fear she wouldn't be able to keep her emotions in check.

Mrs. Ledger pulled Emma into a hug. "Everything will be all right," she whispered. She said it with such tenderness and conviction that Emma almost believed her.

As much as she loved Mrs. Ledger, Emma wasn't in the mood for mothers at the moment. Riley's mom finally released her and returned to her cookies, letting Emma slip away.

What she needed was time alone. What she stumbled upon were voices.

She froze outside the door to Mr. Ledger's study. The door stood ajar, allowing Emma to hear the low, deep voices of a father and son deep in conversation.

"He didn't..." Mr. Ledger paused, as if not wanting to complete his question, "hit her, did he?"

Emma pressed her body against the wall by the doorframe, afraid to breathe, afraid to listen, but unable to leave. She should've known Riley would talk to his dad about what had happened. Riley and his dad were close, as in no secrets, no lies, and no selective disclosure.

"No," Riley responded. "But it was bad. Her brother said so many horrible things, and her dad just stood there. It's so much worse than I thought."

She heard someone exhale like words couldn't explain anything.

"What should I do, Dad?" Riley asked, his voice not as strong as before. "Emma looked so...broken." His voice cracked on the last word, and she felt tears form in her eyes. He shouldn't be in pain because of her.

"Listen to me," his dad said gently but firmly. Emma could imagine Mr. Ledger leaning in to place a hand on his son's shoulder and holding his son's gaze with his own. "You are the best thing in Emma's life. You need to be strong for her. Be her friend. Be there for her. But if something happens with her brothers or her dad or anyone else, you come straight to your mom and me. I don't want you involved, you got it?"

"Yes," Riley said. Silence commenced, and for a moment Emma thought their conversation was over, but then Riley's voice, hardly louder than a whisper, broke through one last time. "Dad, how can he not love his own daughter when she has so much good in her and is so easy to love?"

Emma leaned her head against the wall and looked at the ceiling, no longer able to prevent her tears from spilling silently down her cheeks. She may have been the one broken, but Riley was the one hurting.

◆◆◆

In the Ledgers' downstairs rec room, Emma stared at the darkened ceiling and replayed her brother's words in her head with years of flashbacks flickering through her thoughts to justify them. She thought about Lance. He'd had dreams once. Dreams he'd watched slip away to leave him resentful and bitter.

Hate was a strong word. Every kid knew it. But hate was what she'd seen in Lance's eyes. Hate was what her dad didn't contradict when she'd passed him on the way out of the house. How could she ever go back home and face them?

Emma heard the stairs creak under the weight of someone descending. She watched a silhouette move across the room, but didn't know if she should pretend to be asleep or not. The figure approached her, getting closer and closer before tripping over her feet and falling in a heap on top of her. Riley's grunt accompanied her own.

"Riley?" she wheezed.

"Geez, Em," he said. "Are you trying to kill me?"

"Me? What are you doing?"

He rolled over to situate himself beside her. "I figured you could use a friend."

"Oh," she said simply.

"Why aren't you sleeping in the bed like a normal person?"

How could she explain she preferred the floor, needing something strong and solid beneath her? She didn't answer, and he didn't press the issue. Instead, he unrolled his sleeping bag and climbed inside, fluffed his pillow, tossed and turned, grunted and groaned, until finally becoming still.

"Are you comfortable yet?" she asked.

"No," he replied. "You?"

"Actually, yes." She was warm for the first time all winter in a house that wasn't hers, in a room with carpet.

They remained silent long enough for the clouds to crawl across the sky and split to reveal the moon. Moonlight peeked through the window, illuminating the room enough for Emma to see the ceiling she'd been staring at since she'd turned off the lights hours ago.

"Em?" Riley whispered. "You awake?"

She thought about not answering, but what would be the point? He'd probably seen her open eyes anyway. "Yeah," she whispered back.

"What are you thinking?"

What was she thinking? She was thinking about how her mom wanted something better than her and how her dad and brothers despised her for reasons beyond her control; how she thought basketball could rescue her and take her away from this place, and how her best friend probably saw her as nothing more than a charity case. Was it wrong to love a woman she didn't even know? To hate the woman who had left her, yet desire her comfort more than anything? Was it wrong to want to forgive her dad for everything if he'd at least try loving her as his daughter rather than hating her for his wife's mistakes? Was it wrong to pretend her friendship with Riley was genuine?

"Nothing." She hoped he didn't hear her voice crack.

Riley rolled his head to the side to look at her. A tear slipped from the corner of her eye and down her temple. She felt his arm inch closer to hers, his fingers brushing the back of her wrist before sliding down to grasp her hand, holding on so she wouldn't get lost in the dark.

Nineteen

After a week, Emma had yet to bounce back to her usual self. Not even basketball could dull the pain in her chest and quiet her brother's voice in her head. Something about the way Lance had described their mom seemed off—like he was talking about a stranger. Obviously, his anger had warped his memories of her. No way was their mom the selfish and cruel woman he remembered. Emma had spent the last five years preserving memories of her mom to make sure she didn't get lost and forgotten with time. But sometime in the past week, with her brother's words echoing in her head, Emma had difficulty recalling images of her mom that used to come so easily—images of a beautiful woman, a loving mother, a gentle and kind person. The images were now blurred, sometimes blank, like a reflection on water that rippled and vanished with the toss of a stone. The harder she tried to conjure up the memories, the more they slipped out of reach.

Nothing mattered anymore. Bradshaw had played two games last week—losing both—but she didn't care. Even if they finished the rest of the season with a string of losses, Emma didn't think she'd be able to muster a shred of disappointment. Basketball had lost its flare. She wanted nothing more than to run from the gym and leave it all behind, but she didn't have anywhere else to go. She still hadn't moved back home, and she didn't want to outdo her welcome at Riley's house. It was either endure basketball with girls or wander the streets until she returned to the Ledgers' home. At least the gym was warm.

The girls on the team noticed the change in her behavior and her lack of motivation to lead them on the court. Whatever scrap of respect they'd gained for her in the past two months had vanished. She saw them look at her, she heard them whisper about her when they thought she couldn't hear, but she didn't care. Her confrontation with Lance had changed everything. Not a minute passed when she didn't feel the heaviness of his words mount in her chest and threaten her eyes with tears. She felt like a girl. The emotional, whining, complaining kind of girl, and she hated it.

Gone were her private lessons with Ashley, Shiloh, and Peyton. She'd cancelled those on Monday, not in the mood to teach girls how to play some stupid game for entertainment purposes, and she hadn't resumed them. What was the point? It wasn't like basketball made any difference in the world. No matter how talented Emma proved to be with a basketball, she was still motherless, practically fatherless, and void of worth.

Coach blew the whistle, ending yet another practice, and Emma dragged her feet to the sidelines. Maybe she would sling her bag over her shoulder, exit the gym, and walk the darkened streets, curling up to sleep on some street corner when she got tired, then continuing on until she'd put a safe distance between her and her family. Or maybe she would go to the park and watch the infinite sky turn from dark to light and wish her life would do the same.

"Emma." Coach caught her eye and waved her over.

Or maybe Emma would sacrifice precious time doing nothing by enduring a lecture from Coach. It was only a matter of time. She was surprised Coach had lasted this long without confronting her. Emma seriously considered walking out the door without acknowledging Coach's invite for a one-on-one chat. The look on Coach's face, part anger-part concern, was enough for Emma to run, but she didn't. She obliged and veered her footsteps toward Coach, out of hearing range from the rest of the team.

Coach crossed her arms over her chest. With her head bowed and eyebrows raised, Coach looked at Emma with upturned eyes, as if trying to read under the radar to detect the unabridged version of her problems.

"Everything okay?" she asked.

Emma sighed. "Yep." Not that she would reveal anything anyway.

Coach filled the void between them with nodding. "You've been off all week."

Not something to tell a girl right smack dab in the middle of a crisis. "What do you mean I've been off?" Emma snapped. Even on her worst day she was still better than the rest of the team combined. So she toned down her enthusiasm and didn't take control of every second on the court. Wasn't it time for someone else to step up to the plate?

Coach held up her hand. "Don't be offended. I'm just worried about you."

Worried the team's string of wins would halt to a stop was more like it. "Well don't be," Emma said coldly. "I'm fine."

"You know, if you need someone to talk to, you can talk to me."

"Thanks, but no thanks." Emma didn't even consider the offer. Everyone wore the hat of a counselor lately, devoted to saving Emma from her life. They would tell her how much they understood what she was going through. How she shouldn't feel trapped by the limitations of her family, and how she could do anything. None of it was true.

No one she knew understood what it was like to live in a corner of the garage.

Coach studied her. Emma met her gaze and matched it.

"You have more talent and more potential than anyone I've ever seen," Coach said to her. "But there is no way you'll do anything close to great if you don't believe in yourself."

Emma snorted. Great motivational speech. Believe you're a star and you will be! Too bad she lived in the world of reality. "Just because I can dribble a ball and make a few shots doesn't make me better than anyone else on this team." Lance's words rolled too easily off her tongue.

Coach gave her a sad smile. "Who said I was talking about basketball?"

Walking away, Coach left Emma to glare after her as she collected her things and followed the straggling girls toward the door. What was with these people? Just because their words of inspiration sounded good didn't mean they would change anything. Did they not see where she was from or notice how the entire world sided against her? She couldn't even afford shoes to play basketball. She had nothing to give. On the court or off.

She saw Coach bend over and pick up a ball from the floor. Turning around, she threw an overhead pass to Emma. Emma caught the ball after the second bounce just as the door clinked closed, shutting her alone in the gym. She hadn't been alone in the gym since before she started coaching Ashley. So much had changed since then. Her breath caught in her throat as loneliness closed in on her. It was too big a space for just her.

The silence was too loud. Emma dribbled the ball once and listened as the sound echoed through the gym and faded into the deafening silence. It was a silence that brought images of her mom to the surface. Old pictures of her mom had been buried beneath years of hurt, burned, or shredded during years of mourning until nothing remained. The only picture she had of her mom was the one in her head from her twelve-year-old self. For the first time in a week, the blurred images of her mom became clear, but they were different than before.

Instead of a patient, loving mother, Emma remembered a woman who fought constantly with her husband about money, about having too many kids, about all life had to offer and all she had missed. She remembered a woman who always needed time for herself, who sacrificed moments to hug her children because her clothes would wrinkle. A woman who talked too much about the world beyond, and not enough about the world within, the walls of home. Emma didn't need confirmation from Lance to know these new memories of her mom were the real ones, and the ones she had held onto for so long had merely been her attempts to fill in the blanks with a mom she wished she'd had because it was easier than remembering the truth.

Emma squeezed her eyes shut. Lance had been right after all. If he'd been right about their mom, maybe he was right about everything.

She started dribbling. Right hand, left hand, trying to ward off the thoughts she knew she couldn't stop. A couple dribbles turned into a few more until she zigged and zagged, spinning around the torrent of questions swarming around her. Where was her mom? Did she ever think about Emma or her brothers, or had she started over with a clean slate when she left, never looking back? Would she recognize Emma if they passed on the street? Did Lance truly hate her or was he still dealing with the demons of his past? Did her dad really want her gone? Was Riley's friendship merely an act of pity? They were questions Emma would never ask even if given the chance, afraid she wouldn't like the answers she'd hear.

All of the fear, pain, and loss she'd experienced molded into an invisible opponent. She dribbled, her sorrow flaring into anger. With the ball, she pounded out thoughts of her mom, filling the emptiness inside her. An emptiness only ever filled by basketball. Alone on the court, with a ball in her hands, Emma tasted freedom. Freedom from the limitation and doubt reminding her she wasn't strong enough or good enough or smart enough. On the court, she was flawless.

She played against her invisible defenders, allowing herself to dream about district playoffs and the slim chance Bradshaw had of competing. Was it wrong if she wanted it?

Shaking her head, she spun away from the basket. Sure, she could dream and conjure up the impossible, but what would happen when reality replaced the false image? A life where good things happened wasn't meant for her. She knew it, her family knew it, the entire world knew it, so why did she continue to hope and wish she could slip through the cracks into a new life, a different life? A life that would never be hers. Basketball scholarships given to poor kids who couldn't go to college without them were probably far and few between. Emma didn't know if she was good enough to get one, or if she even wanted one. Lance was right; she was worthless. But, for some crazy reason, she still hoped. It was this hope she played on.

Sweat poured down her face and her breathing came in ragged gasps as she jabbed, spun, drove, and shot, playing against so much more than a cross-town rival. She sprinted the length of the court, twisting and turning with the ball, leaving her defenders behind. She loved to drive to the basket, split the defense, and wrap beneath the basket to fight for a shot, but there was something special about pulling up at the three-point line, firing off a shot, and watching the ball take its journey to the basket and fall through the net.

She went for the three.

The ball swished the net and then bounced on the floor once, twice, then faster and faster until it rolled to a stop. She expected silence to follow.

"I do love to watch you play."

Emma spun toward the voice. Riley leaned against the wall, his arms and legs crossed nonchalantly as he watched her.

She swiped her arm across her forehead to smear drops of sweat away from her eyes. "What are you doing here?"

He seemed unfazed by the caution in her voice. She'd spent the last week living in his house, but they hadn't spent any real quality time together digesting her confrontation with Lance or developing a game plan of what to do next. Most of the time she remained quiet, and although he gave her silence, he was always the same old Riley. Always there, always protecting, always worrying about her.

"Looking for you."

Emma didn't respond. She didn't know how he'd snuck in undetected or how long he had watched her, but she should've figured he would come sooner or later.

"You've been quiet lately," he said.

Now was not the time for this conversation. She wasn't ready yet. She was still stuck in last week trying to process everything. Emma retrieved the ball and dribbled back onto the court, squaring up to the basket. "Have I?"

"Yeah," he said as she released the ball into the air. They watched it drop through the net. "Even with me."

Emma didn't want to explain herself. She didn't want to admit how Lance's words still played like a broken record through her head, how the look in her dad's eyes still burned behind her closed eyelids, or how she continued to question the sincerity of Riley's friendship.

He looked at her, head tilted to the side, eyebrows raised. "Want to tell me why?"

Persistence. When it came to her, patience was not his strongest quality. "There's nothing to tell," she said. "I just haven't had anything to say." Which was true. Even though a million thoughts swarmed in her head, she refused to try and find the words to vocalize them.

He pushed off the wall and walked toward her. "Come on, Em. Talk to me."

"About what?"

"About what's going on with you." His voice rose in volume as frustration fought to have a presence.

She slammed the ball on the ground. "Nothing's going on with me."

"Really?" He knew something. His tone indicated he had given her the opportunity to come clean and be honest with him, knowing she was holding something back, but she wouldn't budge. There was nothing she wanted to share with him—nothing she would share with him.

"Yes, really," she confirmed.

He nodded, not agreeing with her. "Then explain to me why you cancelled practices with Ashley, Shiloh, and Peyton."

Emma tensed. "How did you know about that?" She'd done her best to hide it from him, knowing he wouldn't approve. Teaching girls how to play basketball wasn't number one on her priority list at the moment.

"Ashley came to me and asked what was wrong with you. She said you're just going through the motions at practice, and you cancelled your time with them completely." He held his hands out to the side in a manner to say he lacked answers. "Since you haven't talked to me, I didn't know what to say. I told her you needed space."

Why did it seem like the whole world was in her business? First Coach, then Ashley, and now Riley. Was there a line forming of others? "It's nothing."

He stood in front of her, arms crossed, eyes burning holes in her. "If it was nothing, you wouldn't be skipping classes too."

"Are you spying on me now?" she said, matching the hardness in his tone. Skipping classes was a completely normal and healthy behavior for a high school senior, especially one who had no future.

"If that's what you want to call it," he said. "Or you could consider it as me being worried about you."

"I don't need your worry. I'm fine." She turned away, yearning for nothing more than the silence to cage her again. It was better to be plunged into a life of bad memories than to make new ones with the one person she couldn't stand to lose. She didn't want his pity or his concern. She wanted his friendship unattached by obligation.

"Fine," he repeated.

"Yes, fine," she emphasized.

"No, you're not fine. You've worked too hard and come too far to give up now just because of those stupid things your brother said."

She spun around to face him, her hands balled into fists, her face burning as she let the words fly. "Tell me one thing he said that wasn't true. No matter what I do, I will always be worthless."

Riley took two strides toward her. He secured her head between his hands, making sure she couldn't look away. "That is not true," he said firmly. "You're smart and beautiful and strong and—"

Her chest tightened with every word he said. She broke free from his grasp, tears spilling from her eyes. "Then why did my mom leave?" she choked out. "Why does my own dad hate me?"

"He doesn't hate—"

"Don't," she said, shaking her head and swallowing tears. She didn't need him to lie and paint a pretty picture of her pitiful life to spare her feelings. She wasn't a kid anymore. "You heard what Lance said, and you saw the look in my dad's eyes. You don't know what it's like to look at their faces every day and know they despise you. You don't know how it feels to be left by your mom—the one person who's supposed to love you unconditionally. You don't know what it's like to have to be protected by your best friend because no one else cares about you." She released a shaky breath of defeat, her body two seconds away from collapsing. "I'm tired of being your charity case."

"When are you going to get it?" he said, his voice firm and steady. "No matter what people say, you're not my charity case. I don't pity you. I care about you. There's a difference."

She wanted to believe him. She wanted to know their friendship was real, but how could he be the only person who didn't hate her? "How do I know you're not just saying that because you're a nice guy?"

His eyes softened. "Because no matter what's happened, I've never left you."

"But you will," she said, unable to mask the hurt in her tone or the tears in her eyes. She wished only the best for Riley, but she couldn't help thinking about what life would be like for her when he left. "At the end of the year, you'll leave me, just like my mom did, when you go off to college."

He shook his head. "No," he said softly. "Not even then."

It wasn't what he said, but how he said it. He left no room for doubt, and the genuineness of his words caused fresh tears to fall from her eyes. Her dad and brothers may not have left her physically, but they'd abandoned her in every other way the day her mom walked out. Riley hadn't. She didn't have an excuse not to believe him this time.

"I don't want to be like her," Emma said, her voice small and pleading. "I don't want to go off to college and leave my family because I think I deserve better than them. I can't—" Her words choked off into sobs.

Riley's face twisted in pain as he watched her. For once, he couldn't whip up an answer to sweep all the injustice away. He reached for her. She didn't have the strength to resist him, so she slumped against him, needing his strength and his friendship to remain standing. She buried her face in his chest and cried. Every dream she'd ever had of finding her mom, of gaining her father's love again, of breaking the chains holding her to a life of limitation, shattered. She refused to follow in her mom's footsteps, refused to cause her family more pain, even if it meant living in the garage for the rest of her life.

Riley held her, letting her shed too many years of pent-up tears. He tightened his arms around her, holding her together—always holding her together. When her mom left, when kids teased her at school, when her brothers took their anger out on her, it had always been Riley who held her together.

Even after her sobs subsided, his arms remained locked around her. Never in her life had she imagined having a total meltdown and crying like a girl in front of Riley or anyone else. If it had been Tom instead of Riley, he would have teased her. Jerry would have cracked a joke, never believing his superstar had tears to cry, and her dad and brothers would have ignored her, not knowing or caring what they could do to help.

After a while, Riley slipped out of his coat and secured it around her shoulders. Wiping tears from her cheeks, he pressed his lips to her forehead. "Let's go." He grabbed her bag from the sidelines and slid his arm around her waist to secure her at his side as they made their way across the gym to the exit. The door opened seconds before they reached it, and Ashley appeared before them.

"Hi, guys," she said breathlessly. "I just forgot my—" She stopped when she saw Emma's puffy eyes and tear-streaked face.

Her eyes widened; her brow wrinkled. "Are you okay?"

"She's fine," Riley assured her, tightening his arm around Emma's waist. "She just hates it when I beat her at basketball."

Despite how miserable she felt, Emma smiled. "You wish."

He chuckled and kissed the top of her head. "See you later, kid."

Ashley's faint, "Bye," slipped through as the door closed behind them.

Emma stared out the window as Riley drove through the darkened streets toward his house. For the past week, Emma had done everything she could just to keep herself together. Now she was just tired. Riley didn't say much. He stared out the windshield at the road ahead, one hand on the steering wheel, the other clasping hers. He glanced at her every once in a while to make sure she didn't jump from the jeep and roll away.

They drove by her house, and she couldn't help but look. Through the front window she saw her dad and brothers watching TV together like they did almost every night. They laughed at whatever show they were watching—laughed like for once everything was right in the world. Emma's breath caught in her throat. She turned away, knowing her family didn't miss her absence—they preferred it.

She felt pressure on her hand and glanced up to see Riley smile at her. "It'll be okay," he said, squeezing her hand. "I promise."

Twenty

Someone was watching her. In a hallway full of high school students, the realization didn't come from locking eyes with the perpetrator, but from an unsettled feeling within. Someone was definitely watching her. It wasn't the same feeling as having Riley watch her from the corner of his eye thinking she wouldn't notice, but the full on I'm-so-obviously-staring-at-you feeling. Considering Riley was on his way to fifth period, Emma knew it wasn't him, but the feeling of being watched was so strong. She glanced around to find the culprit.

Ashley.

Emma tried to ignore it—the eyes boring into the back of her head, watching her every move—but she couldn't. "Stop it!" she shouted over her shoulder at the freshman. "I mean it."

Ashley popped up beside her, still staring. "Are you okay?"

Emma groaned. "For the millionth time, I'm fine." Between the time she'd stepped over the threshold into school until the current second, Ashley had made her presence known—by staring. So far, Emma's efforts to make the kid forget about last night's little occurrence were in vain. "I may have had a mini breakdown yesterday, but

I'm over it. So, will you please stop looking at me like I'm going to shatter into a million pieces?"

"I'm sorry," Ashley said. "I've just never seen you cry before."

Emma rolled her eyes. "Yeah, it's amazing to think a person like me actually has feelings, isn't it?" Unlike the rest of the female population, Emma didn't sprout waterworks every other second of the day to get attention, but that didn't mean she was a freak of nature.

"That's not what I meant," the kid protested. "I just want to help."

"Yeah, you and everyone else on the planet." Emma's tone was tinged with more sarcasm than she intended, but seriously, what was with everyone's sudden interest in her? Talk about annoying, suffocating, and downright rude.

Ashley bowed her head. Even with her brown hair casting her face in shadows, Emma saw the kid's chin wobble. Wasn't it illegal for a freshman to look so crushed? Emma's chest tightened. If any tears escaped from Ashley's eyes, Emma would hate herself for eternity.

She never meant to hurt the kid. From the look on Ashley's face, the it's-not-you-it's-me speech wouldn't work, so Emma tried a different approach. "Look, my life isn't exactly..." how could she put it in girl terms without being offensive? "butterflies and roses." She couldn't prevent cringing at the term. "I just needed some space."

"Needed. As in past tense," Ashley stated for the record. "Does that mean we can resume practices? Today?"

If Emma said no, she knew she would regret it. Not to mention the combined guilt trip from Riley and Ashley she wouldn't survive. "Sure, why not?"

Ashley threw herself at Emma, wrapping her bony arms around Emma's waist. "Thanks, Coach."

"I told you," Emma said, wiggling free of Ashley's grasp. "I'm not your coach. Don't ever call me that again."

"Okay, Coach," Ashley said. "I'll tell Shiloh and

Peyton."

"Get out of here," Emma said, lightly pushing Ashley down the hall. The school should implement a freshmen-should-be-seen-not-heard policy. Seniors shouldn't have to tolerate them.

Emma couldn't help but shake her head and laugh as Ashley bounced off one body and then another in her attempt to get to class. She probably wouldn't have had such a tough time if she didn't insist on turning around every five seconds to wave at Emma.

And that was how Emma's life tried to take another step at returning to normal. Whatever normal was.

Monopoly. When played between two people, there was one big winner and one huge loser. Monopoly was Riley's favorite game and it wasn't because he was always the huge loser. No, that would be Emma. No matter what she did, or didn't do, she could never manage a victory in the stupid game. She could have started with two thousand extra dollars and half the properties, yet she'd somehow manage to lose it all to Riley's greedy hands. It was just sad. But on occasion, she would succumb to his pleading and give him permission to break out the Monopoly board. Allowing her to continue invading the privacy of his home was considered one of these occasions.

With the game spread across the living room floor, and the two of them sprawled beside it, she glared at him as he counted his money. He may have been her best friend in the entire world, but one thing he was not was merciful in the game of Monopoly. He played for total annihilation.

"I'm buying four hotels," he said with a smirk.

With a flick of his finger he demolished the houses on Park Place and Boardwalk, clearing the space for his newly purchased hotels, which were sure to send her into bankruptcy with her next turn. Unlike most people, Emma *always* landed on Park Place and Boardwalk, especially after Riley started establishing property on them.

"How is it you always manage to buy hotels before I can buy my first house?" It was the same question she asked every single time they played the stupid game, but she couldn't get over it.

"Strategy, my friend." He had no problem setting his hotels on the properties she would most certainly land on with her next role of the dice.

"Strategy, blah."

Long ago, he had stripped her of all rights to play banker or real estate manager, accusing her of cheating at both. Sorry, but when you get massacred in every single game of Monopoly, one has to implement extreme measures to make the game at least partly competitive. Through time, she switched her focus from trying to actually win a game—knowing it was an impossible goal—to seeing how much she could cheat and get away with before he caught her. She also knew a trick or two about strategy.

A knock sounded on the front door.

Riley pointed at her as he rose from the floor to answer it. "You better not cheat while my back is turned."

Yeah, right. A knock on the front door drawing him away from the board? What better cheating opportunity was there? "I wouldn't dream of it," she said, trying to determine whether she should steal money from the bank to pay his hotel costs or roll the die and flip the numbers to evade the danger zone...or both. She waited for just the right moment to make her move, but he had one eye on her and one eye on the door, which meant she'd have to act quickly.

Riley opened the door, and she watched his smile slip into a frown as his entire focus switched to the visitor.

"Hey, Riley. My sister here?"

Her heart skipped a beat at the sound of Logan's voice.

Riley didn't respond. His hand gripped the doorknob,

his body blocked the doorway, and he gave no indication of moving to allow Logan to pass.

"Please," Logan said.

Emma, her cheating strategy forgotten, stood. "Riley," she said, a warning in her voice. "It's okay."

Riley, his body rigid, glanced toward her before moving aside to let Logan into the house.

Logan stepped in just far enough to close the door. He shoved his hands in his pockets and rocked back on his heels before meeting her eye for a half a second. "Hey, sis."

"Hey." She didn't know if he was here as her brother or as their dad's messenger. If anyone would be sent to tell her she was no longer welcome at home, it would be Logan.

Riley came to stand beside her, keeping a close eye on Logan. She knew Riley wouldn't hesitate to act if Logan said anything out of line to her.

"How are you?" Logan asked.

"She's fine," Riley spit out. "No thanks to you."

Emma slapped him on the stomach. Riley never usually got involved in her family affairs, but after the last incident, Emma knew she wouldn't be able to restrain him. "I'm fine," she reiterated, knowing the small talk didn't matter.

"About what happened between you and Lance," Logan said. "Sorry. You know how he gets."

Of all her brothers, Logan was the one who didn't go out of his way to make her life miserable or make her feel like a complete moron, but he did have an annoying habit of trying to sugarcoat things or dissolve problems with a sorry. She could only take so much sugar before she gagged.

"Yeah," she said, crossing her arms. "I know how he gets, but you didn't see his face. He wasn't just blowing off steam this time. He meant every word he said."

Usually she could let the hatred of her family drip away from her without any permanent damage, but this time was different. This time she didn't want to be the one who shoved everything into a closet and closed the door, hoping it would dissolve with time.

"Emma," Logan said, "Dad wants you to come home."

She took a deep breath and exhaled slowly, trying to remain calm. "Did he say that?"

Logan shoved his hands deeper in his pockets and shrugged. "You know how Dad is."

What little hope she'd had about her dad disappeared. "Yeah, I know how Dad is." Their dad was a man of few words. The likelihood he'd said anything about her was doubtful. Besides, the duration of a week couldn't erase the look she'd last seen on his face. "He doesn't want me at home any more than the rest of you do."

Logan took his hands out of his pockets and took a step closer to her, which caused Riley to do the same, his fingers grasping her forearm.

"You can't expect our family to be perfect—"

"Who said anything about perfection?" she yelled. "I'd settle for functional. You keep your nose in a book and a blind eye to everything going on, Lance lashes out at me any chance he gets, Dad hates me for Mom leaving, and Lucas and Lenny treat me more like a ghost than a sister. You come here telling me Dad wants me to come home, but the last time I looked him in the eye, I was the last person he wanted to see."

Logan looked at Riley, then back at her. She sensed his nervousness growing. He didn't like conflict, and she was in no mood to avoid it.

"The decision's yours." Logan cast another glance at Riley, his eyes hardening. "But you don't belong here."

She flinched as if he'd slapped her. It was the first time she'd heard Logan speak with Lance's tone, the first time she'd seen him own his brother's scowl. It didn't matter if her dad sent Logan to retrieve her or not, she knew the real reason for his visit. Even though Riley had always been a permanent fixture in her life, none of her brothers had befriended him. After Lance's accusations, Emma finally understood why. Riley stood for everything they hated: money, perfect families, and unlimited opportunities. No matter how much they despised her, they despised Riley and his family more. They may not want her at home, but they sure didn't want her living with Riley and his parents. Logan had come to remind both Riley and Emma that she didn't belong with the Ledgers—she wasn't good enough for them.

Logan's behavior convinced Emma that he, like Lance, resented her. Logan was just better at hiding it. She watched her brother let himself out, leaving her and Riley to stare after him.

"The nerve of him coming over here and telling you to go home," Riley practically yelled, his fingers tightening around her arm. "He's no better than the rest of your family."

"Riley, relax. He's just—"

"I won't relax!" he shouted. "Em, he sat there the entire time Lance ripped you apart and did nothing. He's never protected you, he's never voiced his opinion on anything, and yet he comes over here after your family rejected you, says you don't belong here, and tells you to come home?" He shook his head. "That's not okay with me."

She opened her mouth to speak, to stick up for her family in some way, but he cut her off. "Don't you dare defend them. They don't deserve it."

Maybe he was right, but she couldn't help it. She freed her arm from his grasp. "Then stop putting me in a position where I feel obligated to defend them."

"I'm sorry," he said without conviction, "but when someone messes with you, they mess with me too."

"How heroic of you," she said sarcastically. "You're a real knight in shining armor."

Without warning, he grabbed her around the waist and pinned her against the wall. She didn't know how to respond to being trapped, so she just looked up at him, looking down at her. "You know I would do anything to protect you, especially from your brothers. If that means I have to be your knight in shining armor, then so be it." He ended his declaration with an arrogant smile and she laughed, knowing he refused to let her family drive a wedge between them.

"Don't you need a white horse for that?"

He shrugged. "Technicalities."

Their faces were only inches apart, and if he wanted to, Riley could have kissed her again—he looked like he wanted to—but he released her instead.

"And you do belong here," he said, stepping back. "The Ledgers are Emma Wrangton's number one fans."

She should have laughed at his corny comment. She should have rolled her eyes or playfully pushed him, but she knew he was right. The Ledgers had always been there for her. No matter how rough things got with her family, Emma knew she could always come home to the Ledgers. Maybe it was because of this she found the strength to return to her family to face whatever came next, rather than hide out in fear of getting hurt again. Two days later, despite Riley's protests, she found herself packing her things.

"You sure this is a good idea?" Riley asked as she picked up her stuff and shoved it into her backpack. He sat on the couch holding her sweatshirt in his hands like it was a teddy bear he didn't want to give up.

"Good idea?" she shrugged. "But I can't stay here forever, Riley."

"Why not?"

"Because I can't keep hiding from my family. You deserve your privacy, and your parents don't need another teenager around the house." She pointed to herself. "Especially not this teenager."

"You're always welcome here, you know that."

She held out her hand for her sweatshirt, but instead of returning it, he grabbed her hand and stood. "You promise if things get bad you'll come back?"

"I don't promise anything." The last thing she wanted was to burden the Ledgers when they'd already done so much for her over the years. "Besides, they're my family. They won't hurt me."

"They already have," he said, his voice low and fierce.

"Physically, I mean."

"Sometimes it's not the physical stuff that inflicts the deepest wounds."

She couldn't refute his comment, especially not with the way he looked at her, seeing through her tough exterior to the pain and fear she'd always tried to hide from him.

Riley cupped her face in his hands. "Do you want me to come with you? Just to make sure everything's okay?"

She shook her head. As much as she wanted him beside her, she couldn't allow him to be there. It was impossible to know what kind of reaction her homecoming would elicit, and if things went badly she didn't want him there to witness it. She had to protect him somehow and subjecting him to her family wasn't the way. "I'll be fine."

He crushed her against him in a hug like the last thing he wanted to do was let her go.

◆◆◆

Logan had said their dad wanted Emma home, but he had a funny way of showing it. In the twelve hours since she'd returned to the house, nothing had changed. There were no apologies, no forced conversations, and no family meetings on how to better treat each other. Only silence and rejection met her.

She walked into the kitchen the morning following her return. It was the first time since Riley had pulled her out of the house a week ago that she was in the same room with her dad and all four of her brothers. Their talking stopped as soon as she entered. She wasn't under the illusion they were talking about her. She sat at the table and poured herself a bowl of cereal. Her dad remained at the counter, his coffee mug in his hand but not drinking from it. Lance hunched over his food, not even glancing in her direction. Not that he was capable of regret or anything. Logan peered at her over his book as if to say, "Well? What did you expect?" Even Lucas and Lenny were unusually quiet.

She pushed away from the table and approached her dad. She wasn't an idiot; she wasn't going to confront him or anything. The last thing she wanted was to look in his eyes and see the truth all over again. She approached him with the sole purpose of asking, one last time, for him to come and see her play. Even if he only stayed for five minutes, it would be enough to convince her there was hope for her family. "Dad, I—"

He cleared his throat, set his mug on the counter, and took a step away from her. "I, uh, have to be to work early. Logan, make sure your brothers stay out of trouble today, please." Without another word, her dad left. Left her standing there as he walked out of the house—away from her.

Her dad's rejection made her eyes sting with tears, and she slumped against the counter, unable to remain standing without support. Was this how it would be from now on? Her dad unable to remain in the same room with her? She looked at her brothers, sure she would see them smirking, but Lenny and Lucas stared quietly down at their bowls, and Logan was watching Lance, who was watching her. It had been a while since she'd seen anything but hatred in his eyes, but now, she saw what appeared to be fear. Fear, maybe, because he realized his outburst had done more damage than expected.

Lance tore his eyes away, and in that moment, something changed within her. She'd been treading water for years, waiting for her family to love her, to accept her, to give her some indication they cared about her. Only now did she realize the spark of hope she'd nurtured for so long hadn't been keeping her afloat, it had been drowning her. No matter how much she tried to deny it, her entire family had abandoned her years ago. Her mom fleeing in the middle of the night, her dad's inability to meet her eyes, her brothers preferring her absence. She'd lost them and they weren't coming back. All this time she'd been alone, without her family's love and without their acceptance. She'd endured years of their ridicule and rejection, yet she'd survived.

Maybe Riley was right, maybe she was strong enough. Strong enough to be defined by something other than her family. Strong enough to tread her own path.

She took a deep breath, her hands gripping the edge of the counter. She didn't know what to do, so she did the only thing she could.

She left.

She left by the same path Riley had led her a week ago to take her away from her family. She bounded down the porch stairs, hit the yard at a sprint, and turned right at the sidewalk, knowing, for once, her destination.

Yes, something had changed within her—something she couldn't explain—but she knew it was time to take action. She was tired of living her life based on the limitations others set for her, tired of feeling trapped by a family who seemed determined to hold her down, tired of standing on the sidelines of a life she was supposed to be living.

She was ready.

Ready to light her world on fire and watch it come alive, rather than waiting, hoping, for things to get better.

Knowing the Ledgers were early risers, even on Saturdays, Emma wasn't afraid of waking them when she pounded on their front door moments later.

She smiled like a girl when she heard Riley's voice on the other side of the door. "I got it."

He opened the door, pulling a sweatshirt on over his head and matching her smile. "Hey, Em. What's up?" If he was surprised to see her alive and unharmed after her family reunion, he didn't show it.

"I need your help," she panted, still trying to catch her breath after running.

His eyebrows pinched together in confusion. "My help for what?"

She wrung her hands together in excitement, ready to demonstrate the kind of strength she never thought she had. "It's time my two worlds collided."

Twenty-One

Boys.
Girls.

For the better part of two months Emma had fought to keep her worlds separate, but now, with the rematch against Evergreen looming in the near future, she decided to change the game plan. Basketball may not have been the most important thing in the world, but it was the only thing she had. She could wait for eternity for things to change with her family, for hope to peek through the years of pain and shine light on the future, but for all she knew she would wait in vain. Basketball was here and now, and it was time she stopped detesting the girls and embraced them as teammates—not in the literal sense, of course.

Emma's toughness on the court had not appeared overnight, nor was it the result of playing one-on-one with the boy down the street. Resentment yielding to respect from a handful of neighborhood boys determined to make or break her was what had formed Emma as a basketball player. Each time the guys tripped her, elbowed her, fouled her, or humiliated her, she picked herself up and plunged back in, determined not to let them beat her. If the guys had helped her, they could help the girls too.

The Bradshaw girls' team was good, but if they wanted to beat Evergreen, they needed to up their game. It was time to turn the girls into real players. Of course, they'd never listen to her. At least not without a little incentive.

Ever since the stupid slumber party, the girls had shown up religiously to the court on Saturdays to watch Emma and the guys play hoops. Huddling together on the aluminum bleachers, they whispered and giggled with their eyes and ears focused on the guys, no doubt trying to pick up on the gossip frequency of male bonding. Emma had never given the girls an opportunity to integrate. They were spectators, not players.

Until now.

They perched on the bleachers like birds on a telephone wire, gawking at the court and all the guys like they had for weeks. Emma usually ignored them and pretended they didn't exist, but not today. Today, she walked over to stand in front of the girls and spoke loud enough for all of them to hear. "You girls up for a game?"

Madison flinched upright as if on high alert, while Lauren and the rest of the girls froze.

"If we're going to have a shot against Evergreen, we need to learn how to play smart, no matter how rough things get on the court," Emma said. "The guys are willing to help us out, so what do you say?"

"Is this some kind of joke?" Lauren asked.

"No, no joke. I promise." If she'd ever been a Boy Scout, she would have signaled the sacred promise, but since she hadn't, her word would have to do. "I want to beat Evergreen just as much as the rest of you, and I'm willing to do whatever it takes."

"We're waiting on you, pretty girls," Tom hollered from the court.

Madison stood and hopped off the bleachers. "I'm in."

"Wait." Lauren reached out and grabbed Madison's arm before connecting her hateful eyes on Emma. "What's the catch? You've ignored us since the day we showed up here, and now you suddenly want to include us? Why should we care?"

Madison whirled around to face her best friend. "Shut up, Lauren. Emma's the best basketball player I've ever seen, and if she's willing to help us beat Evergreen, well, then," Madison broke free from Lauren's grip and clamped her hand down on Emma's shoulder, "I'm in."

Madison joined the guys on the court and received a round of high fives. It didn't take longer than a minute for the rest of the team to join her. Girls were too easy. Dangling a guy on the end of a rope was all the motivation they needed. Emma couldn't help but smile and shake her head. Lauren, watching her friends abandon her and join the guys on the court, finally gave in too.

"Here's the deal," Emma said, gaining the attention of the guys and girls scattered across the court. "We play. Real basketball. Girls against guys. Girls, I expect us to win. Guys, bring all you've got."

Emma took the ball at the top of the key, hoping her plan to collide her worlds didn't blow up in her face. The last thing she wanted was to have the guys showing off and the girls playing damsels in distress. Riley matched up opposite Emma. She started to protest, knowing he had so much to offer the other girls, but he shook his head. "You're the biggest threat on the girls' team. I'm not leaving you half-defended." He winked at her. "Besides, I can still teach you a thing or two."

She matched his smile. Oh, this will be good, she thought.

Emma slapped the ball to initiate the game and watched the girls freeze, like they'd forgotten everything they'd learned in the past two months. She thought she'd have to wait for an eternity for them to break out of their trance, but then she saw the blur of a figure sneak through the defenders. Passing the ball into the key, Emma watched Ashley snatch it from the air, spin toward the basket, and sink a jump shot before any of the guys could react. Riley glanced at Emma as if to ask, "What was that?" but Emma just smiled and said, "That's my girl."

The girls snapped out of their catatonic state, and the guys received a reality check by the freshman's single act of awesomeness. With the girls two points up and the guys looking to score, Emma's two worlds collided in a game of basketball. No cheap shots, no showing off, and no pride divided the teams. Emma shouted instructions to her teammates, telling them where to move, when to pass or shoot, and what to watch out for to prevent the guys from controlling the court. She stopped the game a few times to show the girls how to pin a defender behind them, how to spin off a screen, or how to read the defense, but otherwise they played. Emma heard the guys whisper instructions to the girls on various plays, and she saw the girls obey. Sometimes. At other times, the girls stuffed the advice into their back pockets to use later so they could execute a move of their choice to show the guys they did, indeed, have their own skills.

For years, Emma had played basketball with the guys. They taught her about strength, strategy, and how to stand strong. They taught her about teamwork, loyalty, and trust. But when she found herself on the opposing team—the girls' team—Emma spotted an indefinable difference. Maybe girls played with less aggression and more grace, or maybe it was their confidence that forced them to play more like a team and less like a one-man show. Whatever it was, playing on a girls' team was different. No way was playing with girls better, but it wasn't necessarily…bad.

The game lasted for hours. By the time Madison snapped the final pass to Shiloh, who went head-to-head with Ben and beat him with his own move, they'd all lost track of the score, but it didn't matter. Emma watched her teammates move on the court, and she knew they were ready—ready for a rematch against Evergreen and for a second chance to prove to everyone they weren't a bunch of losers.

Emma turned her back on the guys and girls, unable to prevent the smile growing on her lips. Who would have thought these girls—these whining, crying, drama-stricken girls—could actually play a decent game of basketball?

She settled herself on the bleachers, expecting the girls to disappear, but they surprised her and stuck around. For once, more interested in basketball than boys.

As she looked around the court, she saw Tom instructing Lauren on how to draw an offensive foul, Ben showing Shiloh how to execute a blind pass, and Jerry teaching Ashley a few tricks on how to defend someone twice her size without getting pummeled.

Riley climbed the bleachers and sat beside her. "Hey."

"Hey yourself."

He propped his feet up on the bench below them and rested his elbows on his knees, turning his head to look at her. "You know you're brilliant, right?"

Emma shrugged.

Bringing her two worlds together had turned out better than expected. She watched the girls and guys interact on the court. Two months ago she didn't think any of the girls would be able to pull off a decent jump shot, much less drive to the basket and score with some fancy move against a guy. Ashley surprised her most. Jerry had pulled Cy over to play two-on-one against Ashley, so she could get more practice at facing off under the basket.

Riley followed her gaze and nodded toward the court. "You did an amazing job with the freshman. She looks like she's been playing for years."

She laughed, knocking her knee against his. "Did you ever doubt me?" she joked.

He shook his head. "Not even for a second." They watched Ashley hold her own against the two boys twice her size. A couple months ago they would have eaten her alive, but now she found her way to the basket each time, no hint of fear holding her back.

Riley nodded toward Ashley. "The freshman reminds me of you."

"Oh, yeah?" Emma rolled her head in his direction, expecting a sarcastic answer. "How so?"

"People take one look at her and think they've got her all figured out. She's clumsy, small, inexperienced, and no one expects much from her, but after a while, they realize how much she has to offer." He turned to look at Emma, and she froze beneath the intensity of his eyes. "Kind of like you. On first glance people may see a tomboy, a poor kid, a girl without much to offer the world, but then they take a closer look, and everything about you changes. They see what I always see."

Emma's breath caught in her throat, and she couldn't do anything except stare back at him, her heart swelling in her chest. He held her gaze for a minute longer before switching his attention to the guys and girls on the basketball court. "Most people have a hard enough time getting past one defender, but you take on two, sometimes three, without fear. You weave through players like they're wooden posts, you dribble like the ball is a part of you, and every shot you take is a testament of grace. Your determination and strength, your love of the game—when you play, you capture basketball at its best." He paused and reconnected his eyes with hers. "You make it a game worth watching."

His words shocked her into silence. How was she supposed to respond to that? She'd seen enough basketball games and watched enough players to know what he was talking about. Basketball was about the passing, the shooting, the breakaways, the impossible shots made at the buzzer, coming from behind to win, and every other moment that caused a person to jump up from their seat to cheer. However, sometimes it wasn't basketball but a player that made the game worth watching. A player whose insightfulness and execution of the game caused spectators to shake their head in amazement. A player who drew the interest of non-fans to the sport. For someone like Emma, there was no greater compliment than Riley's, especially considering players like that didn't come around that often. It wasn't the kind of praise he would give to just anyone unless he truly meant it. Emma didn't know if she measured up to his claim, but it was nice to know how much he thought of her.

Their attention returned to the court. Emma couldn't take her eyes off the freshman. Ashley beat Jerry with a crossover to the left, saw the slight delay in Cy's approach, and slipped between their double-team for the open shot. "She learned that from you," Riley said.

Emma looked at him. If she didn't stop Riley's stream of compliments, she'd probably start blubbering like an idiot. "If I didn't know better, I'd think you were jealous."

"Jealous," he repeated with his eyebrows raised.

She nodded. "Jealous of my mad skills."

"Oh, I'll show you mad skills." His arms encircled her as his fingers found her ribs and started tickling. She laughed, trying to squirm out of his grasp. No such luck. Her escape tactics were no match for his strength and tickling ability.

"Okay," she gasped. "Mercy."

"That's what I thought," he said smugly, pulling her against him as he leaned back against the edge of the seat behind him and crossed his feet on the one below.

She settled herself into the crook of his arm—the one place she felt safe, protected, loved—and leaned her head against his shoulder. For the first time in years, she felt completely content.

"Hey Em?"

She tilted her head up to look at his profile.

"For the record," he looked down to meet her eyes, "there is no better than you."

For a moment she didn't know what to say. She didn't

understand why Riley's faith in her never faltered, why he'd chosen her as a best friend, or why he didn't leave when she tried to set him free from her, but maybe she wasn't supposed to understand. Maybe she was just supposed to be grateful for him.

Letting the girl in her take over, Emma kissed his cheek, regretting nothing. "Same goes for you."

♦♦♦

The small crack in time between the end of lunch and the beginning of class was not to be wasted doing homework or scoring points with teachers. It was about squishing in a little more time with friends to gear up for the second part of the school day. The hallway buzzed with chatter and the slams of locker doors. Emma loved this time of day.

Tom told a joke. Emma and the guys laughed. It wasn't much different than usual except for the part when Madison plowed into their huddle.

"We have to win tomorrow." No greeting. No forewarning of the interruption. Just Madison's face, inches from Emma's, stating a fact everyone already knew.

"Okay," Emma said slowly. She had no idea where the conversation was headed or if it even had a destination, so she took a step away from Madison and let the girl speak.

"Evergreen High School has destroyed our team for the past three years. We can't let them beat us again." Madison's hands clamped down on Emma, her fingers digging into Emma's shoulders, causing Emma to wince. "We have to *win*. We have to crush them and beat them into the ground and—"

Emma would've laughed if the girl hadn't been so intense. Madison and violence? Not a good combo. "With that much aggression we'll be thrown out of the league and banned from the sport forever," Emma said.

"But—"

"Madison!" Emma nearly shouted. She pried Madison's fingers from her shoulders and stepped out of the crazy girl's reach. "Relax. We're going to be fine."

"Fine?" Madison looked at Emma with crazed eyes and flaring nostrils. "What kind of answer is fine?"

Seriously. What did Madison expect her to say? She looked to the guys for help, but they kept staring at Madison like they wanted to clone her and set her loose on the football field.

"Okay, how about this." Emma straightened to her full height and met the intensity of Madison's gaze with one of her own. "You want to win? Leave the girl drama at home and come ready to play, ready to fight for our win. Evergreen may be good, but they have no idea what kind of team we've become. We're going to pounce on them from the beginning and not let up until the final buzzer sounds. And when it does, we *will* have our victory." Emma left no room for fear or doubt. She hadn't worked so hard, endured girls, and suffered multiple moments of humiliation for two months only to lose twice against a cross-town rival. No way.

Riley grabbed both of her shoulders from behind and shook her in excitement while the other guys whooped and hollered, giving each other high fives.

Straightening out of her crazed maniac stance, Madison creased down the front of her shirt, raised her chin, and then placed a hand on her hip. "Okay," she said, returning to her usual superior self. "Good. I think we're done here." Without another word, Madison whipped around and walked away.

"Do you think you girls have a real shot to win tomorrow?" Cy asked.

"You bet they do," Tom said, holding up his hand to give Emma a high five.

Emma smacked his hand, and then looked around at her

friends, needing their support for the most important game of the season. "I didn't join the stupid team to lose."

♦♦♦

Inside the locker room, all was silent. Emma had meant every word yesterday when she told Madison they would win this game, but now, confronted with the actual task of playing Evergreen, doubt crept into Emma's thoughts. Anything could happen. She knew only too well how an off day could swap perfect shots for air balls and passes for turnovers. The rematch against Evergreen wasn't just a game. It was a defining moment in their season and in their lives. Two months ago no one had expected anything from the Bradshaw girls' basketball team, but now that they had secured a sizable number of wins under their belt and showed people what they could do, things were different. Different because this was the first time in over a decade that Bradshaw had a shot of beating Evergreen.

Everyone felt the pressure.

Emma tried to remain calm, knowing once she stepped on the court she could just play basketball and leave the doubt behind, but until then there was nothing she could do except create a list and check things off.

Braids. Check.

Red armband. Check.

Game face. Check.

Beside Emma, Ashley clasped her hands together in a death grip and her leg jiggled a mile a minute as she stared wide-eyed at the floor. The kid was petrified. Emma reached over and put her hand on Ashley's knee until the shaking stopped and Ashley looked at her. Emma gave her a smile. Ashley tried and failed to give one back.

Even Coach, with her clipboard tapping against her thigh, wasn't free of fear. She tried to give the pre-game speech of her life, but her voice shook with every word and she talked in circles, so no one gained an ounce of the motivation they needed to take the court. Maybe that was why the first half of the game went nothing like how they'd planned. Evergreen sought revenge, Coach Knowles second-guessed every decision she made, and Bradshaw failed to live up to their winning reputation.

The buzzer signaled the end of the first half. Trailing by twenty points, the Bradshaw Lions sulked as they made their way off the court. With half the game left, Emma wondered what tricks Coach had up her sleeve to pull the team together. They weren't playing badly, things just weren't going in their favor. Their shots weren't falling, they couldn't get inside for the rebounds, and the refs let half the fouls go uncalled.

Coach ushered them into the locker room just as her cell phone rang.

"Hello?" Coach propped the door open with her foot to let the girls pass and held one finger up to tell Emma she needed a minute to take the call. "Yes, this is she. What can I—"

Her words cut off as the locker room door closed, leaving Coach on one side and the team on the other. Looking around at the sullen faces of her teammates, Emma didn't think they had a chance to win. It was tempting to jump onto a bench, tower over her teammates, and yell at them to get their heads in the game. Yes, the image tempted her to smile, but she knew it wasn't what her team needed. They sat in silence, waiting for Coach to appear and voice words of wisdom and strength to inspire them to return to the game and fight for their victory.

Waiting.

No one spoke. For the first time, surrounded by seven girls, there was merely silence. No whining, no complaining, no blaming each other. Just silence. Emma looked at each of her teammates. Shoulders slumped, heads bowed, eyes closed. The team had already given up. They were ready to give in to the pressure pushing against them and hand the win to Evergreen. Emma didn't think things could get any worse.

She was wrong.

Twenty-Two

The locker room door flew open and eight girls turned to look at their coach, but it was not her slim, pale figure that stepped through the doorway. Lauren's dad took center stage instead. His tall lanky frame and head full of thick black hair didn't belong center stage in the girls' locker room.

"Hi, girls," he said.

His false sense of assurance didn't fool any of them.

Emma's thoughts snapped back to the phone call Coach had answered as the team entered the locker room, and her heart stopped. She stood, not taking her eyes off Mr. Thompson. "What's wrong?"

The eyes of her teammates bounced from Emma to Mr. Thompson.

"Nothing, nothing." Mr. Thompson waved away her question with his hand. "There's just been a change of plans, that's all."

Change of plans during halftime of the biggest game of their lives when they were losing? Seriously?

"Ms. Knowles has been called away, something about a family emergency, so it looks like I'll be filling in for her." His eager smile revealed how much he totally underestimated the role he'd stepped in to fill. This game wasn't a pre-season practice game, nor was it merely a matter of scoring more points against some opponent. This was Evergreen High School!

The girls exchanged glances.

"You're joking, right?" Emma couldn't resist. This was not a time for jokes.

"Emma." Ashley's warning tone sounded too much like Riley's.

"What?"

"No, Emma's right." Lauren elbowed her way to the front of the group. "Dad, you don't know anything about basketball."

His laugh didn't depict nervousness, which was bad. His laugh should have been thick with nervousness.

"Oh, sure, I do," he said. "How hard can it be, right?"

How hard can it be? For a team that had gone from nothing to something in two months, they knew all about how hard it could be. The girls stared at Mr. Thompson. He nodded and kept nodding as he looked around the locker room, either mentally giving himself a pep talk or just taking in the scenery.

"Okay," he said, clapping his hands. "You girls are doing great. Go out there and keep doing what you're doing. Now, who wants to play?"

No one volunteered. Was this seriously how the game would end? With Mr. Thompson steering the wheel? They'd crash for sure.

"Uh…how about," he scanned their faces and started pointing, "You, you, you, and you."

Four against five. Great strategy…for slaughter.

"Dad!" Lauren shrieked. "You only picked four players, none of whom are guards."

"Oh, well, of course I did." He patted his daughter on the shoulder. "I was just joking, sweetheart."

Totally *not* convincing anyone.

Mr. Thompson glanced at the blank clipboard in his

hands. "How about we start off with whoever just came off the field?"

Field? Seriously?

They shuffled out of the locker room, their first half low plummeting to rock bottom.

"What are we going to do?" Madison whined.

"Lose," Emma said without a doubt. "Lose big." They'd worked so hard only to be creamed by their cross-town rival...again. Bradshaw was good, but they needed direction. Direction from someone who actually knew the game and what to look for. Someone who was not Mr. Thompson. How could Coach abandon them at a time like this?

Abandonment. The memories of her mom fleeing in the night in search of something better came back so strong it almost knocked the wind out of her. The rest of the team sauntered onto the court to shoot before they resumed the game, but Emma's feet stopped at the sideline. Five years. Five years since the woman she loved and trusted disappeared with no warning. Just like Coach had done moments ago. Yes, Coach Knowles had a lot to learn about coaching, but she'd built the team into something. She'd gained the trust of all the girls, only to abandon them when it truly mattered.

Emma was blind to how her teammates cast her sideways glances, wondering why she stood frozen like an idiot on the baseline. She was deaf to the chaos of the gym as the pulsing notes of the band rallied fans for the second half. She was numb to the hammering of her heart as it tried to propel her feet forward. It was one thing to accept her family's abandonment, but would everyone else she'd learned to trust abandon her too? If so, what was the point of trusting anyone?

She remembered the first game of the season and how she'd stood on the same line. It had been so easy to run then, just like it would be so easy to run now. With no coach and the certainty of a loss hanging over her head, her presence wouldn't make much of a difference. It wasn't like she had much to offer anyway.

Emma stepped backward—one step away from the baseline, one step toward the exit.

"Em, you okay?"

Shiloh's voice froze Emma in place and snapped her attention back to her teammates. Ashley and Shiloh stared at her, questioning her. Doubt and fear flickered in their eyes as they waited for her to respond.

She didn't know what to say. Looking at her two teammates, Emma realized Coach hadn't just left her, she'd left the entire team.

Ashley held a ball out to Emma, willing her to take it. "You comin', Coach?"

Emma's eyes locked on the kid's, and she knew. She knew she couldn't abandon her teammates. She couldn't—wouldn't—follow the same path others in her life had taken.

Taking a deep breath, Emma shoved Coach Knowles and her lifetime of nightmares aside and stepped onto the court to join her teammates. She took the ball from Ashley and sunk a few shots, doing her best to gear up for what would be the worst second half in history.

One misfired shot, one second with her back turned to rebound the ball, and Emma found herself surrounded by Lauren and the rest of the girls. Great, she thought. Not only was Lauren's dad in charge, but now Lauren was going to get her wish and tar and feather Emma in front of hundreds of people. No way was Emma going down without a fight.

"This is a disaster," Lauren stated for the record. "My dad? Seriously? Let me assure you, what little athletic ability I may have did *not* come from him."

Not exactly the greeting Emma had expected, but okay. Just to be on the safe side, Emma shuffled back a couple of feet.

Lauren nodded at Emma. "You're up."

Emma's breath caught in her throat. She didn't like Lauren's tone. Not. One. Bit. "What do you mean I'm up?"

"We voted." Lauren gestured to the girls surrounding her, a smile growing on her lips. "You're the coach."

"What?" Emma exclaimed. Girls—all of them—needed to be committed to the insane asylum. Immediately.

"You know this game and this team inside and out," Lauren said. "You made this team what it is. If we want to have any chance to win today, we need you to do this."

Emma said the first word that popped into her head. "No."

Lauren crossed her arms and cocked an eyebrow. "No, is not an option. Besides, you're outvoted."

"I don't care if I'm outvoted by a million," Emma said through clenched teeth. "I'm not doing it. Coach left your dad in charge. Not you and not me. We have to trust her decision." Not that Emma believed Coach's decision was for the best, but she wasn't going to let the team ambush her and force her into the coaching role. No way.

"Coach left us," Lauren said. "So, in my opinion, she doesn't have a say in the matter. We have to do what is best for the team, which means you're the coach."

Emma waved her hands in front of her face, trying to ward off the demons. Lauren and the rest of the team stood in agreement. Against her.

Ashley stepped forward out of the circle. "Emma, it's brilliant."

Emma pointed at the freshman, her shock changing to anger. "You stay out of this." She turned back to Lauren. "My answer is no. I don't know the first thing about coaching. If you're dad won't work, then how about—"

"What do you call Saturday practices?" Madison said, cutting her off and stepping beside Lauren.

"Scrimmaging. And it was the guys helping, not me."

"What about post-practice sessions?"

Despite the assurance in Shiloh's voice, Emma refuted

her too. "Show and tell."

"We need you," Lauren said with so much conviction Emma believed her. Almost.

Gone was Lauren's disgust of Emma and her reluctance to place Emma in a position of authority over her. "No one knows this team like you do," Lauren confirmed. "You know how we work and when things need to be changed up. You can do this. You've been doing it."

"No!" Emma pushed through their barricade. No way could she do what they asked. No matter what they thought, she wasn't good enough, strong enough, or smart enough to coach an entire team. Playing was one thing, but coaching was completely different. Especially against Evergreen.

"Emma," Ashley said softly, appearing beside her.

"Don't start, freshman." Emma snatched a water bottle from the bench. She chugged down water for the sake of doing something.

"You can do this," Ashley continued anyway. "You've been coaching me and the other girls all season, and you know you've done an awesome job. Lauren's right. If we want to have any chance to win today, we need you to coach us."

Emma's eyes were drawn to Ashley. Not even Riley could muster that much faith in her with a single look.

Mr. Thompson called them all to the bench before Emma could gather the strength to turn Ashley down again. She threw the water bottle to the floor and turned to her teammates. She felt their eyes on her as they huddled. With Madison on one side and Ashley on the other, Emma wished they could skip to the end of their team chat and play. No such luck.

"So, Coach." Lauren looked straight at Emma. "What's it going to be?"

"I already told you no," Emma growled. "Now, drop it."

"Okay, girls," Mr. Thompson said. "Let's see here." He

had Coach Knowles' clipboard in one hand with the marker in the other. He bit the cap off the marker and, holding the cap in his teeth, tried to give some sort of undecipherable pep talk as he doodled like a first grader on the clipboard. When he realized no one understood him, he tried to take the cap out of his mouth and somehow dropped the clipboard and the marker in the process. All eight girls grimaced. The fate of their game lay in the hands of Lauren's dad, Mr. Basketball Illiterate.

Emma closed her eyes, biting her tongue hard enough to draw blood. Peer pressure was an evil; she would *not* succumb to it. Nope. No way. Coach left Mr. Thompson in charge, so Mr. Thompson was in charge. They would just have to endure the consequences. No ifs, ands, or buts about it.

Opening her eyes, Emma took a deep breath. As long as she didn't look at Ashley, everything would be fine. From across the huddle, Lauren caught Emma's eye and raised her eyebrows, all joking gone. Lauren was asking Emma for help. Emma. Poverty child. Loser. Poor girl. Tomboy. Some may have considered it a bonding moment between enemies, but not Emma. She glared back at Lauren, shaking her head and scolding herself. "Lauren, Madison, Shiloh, and Peyton. Check-in!" Emma barked.

Smiles spread across their faces and Lauren and Madison exchanged a high five, which deepened Emma's scowl. "The rest of you be ready to sub in. Let's see what they do with a full-court press the first time down the court and then pick them up at half court with man-to-man defense. We need to keep the ball under control and run the offense. Make them fight for each and every rebound. Don't give the ball away for free. If I see any of you lagging out there, you're benched."

She shoved her hand in the middle of their huddle. "Team on three."

Lauren bumped Emma's shoulder as they filtered onto

the court, a smug smile spread across her face.

"You're going to pay for this," Emma said.

Lauren laughed. "You've been nothing but a show-off all season. Now it's your time to prove yourself and live up to your potential."

"And what would you know about my potential?"

Lauren rolled her eyes. "I'm not an idiot."

Was that, like, a compliment? From Lauren? Emma shook her head. "Just don't blame me if we lose."

"No chance we'll lose, Coach."

Emma scowled. What was with girls? First they detested her, then they humiliated her, then they detested her some more, and now they trusted her. Emma couldn't keep up with them, nor did she want to exert the effort to try. Somehow, she had to figure out how to survive the rematch with Evergreen as a coach and a player.

She searched the stands for Riley, knowing he couldn't help her out of this mess, but desperately wishing he could. For the first time since she'd known him, Emma was flying solo. *This should be interesting*, she thought. All these girls relying on her, expecting her to pull off a miracle by leading them to victory against the best team in the league. She hoped they prepared themselves for disappointment.

She found Riley and hoped he would come barreling out of the stands and whisk her away to safety. Her eyes pleaded with him to help her, but he just laughed and flashed two thumbs up. Emma knew it was his way of encouraging her to face this challenge head on, but it did nothing but confirm she wasn't ready for this.

The court seemed smaller than it had a moment ago. It provided no place to hide and no alternate solutions for a girl forced prematurely into a coaching role. Emma searched the stands, the court, and the sidelines looking for an escape route, but all she found were hundreds of eyes focused on her. She was trapped—trapped within the black rectangle of the court with a bunch of girls whose hatred of her had somehow turned into trust. She closed her eyes and shook her head. What other choice did she have but to coach her teammates and hope they didn't get slaughtered under her reign?

◆◆◆

It took the world about two seconds to figure out Coach Knowles was MIA and Emma was calling the shots. Sure, Mr. Thompson was the adult on the sideline clutching the clipboard as if his life depended on it in case someone tried to argue that a seventeen-year-old girl wasn't qualified to coach her peers in the most important game of the season, but Emma was the one in the driver's seat. She hollered orders and whispered pointers to her teammates between plays, expecting them to dismiss her callous tone and swallow their whining long enough to listen to her. For once, they obeyed without protest. They had already accepted Emma as their coach.

The transition was not so smooth for Emma.

Playing was tough, coaching was torture, but doing both at the same time was excruciating. A different mentality was required for each, but when both were required at the same time it took all the strength Emma had to stay focused. As a player, she could pass the ball to the open player and cut the other way without looking back. As a coach, she had to pass the ball to the open player, cut the other way, watch how the rest of the players shifted, and devise a strategy for the next time down the court.

Every dribble, every shot, every player mattered. Evergreen didn't merely want to beat Bradshaw, they wanted to leave them on the court, battered and broken. The home court advantage couldn't ward off every swinging elbow or strategically placed foot. If Bradshaw wanted to win—if they wanted to survive—they had to fight. Thank goodness for the guys and Saturday practices.

Maybe it was Emma's leadership, maybe it was a newfound burst of energy, or maybe it was refusing to spend another year as the worst team in the league, but Bradshaw finally found their game. Their shots started falling, they managed to block out under the basket and get their hands on the rebounds, and they stopped getting beat on defense. Despite the pressure, Emma started to relax. Maybe Bradshaw did have a chance to win with Emma as coach.

Whether Bradshaw won or lost, Emma should have known they would not survive the night unscathed.

Bradshaw executed their offense perfectly. Lauren slid down the side of the key to set a screen for Shiloh. Emma bounce-passed the ball to Shiloh at the free-throw line and went to set a screen for Madison on the wing at the same time Lauren popped outside for the pass from Shiloh. Madison sprinted to the top of the key to catch the pass from Lauren as Shiloh resumed her original position under the basket. Madison shot the ball and followed it to the basket, ready for the long rebound.

Emma watched Madison jump into the air, secure the ball between her hands, and let gravity bring her back down to the court. Instead of powering up for another shot, Madison crumpled to the ground with a scream.

Emma cringed.

The shrill of a whistle stopped the clock and the game. Emma didn't know what to do except crouch beside Madison and put a consoling hand on her shoulder as Madison clutched her leg and cried. Just because Emma had the title of coach hovering over her head didn't mean she knew anything about injuries and comfort and snatching back time for a do-over.

Bradshaw's trainer hustled over from the sideline and kneeled beside Emma to assess the situation. "What hurts?" he asked.

"Ankle," Madison gasped, tears streaming down her face.

"Can you stand?" the trainer asked.

Madison shook her head. "I don't think so."

The trainer exchanged a look with Emma. "Help me get her to the bench."

They carried Madison off the court to the sound of applause and set her on the bleachers so the trainer could do his thing. Emma watched the situation and couldn't prevent the guilt from building inside her. Did all coaches feel personally responsible when one of their players went down? Not wanting to dwell on Madison's injury, Emma took a step back. She had a team to coach.

"Emma," Madison whimpered, grabbing Emma's wrist as she turned to leave. "Emma, I am so sorry. I don't know what happened."

"You played great basketball, that's what happened." Emma squeezed Madison's shoulder.

Emma turned back to the court—turned back to her six remaining teammates staring at her, waiting for the plan. What do you say to a team who just watched one of their starters be carried off the court? They all knew Madison wouldn't rejoin them tonight, so what could Emma say to motivate them?

It wasn't supposed to be this way. Jen Knowles wasn't supposed to abandon them, Madison wasn't supposed to be on the bench with an injury, and Emma wasn't supposed to be in charge of the fate of an entire team.

"What do we do now?" Steph asked.

Emma covered her face with her hands and tried to crease the fear from her eyes. Her teammates waited, so she plunged ahead with plan B, making it up as she went. She dropped her hands from her face and took a deep breath. "Ashley, go check in."

The kid looked at her like she'd just been asked to go to war without a weapon. During the first half, Ashley had played a total of two minutes. Maybe. The kid had every reason to be afraid since Coach Knowles hadn't had enough faith to put her in a game for any extended period of time all season. But Emma wasn't Coach Knowles. As a coach—as a player—she needed Ashley on the court with her, not watching from the bench.

Emma nodded toward the sidelines. "It'll be fine. Go on."

Ashley scampered off to check in. As soon as she was out of hearing range, Lauren spun on Emma. "Are you crazy? You put that disaster in and we'll lose for sure."

The rest of the team nodded in agreement, ready to throw in their protests.

After everything that had happened, Emma didn't need any more drama. She mustered what little strength she had left, pretended it was so much more, and confronted her teammates. "You guys put me in charge to coach this team, so listen up. Ashley's ready for this. She's a lot better than you give her credit for, and we need her if we're going to have any shot at winning tonight. She is part of this team, probably dealing with more fear than all of us put together, and she needs our support, you got it?" Emma looked into the faces of her teammates, ready to challenge anyone who opposed her. One by one they nodded, probably going against their instincts to trust her.

As if to mock Emma, Ashley tripped as she rejoined their huddle. A few of the girls rolled their eyes, but Lauren caught Ashley before she face-planted and set her back on her feet. "You can do this, freshman," Lauren said, slapping her on the back.

The ref blew the whistle and both teams ended their huddles and filtered back onto the court.

Shiloh accepted the ball from the ref as Bradshaw stacked up for the inbounds pass. She slapped the ball and the line split. Emma broke free and caught Shiloh's pass. She pivoted toward the basket and secured the ball at her hip in triple threat position. Emma took a deep breath before dribbling slowly downcourt, waiting for her teammates to set up on offense.

"You must be under a lot of pressure as the coach and all," Emma's defender said as Emma crossed mid-court with the ball. It was the same girl who had defended her in their first game against Evergreen, Valerie Hockus. "I hope you don't choke and cost your team the game, especially considering you already have one injured player on your record."

Maybe it was the heightened sense of responsibility that came with being a coach or maybe it was the past-due decision to stand up for herself, but Emma felt a smile grow on her lips. "I hope you and your teammates are ready to lose tonight."

Valerie's face hardened. "Not a chance."

Emma squared her shoulders to the basket, locked her eyes on her defender, and put up a shot without so much as a defensive hand in her face.

The announcer's deep voice boomed over the speakers. "Wrangtoooooooooon with a three."

"I wouldn't be so sure." Emma skipped backward toward the opposite baseline, knowing the game was far from over.

Evergreen may have been the number one team in the league, but they were far from perfect. The Evergreen coach, perhaps sensing Bradshaw's desire to win, became more vocal and more animated with every second that passed. He paced the sideline, tracking the ball with his beady eyes and waving his arms frantically at his players. His shouts could be heard throughout the gym as he yelled at his players, yelled at the refs, and yelled simply for the sake of being heard.

Evergreen started to falter.

Evergreen's number thirty-seven had the ball just inside the three-point line. She'd given up her dribble and stood cemented to the same spot on the floor. She should have passed to an open player, but with Peyton's arms swinging wildly in front of her face, the girl panicked. She chucked up an air ball.

Shiloh snatched the ball out of the air and fired an outlet pass to Ashley at midcourt. Emma swept up the court from the outside lane and it was two-on-one.

Ashley dribbled downcourt, and the Evergreen defender remained halfway between her and Emma until she determined who would take the shot. She probably figured Emma would get the ball to shoot and didn't commit to Ashley until the kid put her head down and charged to the basket. The kid initiated a layup, but instead of bouncing the ball off the backboard like everyone expected, she underhanded a pass to Emma. Without missing a beat, Emma caught the ball and put up a short jumper.

Shouts erupted from the stands as the ball fell through the hoop and Evergreen set up on offense. Emma pointed to Ashley from across the court and they exchanged smiles. After all the hours they'd spent together in the gym, Emma had to admit, the kid was *good*.

By the end of the third quarter, Ashley proved to be a new problem for Evergreen. She spun off defenders before they had a chance to crush her and plunged into the key against girls twice her size, only to pop out the other side unscathed with her hands up and ready for the ball. Sometimes it only took one dribble, sometimes a few more, for the kid to find a hole in the defense and fire off a shot or pass the ball to an open player. Her size allowed her to slip through holes in the defense undetected, and with her speed she was always a step or two ahead of her defender. Thank goodness she wasn't still tripping over her feet. Ashley's newfound talent, along with Shiloh's rebounding madness, Lauren's aggressiveness, and Emma's knack for coaching in combination with her playing ability, enabled Bradshaw to close the gap in the score and pull within ten points by the end of the third quarter. With eight minutes remaining, it was anybody's game.

◆◆◆

The Evergreen coach probably thought a team entering the fourth quarter down by ten would explode onto the court to make up the difference in score as soon as possible. Emma decided to change things up a bit. Evergreen wanted the ball like kids wanted candy. They wanted to score; they wanted to stretch their lead as far as possible. Cheap fouls with the intent to cause as much damage as possible was the game they played, and Emma decided to take advantage of their desperation. She knew Bradshaw's passing game was strong, so the fourth quarter started with one giant game of keep away.

It worked.

Evergreen, governed by their frustration, forced the fouls, sending Bradshaw players to the foul line where they made one basket after another. Point by point, they continued to close the gap.

The intensity of the game heightened as the clock ticked below two minutes. Emma didn't know what would be worse, being the team down by one needing to secure a lead or being the team up by one needing to retain the lead. Either way, both team's looked for a break.

With thirty seconds on the clock and down by three, the ref handed Emma the ball under Evergreen's basket. She took a deep breath before slapping the ball and setting her teammates in motion. They broke formation, trying to get open. Emma's eyes locked on Lauren's. Considering they were practically enemies, it was scary how much passed between them—how their plan formed without spoken words. Lauren sprinted for the opposite baseline, catching her defender off guard, as Emma cocked her arm back and threw a baseball pass the length of the court. Lauren caught it on the run at the opposite free-throw line, dribbled twice, and went up for the easy lay-in.

Two points, Bradshaw.

The crowd went wild. One point down, Bradshaw needed one basket to win.

Evergreen called a timeout.

Wiping sweat from her forehead, Emma glanced at the scoreboard as she walked toward the sideline. The game, the season, Emma. Everything would be defined in the next twenty seconds.

Twenty seconds.

A time both desired and feared by any true athlete, but most athletes didn't double as coaches. Emma would be lying if she'd said she wasn't scared. Scared of having an entire team and a gym full of people relying on her for the outcome of this game. Somewhere in the stands, Riley, the guys, and the Ledgers cheered for her. Win or lose, they cheered for her. She didn't want to disappoint them, she didn't want to let them or her teammates down, but she was filled with so much doubt. She wasn't a coach. She was hardly a player, yet seven girls looked to her to be both.

Emma didn't know if she was strong enough, good enough, or smart enough to lead her teammates to victory in the next twenty seconds, but she had to try. Somehow, she had to smother the doubt and fear surging within her and be the coach and player her team needed her to be.

She needed the perfect plan.

Mr. Thompson nodded and clapped as the girls came off the court to form a huddle. Even if he had been in charge, there's no way he would have survived. Sweat beaded on his brow and his wide eyes looked on in fear.

All Evergreen needed was to hold onto the ball. They were up by one and the game was theirs. But beating what used to be the worst team in the league by only one point was not acceptable for them—they would look for the shot.

"We need the ball," Emma said. "Let's go with a full-court press and be ready for the long pass. Don't foul, don't reach in, and don't give them the shot. Get the ball. *When* we get the ball, this is what we're going to do."

Emma felt the eyes of her teammates on her as she kneeled in the middle of the huddle and propped the clipboard on her knee. Diagramming the last twenty seconds of the game, she covered the clipboard with Xs, Os, and arrows as she explained their offense. "Whoever gets the ball needs to pass it to Ashley."

Emma looked up from the clipboard into Ashley's eyes, knowing she couldn't trust anyone else to make the last basket count. "You know what you need to do."

Ashley's eyes widened. "What? N-no."

Emma circled an empty space on the clipboard amidst the arrows. "They're leaving the baseline wide open and you've been slipping through the cracks in their defense all night long." She thought back to the look-at-me-I'm-brilliant move Ashley used to beat her in their one-on-one match at practice a while back. It was the perfect plan, the perfect unexpected surprise play to end it all.

"I've only ever done that move in practice," Ashley protested, knowing exactly what Emma expected of her. "And never with an actual defender."

"Then now's your chance."

"Emma, no. It should be you."

"There are twenty seconds left in this game and I'm the highest scorer." Emma wasn't trying to brag. She was merely stating a fact for strategic reasons. "Everyone expects me to take the final shot. That's why it's so much better this way," she said, tapping the clipboard with the marker.

Ashley shook her head. "I can't—"

"Yes, you can," Emma said firmly, not wanting to hear excuses or allow Ashley to hold herself back. "This team needs you out there, focused and confident. You got it?"

Ashley gulped, fear not completely gone from her eyes, and nodded. The girls on either side of her slapped her back, murmuring words of encouragement.

"All right." Emma glanced up and met the eyes of her teammates staring down at her.

At her—not through her.

Emma felt her chest tighten. For the first time all season, she actually felt like she belonged to a real team. A team that could prove to everyone they had what it took to beat the number one ranked team in the league. Did each of her teammates know how much they were needed in the last twenty seconds of this game? Did they know how Emma was, *gulp*, proud of them for how far they'd all come this season? Maybe now was the time to tell them, but she doubted she could cram everything she wanted to say into the remaining five seconds of the timeout. Besides, sometimes words failed to encompass the depth of feelings, especially when there was a chance they would gush forth and make Emma sound like some sappy girl.

Emma thrust her hand into the middle of the huddle. "Let's do this."

Their team cheer was barely heard amid the roar of the crowd. Everyone was on their feet, clapping, stomping, yelling. The stands may not have been filled, but the fans that were there made it seem like it.

Emma dropped the clipboard on the floor next to the bench, knowing she wouldn't need it again. She felt someone nudge her shoulder.

"Win or lose, you've done good tonight, Poverty Child."

"You haven't done too bad yourself, Ice Queen."

Lauren laughed and nodded across the court toward Ashley. "I guess you were right," Lauren said. "The freshman can play."

Emma smiled. "I know."

"You think she can do this?" Lauren asked, no doubt referring to the pressure filled win-or-lose shot.

Emma glanced at Ashley. The girl who had befriended her only two months ago even though Emma had done everything to deter her. The girl who was feisty and annoying, yet somehow too smart for her own good. The girl whose love of basketball was second only to Emma's.

Emma swallowed the lump in her throat, internally scowling at herself for getting personally attached to the kid. "Absolutely," she said in answer to Lauren's question. And she meant it.

"Good," Lauren said with a nod. "Because I really want to win."

Emma laughed. "We all do."

Lauren slapped Emma's back before matching up on defense. Emma took her place opposite Valerie, hoping her plan worked. Evergreen's number twenty-one stood at the baseline with the ball as her teammates struggled to get open. Bradshaw didn't make it easy. Emma and Lauren marked their people move for move, preventing any kind of short pass. With no other option, number twenty-one threw an overhead pass toward the Evergreen post player at midcourt.

The ball reached the height of the arc and started its descent. The Evergreen player held out her hands, waiting for the ball to fall into them. One step was all Shiloh took in front of her opponent to seize the ball and steal Evergreen's one and only opportunity to score.

The transition from defense to offense happened flawlessly. Lauren sprinted downcourt to help Shiloh, while Emma filled the weak side lane. Ashley and Peyton raced to get into position as Evergreen set up on defense.

Five-on-five at Bradshaw's basket with ten seconds left on the clock.

Lauren passed the ball to Emma and set up on the left side. Emma snapped the ball to Ashley on the right and then cut through the key to set a screen for Shiloh. Shiloh retraced Emma's steps to the top of the paint where she snatched the lob pass from Ashley out of the air, while Emma snuck along the baseline and popped out the opposite side. Lauren slid down, set the screen for Emma, and then rolled toward the basket. Emma sprinted to the top of the key where she met Shiloh's pass and Valerie, ready for the final one-on-one face-off as the seconds clicked down.

Valerie crouched low, waiting for Emma to make her move. They looked at each other with sweat beading on their foreheads, faces flushed, and the desire to win burning in their eyes.

Emma dribbled between her legs, jabbing one way only to come back and jab the other way, always in control, biding her time with the clock and checking Valerie's readiness. Valerie, sweat pouring off her face, kept her focus on the ball, trying to anticipate Emma's next move. During their first game earlier in the season, Emma had won their end of game face-off. Now, Valerie wanted revenge. Emma smiled.

Show time.

"You ready to lose?" Emma asked.

"You wish," Valerie growled.

Valerie was shorter than Emma, but she was quick, which probably explained why she felt confident playing Emma so tight on defense, wanting her to fight for the shot or the drive or the pass. Emma lunged forward with a dribble, then pulled back to create space for a double crossover. Valerie was a split second behind as Emma drove by her, but Emma counted on the girl's quickness as she initiated a spin move. Relying on the closeness of Valerie's defensive position, Emma stretched her arm out farther than usual. Instead of completing her move, she executed a behind the back bounce pass behind Valerie. The ball traveled across the key to Ashley cutting up from the baseline. Selling the play, Emma faked the lay-up, and Valerie, thinking Emma still had the ball, jumped to block the shot. Valerie collided with Emma in her desperate attempt for the ball, and they flew out of bounds. With no foul called, Emma watched from the floor as the fate of the game landed on the freshman's shoulders.

Two defenders collapsed on Ashley for the double team, but the kid faked right, drawing one defender with her, before she reversed direction and split between them, cutting through the middle of the key. Another defender popped in front of her, obstructing her path to the basket, and without missing a beat, Ashley executed the same two-step move she'd pulled against Emma. Emma watched as Ashley—the girl the world tried to keep down, the girl no one expected anything from—took flight.

Suspended in the air, Ashley stretched her arm skyward, the ball in her upturned palm. With her face scrunched in determination, Ashley flipped the ball in the air and players and fans watched its journey to the basket as the buzzer sounded.

◆◆◆

Silence.

Silence was all Emma heard. Silence when Ashley's winning shot passed through the net. Silence when the look on Ashley's face shifted from determination to shock. Silence when everything in Emma's world clicked into place.

Of course, in truth, the gym had exploded with sound. Shouts and claps thundered around them as fans flooded onto the court to share in this impossible moment.

Emma pushed Valerie off her and before she took two steps, Ashley jumped into her arms. Words couldn't articulate anything about this moment, so they did what any girls would do: they screamed. The rest of the team, including a hobbling Madison, surrounded them in seconds, jumping on top of one another until they fell in a heap to the floor with Emma on the bottom of the dog pile. Talk about bony knees and elbows! Eight girls who began the season as losers, celebrating now as friends—more or less. Even

Lauren violated their no-touch policy to embrace Emma in a hug.

The moment was not one to last forever. One by one they got picked apart by family and friends until it was only Emma left with a smile of shock on her face.

Bradshaw had won.

Emma had coached her team to victory.

Winning one basketball game may not be a big deal for most people, but for Emma it was monumental. Girls had listened to her, obeyed her instructions, treated her like a part of the team rather than a person wasting space, and here they stood as victors over their cross-town rival, for the first time in ten years.

Maybe she wasn't completely worthless after all.

The weight of Emma's realization almost crushed her. For the first time in her life, she felt like she actually did something good. She didn't know if she should laugh or cry or fall to her knees in gratitude, so she stood in the middle of screaming fans, looking for a familiar pair of blue eyes.

Scanning the gymnasium, she saw the Evergreen players watch in disbelief from the sidelines as Bradshaw celebrated their victory, she saw Mr. Thompson slumped in a chair fanning himself with a clipboard—the pressure of coaching assistant too much for him to take—and she waved to Mr. and Mrs. Ledger who smiled down at her from the bleachers. Hundreds of people surrounded her, but Emma finally found Riley.

Their eyes met at the same time. He smiled, like he knew exactly how much this moment meant to her, and she laughed. Wanting to close the distance between them as fast as possible, Emma pushed through the crowd and jumped into his outstretched arms. It was a good thing Riley was strong, otherwise, her momentum would've flattened him.

"Em, you were amazing." He tightened his arms around her. "I knew you could do it."

A lump formed in her throat, preventing her from

responding, so she just clung to her best friend.

It only took Tom and Jerry and the rest of the guys seconds to surround them. They pulled her from Riley's grasp to give her hugs of their own and congratulate her on her coaching debut.

"So," Jerry said, punching her lightly on the arm. "Now that you can't deny the fact you're a superstar, what are you going to do?"

The guys waited for her answer. Aside from relishing in Bradshaw's victory, she hadn't thought about anything beyond the next five seconds and preserving this moment of perfection. But then she caught Riley's eye from across the circle and smiled. She couldn't explain how the hatred of a group of girls could mold into trust, how a girl with nothing to offer could end up coaching her team to victory, or how a guy like Riley could be interested in a girl like her. But if she was good enough to gain the trust of an entire team of girls and good enough to be a coach, maybe she was good enough to be Riley's friend and his—gulp—girlfriend.

She laughed at the realization, knowing the answer to Jerry's question. "This."

She closed the distance separating her from Riley, wrapped her arms around his neck, and pressed her lips to his, finally feeling like his equal. She felt his initial surprise, but then his arms tightened around her and he kissed her back.

The guys hooted their approval, and she heard Jerry mutter, "It's about time."

When they finally pulled apart, Riley's eyebrows scrunched together in concern when he looked at her. "Em? What's wrong? Why are you crying?"

She hadn't realized she was, but then she felt the tears sliding down her cheeks and she laughed. "I don't know."

"I knew it." He threw up an arm in defeat. "I'm a horrible kisser."

She laughed. They all did. "No, it's not that," she said.

"I guess..." She didn't have much, but when she looked around the gym, she saw her teammates celebrating, the guys—her friends—smiling at her, the scoreboard lit up with the victory of a game she had played and coached, and finally Riley. With one arm still wrapped around her waist, unwilling to let her go, Riley wiped tears from her cheeks, waiting for her answer.

"I guess it's not so bad being a girl," she said. "I guess it's not so bad being me."

Poverty child. Loser. Poor girl. Tomboy. As far back as she could remember labels had defined who she was and what her future would hold. Maybe now she was entitled to add a few of her own labels to the list: Basketball player. Coach. Friend. Girlfriend. And maybe, just maybe, college-bound.

Acknowledgments

A huge thank you to the many people who helped make my dream of writing a book a reality:

Verity Hiskey, my sister and friend, thank you for loving my story from the beginning. Your insight and love of all things good inspired me every step of the way.

Lindsay Paige – For taking a newbie like me under your wing and introducing me to the wonderful world of self-publishing. Your encouragement and expertise were invaluable in getting me here.

Darcie Sherrick – For infusing even more laughter into my life and for constantly reassuring me that my story was good enough even though I wanted to scrap it and start over. Thank you also for your expertise, your honesty, all of your support, and most of all, your fine tooth comb.

To all of my beta readers for taking time to read a stranger's story and helping me see my story with fresh eyes. Your support and feedback were instrumental.

Jennifer Roberts-Hall – Thank you for all of your edits and catching all those pesky details that tried to go unnoticed.

It's often difficult not to judge a book by its cover, which is why I am hugely grateful to Michelle Preast. Ah, the patience you had with me through the many drafts of my cover before you nailed it. Thank you for a beautiful cover.

The journey of writing a book would not be possible without the love and encouragement from my family and friends. I love you guys!!

To all you readers, thank you for taking time out of your busy lives to read this story. I hope you enjoyed reading it as much as I enjoyed writing it.

And lastly, to my husband. None of this would've been possible without you and your unfailing faith in me. Your patience, love, support, and laughter built the foundation for this book and made me fall in love with you all over again.

About the Author

A former three-sport athlete in high school, Samantha grew up with a ball in one hand and a book in the other. From the moment her first grade teacher asked her what she wanted to be when she grew up, Samantha knew she wanted to be an author.

Samantha currently resides in the Pacific Northwest with her husband, a ball-obsessed Australian Shepherd, and a cat that can't get enough cuddle time. Books, writing, sports, music, and marshmallows top her list of favorites.

A Game Worth Watching is her first novel.

SAMANTHA GUDGER